**THE COLLAPSE:**
**FATE'S VULTURES**

# FEAR THE REAPER

## JAMI GRAY

Cover Art: Deranged Doctor Design, www.derangeddoctordesign.com
Publisher: Celtic Moon Press Revised edition, 2021
ISBN: 978-1-948884-58-7 (ebook) ISBN: 978-1-948884-59-4 (print)

First edition, September 2019, Escape Publishing - HarperCollins Australia
ISBN: 978-1-4892-911-58 (ebook)

# sign up for free reads from jami!

Join Jami's newsletter to be the first to hear about new releases, free books, special prices and other nifty events.

Sign up at: https://www.subscribepage.com/jami-gray-books

# what readers say...

**About Arcane Transporter:**
*"Taking a refreshing approach to fantasy magic, this fast-paced, economical thriller is told from a highly likable perspective."* —Red Adept Editing

**About PSY-IV Teams:**
*"This story is an emotional roller coaster, from betrayal, anger, fear, love..."* —InD'tale Magazine

**About the Kyn Kronicles:**
*"...a fantastic paranormal action novel is quite possibly the best book I've read this year. I could not put it down, and had to exercise serious self-control to keep from staying up all night to finish it."* —The Romance Reviews

**About Fate's Vultures:**
*"...if you like your characters with a bit more bite, with secrets, with hidden agendas, and all those sorts of things, and your worlds are a far more deadlier place, then this is for you."* —Archaeolibrarian

# also by jami gray

## ARCANE WONDERLAND

Last Call

Bitter Spirits

Rune & Tonic

## ARCANE TRANSPORTER

Ignition Point (*Prequel Novella*)

Grave Cargo

Risky Goods

Lethal Contents

Collision Course

Blind Spot

Terminal Drift

## THE KYN KRONICLES

Shadow's Edge

Shadow's Soul

Shadow's Moon

Shadow's Curse

Shadow's Dream

Shadow's Fall

Tangled in Shadows (*Short Story Collection*)

# FATE'S VULTURES

Lying in Ruins

Beg for Mercy

Caught in the Aftermath

Fear the Reaper

# PSY-IV TEAMS

Hunted by the Past

Touched by Fate

Marked by Obsession

Fractured by Deceit

Linked by Deception

# BOX SETS

PSY-IV Teams Box Set I (Books 1-3)

The Collapse: Fate's Vultures (Books 1-4)

The Kyn Kronicles Box Set (Books 1-6)

Arcane Transporter Box Set I (Books 1-3)

Arcane Transporter Box Set II (Books 4-6)

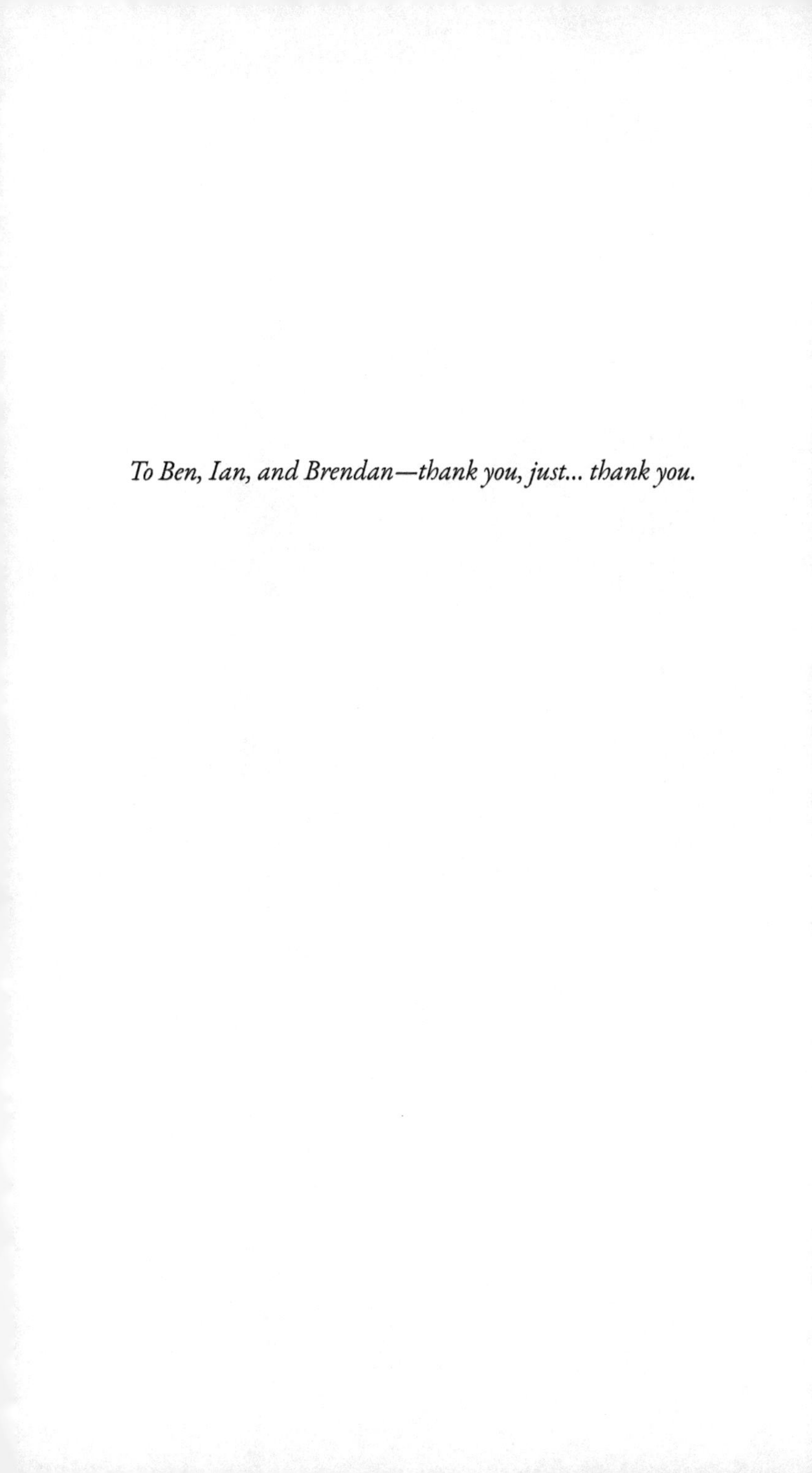

*To Ben, Ian, and Brendan—thank you, just... thank you.*

# acknowledgments

This whole writing journey has been a wild ride and no matter the twists and turns, I've been blessed to have a great support system helping me hold on. As with every book I can never thank my Knight in Slightly Muddy Armor or my Prankster Duo enough for their endless patience with take-out dining options and my tendency to mentally wander off with no warning. To my writing partners in crime—DeAnna, Camille, Dave—love you guys, this wouldn't be half as fun without you. To you, the readers, thank you so much for braving the dangerous world of Fate's Vultures and cheering them on.

# one

As Lilith sat next to her sleeping daughter, she couldn't escape the terrifying truth that a child held her mother's greatest hope and deepest fears. Sweeping waves of love and worry fought against the tide of guilt that eroded her heart. Not for the first time she wondered what good was it to be queen if you couldn't protect the one who needed it the most?

Bitterness rose, but she choked it back. It wasn't easy. Capricious and corrosive, her emotions were a mess, and she blinked away the hot press of rage-driven tears that threaten to escape. Lilith took a shuddering breath and Tabby's sleeping face came back into focus.

*Her baby was alive and here.*

She gently untangled her fingers from Tabby's loosened hold and traced a feather light touch over the endearing scatter of freckles, carefully avoiding the fading shadows of exhaustion under her child's closed eyes. Those shadows and the nightmares that stalked her precious daughter were glaring evidence of Lilith's failure to protect the thing she held most dear.

Once she brought Tabby home, the well-intentioned had offered empty words of comfort not understanding they were only pouring salt into a festering wound. It had gotten so that if one more person made some asinine comment about how lucky Tabby was, Lilith's knife would be buried in their sanctimonious heart.

Yes, Tabby had escaped the Raider's captivity without being physically violated, something Lilith got on her knees in thanks for every damn night, but that wasn't all Tabby endured. The scars left from being kidnapped, beaten, and witnessing another young girl being brutally raped, had shattered her daughter's innocence beyond repair. Her compassionate, outgoing baby had turned quiet, withdrawn, and wary. Lilith's destructive rage at seeing those changes in Tabby frayed her calculated control, and when you wielded as power as Lilith did, that was a dangerous thing.

No matter how long it took, no matter what she had to do, she vowed those fucking Raiders and whoever they were in bed with would pay for what they stole—from Tabby, from Lilith, and from all those other grieving parents whose children didn't come home.

Various scenarios of how to enact her vengeance played through her mind in brilliant, bloody detail because a mother's vengeance was a terrifying thing—merciless and patient. Two of Lilith's defining characteristics. Visualization was a key factor in any successful endeavor, and in this, she would accept nothing less than success.

Tabby's soft whimper derailed Lilith's bloody plans and she hummed a soft lullaby until Tabby settled once more without waking. Lilith waited until Tabby's breathing deepened, then waited a little longer to ensure her sleep remained undisturbed. Finally, she leaned in and pressed a kiss to Tabby's forehead. "Sleep well, baby."

She tucked in the blankets, left the lamp's soft light on as

Tabby didn't do well in the dark, and slipped out of the room, keeping the door ajar. She padded barefoot into the living room, nabbed the blanket off the back of the couch and wrapped it around her shoulders. Then she picked up the half-filled glass from the low-slung table and sipped the watered-down whisky as she wandered to the tall windows that over-looked the nearby forest.

Flames snapped and crackled in the immense fireplace behind her, their dance reflected in the night-blind glass. The outside chill was held at bay from the combined efforts of whisky's burn, the blanket's cocoon, and the press of heat from fire at her back. Clouds passed over the moon and played peek-a-boo with the surrounding trees, the shadows veiled in shades of black. Wild and dark, it matched her mood.

The isolated cabin was her private retreat. Built decades before by a paranoid bastard with more money than sense it backed into the mountain, which left a winding, narrow trail as they only approach, and blended into its surroundings effortlessly. It hid a collection of special properties—hidden arsenals, solar generators, a panic room, bullet proof, non-reflective glass, and camouflaged escape routes.

Known only to her and one other, it was the perfect safe house, which was why she brought Tabby here. It was an escape from the wagging tongues that plagued their day-to-day existence. Her daughter needed time to heal, Lilith had decisions to make, and both of them craved privacy.

Years of being submerged in the demands of her position and the weight of responsibilities had left Lilith emotionally empty. The hollowness that threatened to swallow her whole only disappeared when she was with her daughter and finding time to spend with her daughter was a damn crapshoot.

Lilith's role required burying and keeping a variety of secrets, and one of the biggest was Tabby's familial connec-tion. Staying quiet was far from easy and required ugly concessions, the kind that coated a layer of grime over Lilith's splintered heart. For years, the truth drove her every decision, because Tabby's well-being was more important than Lilith's soul. Then came Tabby's abduction and every devil's bargain fell by the wayside as Lilith's skewed priorities came home to roost with brutal talons.

*God, she sucked as a mother.*

Her darker emotions slipped guilt's hold and surged forward, hungry for acknowledgement. Hundreds of 'what-ifs' echoed in her head, each dragging along an alternate scenario until she wanted to scream in frustrated fury and self-directed disgust. Instead, her fingers tightened on the crystal glass in her hand. She fought back the urge to throw it against a stone wall and watch it shatter, because the clean-up would be a bitch. Instead, with disciplined control, she raised the glass to her lips, the bitter bite of whisky a twin for her thoughts.

She wallowed in her self-pity for a heartbeat, maybe two, then kicked the entire mess back into a dark hole. It was time to focus and move forward, starting with her top priority—her daughter's safety.

*"Better late than never,"* a snide little voice mocked.

Her lips curled in a silent snarl, but she froze, her inner turmoil silenced, when a flash of light hit the glass. Another burst hit, and this time she caught its direction—behind her. She turned and zeroed in on the silent, repetitive signal coming from the lamp next to the couch.

The silent alarm was triggered when someone found their way through the abandoned mines that seeded the nearby mountain and breached the basement escape route. The maze of unmapped tunnels was daunting and dangerous, so for a visitor to make it all the way to the basement meant they should be friendlies. However, 'should be' wasn't good enough for Lilith, not with Tabby asleep down the hall. Her

muscles coiled and her senses sharpened with predatory anticipation.

She crossed the room to the mantel, set her drink down, and then went to crouch by the coffee table in front of the couch. She let the blanket fall to the floor and pressed a finger against the hidden lever underneath the table's edge. There was a quiet click, and then she shoved aside the thick wood top and reached into a hidden compartment to retrieve the gun inside.

She checked the magazine, then the chamber with prac-ticed ease before thumbing off the safety. She straightened, crossed the flagstone floor, her bare feet silent, and brushed her fingers over the old tech security panel. The locks released with a muffled thump.

She pushed open the thick door that led to the basement and was greeted by a cool darkness. With the gun held ready in one hand, she slipped inside, reached back, and eased the door shut behind her. She activated the security by memory and locked the door behind her. Old tech or not, it would offer an impenetrable layer of protection for Tabby.

She glided down the stairs, her eyes adjusting to the shad-ows. She hit the bottom step, ignored the light switch, and relied on the darkness to mask her presence. She crossed the room and utilizing her memory of the room's layout, avoided the furniture. When she reached a heavy, reinforced door set in the back wall, she stepped to the side of an empty fireplace. With her gun aimed at the floor, she used her other hand to unlatch the well-oiled lock.

She slowly twisted the knob, then pulled the door open just enough to squeeze through. She stood inside the stygian darkness at the top of a short flight of stairs, and carefully closed the door behind her. The darkness was deeper, heavier than the one on the other side of the door. Cool air curled around her and carried the familiar scent of the Colorado

Mountains, leaving a whisper of chill against her skin. A sixth sense, the one that warned when you were being hunted, kicked into high gear.

Someone waited below.

She cupped the gun, raised it, and with her arms bent and her finger soft against the trigger, she inched down the stairs, letting the barrel lead. She made it two steps before grit shifted under her bare heel, the sound overly loud in the humming quiet. She stilled, waited, and barely dared to breathe.

"Lilith?" The low question emerged from the darkness.

Her name in a familiar voice shifted her finger from the trigger to rest along the slide. As tempting as it was, it did her no good to shoot her unexpected visitor. "A little late to be visiting, isn't it, Charity?"

A soft click was followed by a spill of light as Charity a solar lantern. "I wasn't expecting you to be here." As a shadow within the shadows, Charity remained just out of the light's reach.

As Charity was the only other person in the know about this safe house, Lilith couldn't fault her for using it. Still. She stifled her sigh, moved down the last few stairs and dropped her gun to her side. "Considering your entrance—" she tilted her head towards the opening that stretched behind the other woman, "—I kind of figured." When a few feet separated her from the road-stained blonde, Lilith stopped. "What happened?"

Covered in signs of a long, hard journey, Charity's normally electric blue eyes were dark with exhaustion. Dirt, sweat, and dust left her hair a lank mess. "Ran into a situation."

"Did you now?" Lilith murmured.

The sound of someone approaching shifted her attention to the tunnel. She reached past Charity and grabbed another lantern from the shelf on the wall. After twisting it on, she held it up to illuminate the earthen passageway. The shadows that lurked just outside the edge of the light morphed into distinctly human shapes. "I see you brought the situation with you."

Charity went and stood on the other side of the opening and the additional light from her lantern revealed her tag-alongs. "I didn't have much choice." An edge of an apology rode her voice.

Lilith's attention sharpened on the figures coming up the tunnel. Shadows and light battled it out as the figure in the lead came into view. Her heart seized as Karma proved the ulti-mate bitch when the one man guaranteed to upend her life strode into view. "What the hell?"

"Hello to you too, babe." Reaper's sardonic drawl was unmistakable and highly unwelcome.

Yet Lilith couldn't stop herself from taking him in, from his devil dark eyes, to the inky strands tied back at his neck, to his equally dark beard, age had only refined his allure. He stepped out of the shadows and filled the space with his wildly dangerous presence and a tiny part of her purred in antic-ipation.

"There's a bounty out on the Vultures," Charity explained. "They needed a place to lie low."

*Oh, hell no!*

She bit back her automatic protest and caught the unmis-takable mix of frustration and defiance shading Reaper's face. Obviously, she wasn't the only one unhappy about this situa-tion, but his discomfort was clearly not going to keep him from insisting on invading her privacy.

*Typical Reaper.*

Resentment strained her self-control, but she refused to reveal how much his presence bothered her. "So naturally, you bring them to my door?"

Reaper stopped by the tunnel's entrance, shifted to the

side, and waved the ones behind him forward without looking away from Lilith. "Alliance, remember?"

She held his mocking gaze. "As if I could forget." It wasn't like she need the reminder since the alliance was her idea in the first fucking place. A necessary evil at the time, but now, she was rethinking things. Unfortunately, she couldn't give in to her urge to kick his ass out of her cabin because she wasn't her own person. Hadn't been for a long while.

Charity braved the tense silence and pointed out, "The last place anyone would think to look for them is here."

Lilith didn't comment as two more men, one a shorter haired version of Reaper, the other lean and mean with a wild tangle of gold-streaked brown strode forward and into the basement. Recognition came quick—Math and Ruin. Both looked decidedly worse for wear but were upright and moving under their own volition. Whatever trouble trailed them had taken its toll.

Denying the bedraggled group sanctuary wasn't nice, nor was it a smart play. In resigned acceptance, she shifted aside so the two could move further into the basement. When Ruin caught her eye, he tilted his scruff-covered chin in silent acknowledgement, and then beelined to Charity.

Reaper's almost twin, Math, flashed her an impudent grin and wrapped his arms around her in a tight hug. "Surprise."

Lilith returned Math's affectionate squeezed and ignored the scent of night and travel that clung him. Luckily, she managed to hang on to the lantern and gun throughout the exchange. "You look better than expected."

He pulled back and let her go, his dark eyes serious above his fading grin. "You listening to gossip again?"

"It's not gossip if it's truth." Even though they hadn't seen each other in close to a year, she easily fell into their familiar, teasing byplay. "You find what you were looking for?"

The assassin lost his amusement and regained his normal grim demeanor. "And then some."

"Play catch up later." Reaper bit out in an irritated demand.

Lilith stiffened, but before she could snap back, Math, who stood in front of her with his back to Reaper, rolled his eyes. Then, likely to just to get under his brother's skin, he pressed another quick kiss to Lilith's cheek before he turned and joined Charity and Ruin off to the side.

Lilith's attention shifted back to Reaper, and she replaced her intended sharp retort with a question. "What happened?"

Reaper frowned and folded his arms over his broad chest. "We found the mole in Pebble Creek."

That was not the answer she expected, and curiosity hit hard. "Who?"

"It's a long story," Charity said and gained both of their attention. "A story that can wait until the others catch up."

The "others" were the rest of the mercenary arbitrators that made up Vultures—Vex, twin sister to Charity's man Ruin, and Havoc, Reaper's second-in-command. "Where did you leave Vex and Havoc?"

Ruin wrapped an arm around Charity's waist and answered, "They're hanging back with the bikes."

As her plans for a few quiet days to make life-altering decisions went up in a puff of smoke, Lilith let out a soft, resigned sigh. She set the lantern on a nearby shelf. "Who's going to go get them?"

Math stepped forward. "That would be me."

"Make it quick," she ordered. "I don't want to keep this passageway open for long." The faster she could get them in and upstairs, the faster she would get some damn answers. Then, if she was lucky, she could them settled and make her escape from Reaper's disquieting presence. "Pull the bikes beyond the first bend. That should be enough to keep them out of sight."

Math jerked his head in acknowledgement, and then shared a look with Reaper, who tilted his head back the way they came in an unmistakable command. Math heaved a sigh, reached past Lilith, took the lantern she set down, and then headed back into the tunnel.

As everyone watched Math disappear, silence reigned. When his light wasn't much more than a memory, Lilith turned to her unexpected guests. "Don't make me regret this."

Reaper's grin was fierce. "No promises."

## two

Reaper stepped out of the shower and into the steam-filled bathroom. At least there was one pro to dealing with Lilith and all that was her—hot water. He grabbed a nearby towel and dragged it over his body, grateful the chill that settled in his bones had faded. He wrapped the towel around his hips and shoved his wet hair out of his face.

*God, it felt good to be clean and warm.*

That thought barely cleared his brainpan before it was followed by another.

*Shit, I'm getting old.*

Maybe, or maybe he was finally hitting the end of his rope. God knew between running herd on the supply routes, disrupting the depraved Raiders flesh trade, uncovering moles, and navigating the dirty waters of power and politics, it had been fraying for months.

He should have known when he got Crane's panicked call, the end results would be a cluster. But instead of hanging up, when the man who controlled the Central Territories asked for help, Fate's Vultures aimed for Pebble Creek, hit the road, and drove straight into the bloody aftermath of a Raiders' ambush. The settlement was left reeling from Crane's death and Simon's kidnapping, which forced Reaper and the Vultures to step in and hold shit together—a role none of them asked for or wanted.

If it had been anyone else other than Simon and Crane, Reaper might have made a different decision. But it wasn't and Pebble Creek was too critical to the western supply routes to be left undefended. So, yeah, they stuck around until that damn bounty of Greer's hit and shoved them out. Now they were so far up shit's creek with no paddle in sight, it wasn't even funny.

He rubbed both palms over his face and blew out a breath, the stress of it all sinking its claws a little deeper. After two days on the road and a brutal run-in with unfriendlies his patience was AWOL, and his collection of aches and bruises was daunting. While his shower eased his body's complaints, his patience was nowhere to be found. There was one win in this mess, everyone was still breathing.

Exhaustion cracked his mental vault and memories rushed the unusual breach. He braced his hands on the stone counter and gave headspace to what brought him back in contact with the one person he'd sell his soul to avoid. Lilith. He couldn't decide if he wanted to bury her in blame or burn rubber to get the fuck away, but either way seeing her again raised old ghosts. He warned those ghosts off with a low growl and they retreated, not by much, but enough to create a workable distance so he could focus on more immediate concerns.

A faint hope circled that a solution would fall into his lap, but when it fluttered off, his bitter bark of noise escaped. Reaper would drop in shock if Lady Luck decided to favor Fate's Vultures. Her mercy was in short supply, as evidenced by the fact the Vultures currently topped every mercenary's to-do list. It was a hell of a reality shift going from hunter to hunted, but it was far from unexpected.

Nowadays, change was life's only constant. Seventy, eighty years ago Mother Nature taught humanity a vicious lesson and then left them to deal with the horrific aftermath. Man barely survived her temper or the raging wave of viruses and famines that dropped humanity to its knees before the massive economic collapse shattered what remained of the global governments. But humans were stubborn bastards and once the world was nothing but ash, they shoved to their feet and rebuilt. Decimated populations scattered, and world powers disappeared, replaced by territories ruled by those who could hold them.

In humanity's current rendition of society, survival was a risky bet, but it was a skill Reaper honed to perfection. It hadn't been easy, but those things never were. He chose his own path after he learned the hard way that right and wrong was a matter of perspective and rules were a joke. Disgusted by the arrogance of those bloated with power, he picked the one role that meant he didn't have to play by anyone's rules—mercenaries, vigilantes, however you named it, it amounted to the same thing—freedom from authority. Authority like the powerhouses that divided the land west of the Mississippi.

And there were plenty of players to choose from.

Once the rising oceans devoured the western coastlines and widened inland rivers, the collapsing infrastructure of what used to be the western states was divvied up. Now it was held by three people: Michael, Lilith, and, Crane's successor and latest addition, Simon.

Michael's Northwest Territories spanned from the Northland border and encompassed Washington, through Oregon, into California, and down into the Tahoe Forest. Lilith's Rocky Mountain domain stretched from Colorado, into the unclaimed portions of New Mexico and Texas, reaching all the way to Albuquerque and to the coastal town of Houston.

This left Simon with the Central Territories, hub of the

western supply routes that spidered out from Idaho and crawled all the way down into Utah and into northern parts of Arizona, while other tendrils stretched from the west coast to east at the Mississippi, and up over the Northland border.

They weren't the only players, and smaller ones swam in the cesspool.

When the dams that supplied much needed water to the desert climes failed, two other groups emerged. When the biggest dam on the Colorado River failed, the Raiders, a violent collection of psychopaths, set up shop in the bones of Nevada and played havoc with the supply lines, hence the importance of the Central Territories.

The Free People, led by Istaqa, salvaged the smaller dams that kept the water flowing to the Southwest deserts. Istaqa was a strategic leader elected by the First Nation people and he managed to keep his people neutral, for the most part. Unfortunately, recent events were forcing his position to shift, creating unusual alliances.

All of the upheaval left a swath of the Southwest open—from Lost Angels, to Phoenix, and encompassing El Paso and San Antonio—until twelve years ago when the Mexican Cartel families ruthlessly recaptured during the tail end of the Border Wars.

All in all, the western half of what used to be the U.S. was a crowded fucking pool, and Reaper, with a justified hard-on for one of the players, was determined to reduce the numbers by at least one. The bastard himself—Michael. His betrayal still haunted Reaper's nightmares and those demons threatened to drag him down into hell if didn't find the vengeance he craved.

To find that vengeance, Reaper created the role of arbitrator, and occasional executioner, in hopes of balancing the karmic scales. He and the other members of Fate's Vultures had carved out their place without owing their allegiance or souls to anyone.

With Havoc, Ruin and Vex at his side, they traveled the Western Territories and offered their services. Sometimes for a price, sometimes because it was simply needed, as was the case with Crane and Pebble Creek. This time, doing a good deed dumped him here, hiding out from the bastard he hunted with the one woman he didn't dare trust. He tried that once before with painfully shitty results.

Knuckles rapped against the door and his name followed, jerking him out his head. "Yeah?"

"You done?" Math's voice was muffled.

Reaper pushed away from the counter, turned, and pulled open the door. As with every time he saw his kid brother's face, it was like looking into a mirror from the past. "Yeah," he stepped around Math, "it's all yours."

"'Bout damn time." Math slipped inside and closed the door behind him.

"You're welcome," Reaper called back, too tired to check Math's attitude. It wouldn't do any good anyway. To bridge the years-deep rift would take more than a matter of days and a handful of bonding moments over the bloodied remains of mutual enemies.

Reaper headed to his saddle bags propped against the couch and got his first good look at the piece of furniture. He gave silent thanks that Lilith lost her earlier bid to banish him to the basement with Havoc because there was no way he could comfortably crash on that.

Lilith.

This time his curse was audible and followed by a soft huff of sardonic humor when he recalled Lilith's frustration at discovering each of the Vultures, except Reaper, was paired up into couples. A fact that blew his mind. Seriously, a few months ago, the Vultures only had themselves to worry about.

Now? Ruin was tied up with Lilith's master spy, Charity. Havoc got tangled with Mercy, an assassin, who just happened to work for Reaper's brother, Math, who somehow managed to snag the prickly heart of Vex, Ruin's twin. The lovefest was enough to make a man consider becoming a hermit.

*Who needed that kind of shit?*

Through the still open door of the past, memories of soft laughter and softer skin drifted out to tease and tempt, but he refused to acknowledge them.

*Nope, never again.*

Since no one else was in the basement, he tossed aside the towel and pulled on a pair of jeans, going commando. He fastened the last button, and his stomach issued a loud, demanding growl. Right, next stop kitchen. He grabbed the damp towel and his bag, then headed for the stairs.

He paused on the main floor and took a quick recon of the layout. There was movement upstairs indicating the others were settling in, but down here remained quiet. A little nosing around and he found a pile of dirty clothes in a small utility room and added his towel. He went back to the living room and dropped his bag behind the couch. He skirted a blanket puddled next to the squat coffee table, paused, turned, bent, picked it up and toss it on the couch, then he aimed for the kitchen.

His bare feet met cool tile and he hit the wall switch just inside the entryway. Light bounced off the fridge, illuminating his goal. He bypassed the island with a sink, pulled open one of the metal doors, and stood there as chilled air brushed his chest. He considered his options, and then started to collect the necessary items for a sandwich. He amended that to two sandwiches when another growl erupted from his stomach.

He dumped the sandwich makings on the counter, then searched the cabinets to unearth a plate. It took him a few minutes to put everything together, then he returned the perishables to the fridge, grabbed a bottle of home brew hiding in the back, and closed the door. There was an apple in a bowl on the counter. He snagged it, sank his teeth in to hold it, and then used his free hand to pick up his plate. Hands and mouth full he headed to the couch.

He was so focused on his destination, he almost ran Lilith over. Their bodies collided and her unexpected squeak was drowned out by his muffled grunt. Curves and heat jolted his system, lit up his nerve endings, and blasted through his iron-control. His dick sprang up in hopeful attention, even as a storm of curses ran through his over-stimulated brain.

She jerked back, one of her hands pressing against his stomach to brace, and the heat of her touch seared through him. His muscles contracted violently, but somehow, he kept his plate and drink safe. Since his mouth was full, he resorted to glaring at the redhead who was now frowning up at him.

"Watch it," she snapped. Her palm pressed deeper into his bare skin as if to push him away.

Fire roared under his skin and ignited a dangerous hunger. He ruthlessly smothered it and despite the apple in his mouth, managed to curl his lip.

She met his glare with one of her own, dropped her hand, and brushed past him.

He turned his head to watch her ass twitch all the way to the kitchen. In his defense, it was a gorgeous ass.

*Too bad the woman attached could be a bitch.*

Despite the uncomfortable ache of his disappointed dick, he finally made it to the couch and settled in. He kicked his bare feet up on the coffee table and worked his way through his food, forcing his body back in line, all the while he listened to the noises coming from the kitchen.

He took in the massive space and had to admit it was the shit. The furniture's heavy wooden frames and supple leather clearly indicated it was custom-made for the room. There was a set of chairs on either side of the oversized couch. A large coffee table was partnered with matching end tables, and everything was arranged to take advantage of the view.

And it was a hell of a view, even at night. The wall of windows framed the stunning panorama of the surrounding mountain's wild beauty, and there was no doubt it would be breath-taking during the day. The smooth blue-grey toned stones of the river rock fireplace stretched up the wall, ending when it hit the wood beams lining the angle ceiling. Inside, a fire burned, the soft snap of wood was accompanied by the faint bite of cedar, adding to the cozy atmosphere.

He settled back into the sectional couch that was quickly becoming a favorite. At six foot two, finding comfortable furniture was a challenge. But this piece would work for tonight's bed. It was way more comfortable than the floor and his feet wouldn't hang off the edge.

The noises in the kitchen stopped, and the light flicked off. He turned his head in time to see Lilith set a shoulder against the archway between the living room and the kitchen. Steam rose from a stoneware mug cradled in her hands and she tilted her head to the side to study him.

There were new strands of white weaving through her tangle of burnished copper, and the colorful beads threaded on the tiny braids scattered throughout her wild mane added an untamed element to her beauty, turning it borderline feral.

He didn't want to admit it, but he liked that look on her.

She took a sip, her thick lashes veiling her eyes even as they did nothing to dampen her stare. She was good at hiding her emotions, and age seemed to have honed her inscrutability. But once upon a time, he was damn good at reading her. Given enough time with her now, he had no doubt he could rediscover those skills.

Tension coiled between them, and he asked, "Scheming?"

She didn't do the expected and snap back, instead she took

her time lowering her cup. "No point in making plans until I know what I'm dealing with." She pushed off the wall, strolled over to the chair closest to her, and set her cup on the table nestled next to it. She sank into the chair, threw one leg over the leather-wrapped, cushioned armrest, and bent the other into the seat as she positioned to watch him. "So, your mole? Who was it?"

Not the least surprised she chose to focus on that first, he finished off his apple, dropped the core on the plate, and set it aside. He grabbed his bottle, settled back, and brought it up to his lips. "Doc Mandy." Then he took a drink.

Stunned shock wiped Lilith's expression clear. "Come again?'

Yeah, that was his reaction when Vex and Math shared that unexpected nugget. Mainly because Doc Mandy was a trusted member of Pebble Creek. Years ago, the doctor's family had been slaughtered, and where most would be left shattered, Mandy survived.

Probably because Crane gave her a reason to keep going by having Mandy serve the community of Pebble Creek. But even that wasn't enough to stop her from turning on everyone. Just added proof of something he already knew—everyone, *every-fucking-one*, had a price. "Long story, but highlights are Mandy's son isn't dead, which gave Michael's right hand bitch, Greer, leverage over Doc. Leverage Greer used with a heavy hand to force Mandy to share information on Pebble Creek, its supply routes, and to set up Crane to be taken out by Raiders. All because Crane took exception to the Raiders transporting kidnapped kids and women to the highest bidder."

As he spoke, some unnamed emotion washed through Lilith's face and there was unexpected sympathy in her voice when she muttered, "Poor Mandy."

"Save your sympathies for someone who deserves it." Yeah,

it was harsh and cold, but Doc's betrayal was way too fresh. Besides, *what the fuck?* One of those kidnapped kids was Lilith's.

Lilith eyed him and tension crept into her languid pose. "You don't think she's deserving?"

"Not a damn bit."

She frowned. "That's harsh."

If Lilith thought he'd back off his opinion, she'd forgotten who she was dealing with. His silence spoke volumes and stated his position loud and clear.

She didn't miss his unforgiving silence and her face stilled, something deep working behind her mask. "She's a mother. A mother will do a great many things for her child."

Something about her reaction bothered Reaper, and he couldn't pinpoint why. He didn't alter his sprawled position but kept his attention sharp. "Yeah, I get that."

"Then why can't you cut her some slack?"

For a moment he wasn't sure he heard her right. "Are you seriously asking me that?"

She didn't elaborate, but sat there, eyes trained on him, and her full lips compressed into a thin line of disapproval.

He dropped his feet from the coffee table and sat up, arms braced on his knees. "She found out that bitch had her kid and instead of trusting those she called friends, she betrayed them in the worst possible way. She's a damn doctor—sworn to save lives. Her betrayal led not only to Crane's death, but several others who were doing nothing but going about their day. They hadn't done a thing to her. Hell, Crane saved her but that didn't stop her from making that decision. So, no, I can't cut her slack." The last word was packed with disgust and sarcasm.

The delicate line of Lilith's jaw grew more pronounced as her chin lifted in a telling move. She was digging in for the underdog. "It was her son. What would you have her do instead?"

"Ask for help," he bit out.

She didn't back down. "It's that easy for you? Risk your child's life on a slim chance that someone would help?"

"Yeah, it is." He held her gaze and his voice dropped into a low tone as unforgiving as he felt. "The chance was far from slim. One word and Crane would've moved heaven and hell to help her get her kid back, but she didn't say word one."

Lilith shifted in the chair and unhooked her leg from the armrest so she could come up on her knees in the seat's deep cushion. "Don't be naïve, Reaper." She dug her fingers into the armrest as she matched his tone. "Crane would've only made that move if it didn't jeopardize him or his territory."

For two days Reaper did his best to ignore what Doc did, but faced with Lilith's defense of the woman's actions, his simmering fury flared. "Just because you put your position above others, doesn't mean everyone else does."

"Yeah, it does." Anger glittered in the jade depths of her gaze and color swept under her cheeks, provoking an unfamiliar reaction he had no desire to admit to. "Who do you think I learned it from?'

"Crane?" Reaper loaded his question with disbelief and followed it with a snort. He deliberately sat back, hitched one leg on the sofa, laid his arm along the couch's back, and shook his head. "Nope, not buying it. Especially considering he's dead because he went after those fuck widgets that were selling kids. Ruthless dicks don't do that."

"They do if it means removing a threat to his supply lines, and trust me, those Raiders were seriously screwing with his business." She released the armrest, reclaimed her drink from the side table, and resettled in the chair. She cradled the cup as she lifted her gaze to his. "Don't fool yourself. I wasn't the only one upset with his recent inability to ensure secure deliveries. And if helping Doc meant going up against Greer and ultimately crossing Michael, Crane would've left her in the wind." She lifted the cup and took a sip.

He hated the inescapable ring of truth in her voice that made it hard not to believe her.

Crane had screwed Lilith on an arms shipment, and if he made the mistake of crossing a woman most took great pains to keep happy, there was no telling who else may have been seriously displeased with Crane before his death. Which meant the simplest way to get rid of a fuck up was find leverage and apply pressure. So, he reluctantly admitted if it hadn't been Doc, it could've easily been someone else. Not that it justified how Crane died, or why, but that was the thing when playing with powerhouses, if you weren't careful, you would get sucker punched when you least expected it.

Still, Reaper couldn't help but poke at her. "Pity we can't ask Crane his take, considering he's dead and all."

"Pity," she agreed without rising to the bait. She waited a beat and switched gears. "What happened to Doc?"

"Turned her and her kid over to Simon with a warning to watch his back."

Lilith arched an eyebrow. "Let me guess, you lost Greer?"

He managed an unconcerned shrug even though he was far from indifferent. "Math and Vex had her pinned, managed to nail her with a couple of bullets, but the bitch went out a two-story window. When Math checked where she fell, all that was left was some serious bloodstains."

She stilled. "No body?"

He shook his head.

Frown lines marred her forehead. "Explains the bounty." She studied him for a moment, her mind clearly elsewhere. When it came back, she asked, "Do you have a plan?"

"Yeah."

She held his gaze, something working behind her eyes. "One that doesn't include a suicide run at the easiest target?"

It was his turn to frown at the unexpected direction of her question. "What the fuck does that mean?"

She rolled her eyes. "Oh, for god's sake, Reaper! It's no secret you have it out for Michael. This—" she waved one hand in the air, "—gives you the perfect excuse to do what you've wanted to do for years."

Her exasperated tone tripped his temper, and he didn't bother reining it in. "Maybe it does, but is that so wrong? After all he's done, the blood he's shed, why the fuck shouldn't I take this opportunity and make the most of it? The world would be a better fucking place without him."

# three

Reaper's cocksure and furious answer hit Lilith's unsettled emotions and ripped open old hurts. She hated the fact that some part of her still cared about him, and forced the question, "And you? Would the world be better without you?"

"Don't."

Undaunted by his clear warning she used mockery to hide years-old pain at his familiar rejection. "Don't what? Challenge the almighty Reaper?"

His bare feet dropped to the floor, and he sat forward on the couch, bracing his arms on his knees. The muscles along his arms tensed as he curled his hands into his fists and the anger in his voice spilled into his face, turning it dark. "Don't pretend to give a fuck about me."

His verbal blade was coated in glacial animosity and sank through skin and bone to slice a lethal blow to her heart, rattling the rickety foundation of what they once built. His certainty that he meant nothing to her hurt to the point of breathlessness and left her stunned.

He didn't give her a chance to respond. "We both know how that game ends."

Her hands tightened on the cup until some part of her worried it would shatter under the pressure. She carefully twisted and set down her cup. *Don't go there, don't go there.* The words beat in her skull like a childish chant to block out the pain and roughened her voice. "Nothing ever changes with you, does it?"

She uncurled, rose from the chair, and walked around the coffee table to grab the blanket tossed over the far edge of the couch. She refused to look at him, afraid if she did, all those ugly things she never got a chance to say when he left her would come tumbling out, taking them someplace they shouldn't go. But there was one thing that needed to be said, because this time, there was more than just the two of them on the line.

"You may not care if you live or die, but there are those who do. Even now." She wrapped the blanket over shoulders like a shawl. "You taking on Michael is like putting a gun to your head and pulling the trigger." She moved as she spoke, afraid if she or the words stopped, the storm of fury and hurt raging in her chest would escape and have her taking her fists to the arrogant ass watching her. "But, just like before, you don't care. Hell, so long as you got what you wanted, you never did." She ruthlessly locked her emotions down and finally looked at him. "And just like before," her voice carried a distinct mocking chill, "the rest of us just have to deal with it, whether we want to or not."

His lip curled and despite the goatee and beard, his derision was clear. "The only one who doesn't agree to taking that bastard out is you."

He was so wrong. She wanted Michael's blood with a frightening hunger. Always had. The self-appointed king of the Northwest had destroyed her chance at happiness, and now he threatened her child, but sharing that with Reaper wasn't safe. Hell, thinking it wasn't safe.

She shook her head, turned away, and walked to the wall of windows, pulling the blanket tight. She stared into the night-blind glass and tried to hold on to her fraying temper, but it was a frustrating endeavor.

Behind her, unaware of her thoughts, Reaper kept inflicting his punishment. "Talk about never changing, babe."

She caught his movement as he rose from the couch through the glass and braced as he closed in and stopped at her back. Not close enough to touch, but she could feel him, hovering like a looming storm.

The low lash of his icy voice struck with unerring accuracy. "Here you are, all these years later, still desperate to make the world bend to your rules. Even after your daughter gets taken, you still refuse to wise up to what's barreling straight towards you." He met her gaze in the glass, the dark depths burning with contempt. "Shouldn't surprise me, you put one person, and only one person, ahead of every fucking thing else."

She gritted her teeth.

*Don't fall for it, don't.*

He leaned in without touching her, his breath feathering over her ear, and viciously twisted his verbal blade. "You."

She took the hit, unsurprised how deep it sank. Guilt, resentment, and anger followed in its wake and somewhere deep where she couldn't see it, one last foolish, surviving hope shattered under the impact. She fought back the pain with anger and hissed, "Fuck you, Reaper!"

He held her gaze and his lips twisted into a cruel smile and drove their conversation right into the disaster of their shared past. "Any time, babe, because you know I'm right."

The abused tethers holding her temper snapped. "No. You're not." Her hand holding the blanket turned bloodless and she turned with a studied deliberateness to coldly inform him, "You never were."

He straightened and folded his arms over his chest, his entire body screaming arrogance and disdain.

Her volatile emotions created a pulsing ache in her head and her free hand, under the cover of the blanket, curled into a fist, her nails digging into her palms. It took serious discipline not to claw that cocky superiority off his face. In attempt to refrain from inflicting bodily harm, she sucked in a deep breath, lifted her chin, and met the heavy weight of judgement in his gaze, knowing he was using his height to try and cow her.

*As if that ever worked before.*

"I've always put you first." Her voice was a harsh whisper as it crawled out of the crush of emotions.

His gaze narrowed, his jaw flexed, and he dipped down until they were nearly nose to nose. "I call bullshit." Each word was bitten off.

She sneered as furious disgust filled her. "Of course, you do." Not in the least bit intimidated, she rocked up on her toes, ignoring her flash of satisfaction when he jerked his head back, and drilled a finger into his chest. "But I wasn't the one to walk away."

He curled long fingers around her wrist in a painless, but unbreakable hold and held her still. "Didn't you?"

Intense resentment seared into furious life with his question, and she tugged against his hold. "The door didn't close behind my ass."

Disgust twisted his features as he ignored her struggles. "You didn't leave me much choice. Not with you hand wrapped around my balls trying to turn me into your lapdog."

It took a second for her brain to process his unexpected accusation, but when it did, she could only repeat, "Lapdog?"

"Yeah, sweetheart." Now it was his turn to sneer. "What

else was I supposed to think after your little ultimatum?" He thrust her arm away.

The force of his action knocked her off balance. To avoid smashing into him and falling, she let go of the blanket and slapped her palms against his naked chest. The heat of him seared through her skin and her fingers to curled until her nails bit flesh, but she barely noticed. Fury, resentment, and bitterness roared through her, escaping the iron grip of shackles normally locked tight, as he resurrected the old, stupid argument. "You thick-headed, stubborn dick!" The last came out on a shout.

His spine snapped straight, and he stepped back as if to shake off her touch. "How am I the dick when you were the bitch who wanted me to play second fiddle to your damn position?"

She was physically shaking under the unrelenting onslaught of emotions and self-preservation and control was forgotten. "You're the dick because when all was said and done, you left me, you asshole!"

"And it was the best damn decision of my life," he roared back.

She jerked back as if slapped when the unmistakable truth echoed through the room. She stared at him as a bone-chilling ice swept over her incandescent emotions.

But he wasn't done taking his pound of flesh. "No way was I going to tie myself to a woman who didn't have my back. Good thing I learned your priorities early."

"*My* priorities?" Something bright and bitter rose, cracking the ice. "What about yours, Reaper? You were supposed to be my partner. Do you remember that?"

"Not like you needed me, did you, Rocky Mountain Queen?" He raked her head to toe with a contemptuous look, then met her gaze and curled his lip. "You never wanted a partner, so I gave you exactly what you wanted."

She matched his scathing look with one of her own. "Right, because I wanted a man who bailed on me to get his fucking vengeance." Unable to contain the storm inside, she rocked forward and slammed her hands into his chest, her palms stinging with the contract. "Some fucking partner you are!"

He was knocked back a few steps, his chest marred by red marks. He caught her wrists before she could do it again and yanked her against him. "Knock it off, Lilith."

"No!" She jerked against his hold, but he didn't let her go. She rose to her toes, unapologetically invaded his personal space, and got in his face, not bothering to hide years of resentment and pain. "You left me. I wanted you. I needed you."

Something flared deep in his eyes, but drowning under the riptide of emotions, she ignored it and rode a vindictive instinct she rarely acknowledged and blurted out, "You left me alone and pregnant, so I did what I needed to raise our daughter."

His face blanked, his head jerked back, and his grip disappeared so fast it was a wonder it didn't leave marks on her skin. "Our what?"

"Our daughter." She enunciated each word, driving her point home with ruthless accuracy. "The one beautiful thing you left me. The one thing I won't let you destroy."

# four

Reaper wrapped his hands around her upper arms before she got the last word out, his grip tight enough to leave bruises. He backed her into the window with terrifying speed and intensity.

Her spine met the chilled glass and her heart pounded as whatever hold he had on his temper evaporated.

He held her there, his face set in implacable lines and his eyes burned as he gave her a hard shake. "Tell me you're fuckin' joking, Lilith."

"Why should I?" Her temper was more than a match for his. In an abrupt move she brought her arms up, broke his hold, and shoved her palms against his chest, forcing him back. She took advantage of the narrow opening and sidestepped him. "So you can try and excuse the fact that you're a total asshole?"

He caught her arm and held her in place. "You hide my kid from me and I'm the asshole?"

She glared at him over her shoulder. "I never hid her."

"Didn't you?"

"No." She jerked her arm free and then pivoted until she

faced him. "But it would be hard to see through the dust you kicked up in your rush to leave. Nor did you look back."

"You sure as shit didn't give me a reason to, did you?" His hands curled and uncurled at his side.

She set her bare feet, folded her arms, and angled her chin. "Why should I?"

"If she's mine—"

"If?" Lilith's question was a sibilant whip, and she seriously considered killing him. Instead, she raked a hand through her hair, ignoring the bite of pain when her fingers snagged on the strands. "There's no *if* about it."

He shot her a dark look. "You lied to me once before."

Embers of whatever they once shared turned to dead ash and she slipped behind the coldly imperious mask she spent years creating. She held his furious gaze and her lips twisted as she gave him the bitter truth. "Believe what you want, you always do."

A screaming silence fell and stretched for a long moment. Reaper broke first, muttering an oath before he turned from her to stare out the window. "This better not be another one of your games."

She didn't check her snort of disgust and shared a brutal truth. "You aren't worth that much to me. Not anymore."

Reaper's body gave a small jerk, but his expression was blurred by the dark glass. "You had no right to keep her from me."

"Didn't I? I'm her mother." Because the hurt he inflicted ran deep, she was deliberately cruel. "While you—you're simply a genetic donor." She knew she scored when his head twitched, but she wasn't done. "Besides, if I wasn't enough for you to stay, there was no way in hell I'd risk my baby's heart with you."

A hesitant, "Mom?" dropped into the middle of their argument before he could respond.

Lilith spun around and faced the hall, absently feeling Reaper do the same behind her.

A barefoot, sleep-tousled, Tabby stood there, her freckles standing out in her pale face, her green eyes swimming in tears. "It's him?"

The stricken expression on her daughter's face lanced Lilith's heart and in that moment, as unfair as it was, she knew one of her many pending decisions had been made for her. "Sweetheart, I ca—"

Tabby spun on a heel and dashed back down the hall towards her room.

"Tabby!" Lilith went to follow only to be brought up short by Reaper's grip on her arm. She spun on him with a snarled curse and jerked her arm free. "Let go."

"Lilith—"

"No," she cut him off and shook her head as a door slammed down the hall. "You don't exist. Not until I talk to her."

His face darkened. "Dammit, I have a right to talk to my daughter."

"No, you don't," Lilith snapped, patience long forgotten. "You gave up that right when you left us." Her tone turned harsh. "She's mine to protect, even from you."

"I'm not the one who lied to her."

She didn't give an inch even as she took the deserved hit. "No, you're just the bastard who walked away." She threw out a hand. "Do what you do best, Reaper, and get out!"

Heart-sore and angry, Lilith spun around and headed after Tabby.

This time, it was her turn to not look back.

# five

Reaper stood barefoot and shirtless with his hands braced on the deck's railing, the cool night air doing jack to ease his temper or calm his spinning thoughts. He struggled with the fallout of Lilith's bomb. His mind bounced from memory to memory like one of those old pinball machines where unexpected levers slammed the small ball into unforgiving surfaces, only to ricochet into the next damn hit, as he tried to find what he missed years ago.

The first time he saw Lilith, she was reading the riot act to some underling in the infiltration unit she ran during the Border Wars. As he watched her tear the idiot a new one, he was alternately amused, horny, and curious. Curious enough that he didn't mind working to get her attention. Something that took longer than he initially expected, but then again nothing was ever easy when it came to Lilith.

Their dance had been unusual, at least for him. When it came to women, he didn't have to work very hard for company, even less during the never-ending skirmishes of the Border War. But his dance with Lilith was unusual. She was night and day apart from the camp tramps and he found he couldn't walk away.

At first, he excused his unexpected behavior on his need to win, but in the end that had shit-all to do with it. It wasn't just how he got off on their arguments because neither one was used to bending for someone else, or how the never-ending craving that crawled through his veins that only fucking her would dull, but it was the other times—the ones that existed outside their harsh reality.

Like when they lay skin to skin in the dead of night sharing conversations about their worries, secrets, and dreams. The brush of her hand before they headed out on their separate missions. The way they could set their egos aside to work together as if they shared the same mind. It wasn't until years later that he realized that his anger with her at the end wasn't solely because he felt betrayed by his lover, which was bad enough, but his perceived betrayal by his best friend, which was worse.

*If that wasn't a kick in the nuts, now she shares he has a daughter? What the fuck?*

His fingers dug into the rough wood, and he clenched his teeth as he swallowed down his furious growl. *What kind of woman doesn't tell a man he has a fucking kid?*

As if waiting for the question, Lilith's voice echoed in his brain and sank a vicious fist into his gut. *I did what I needed to raise our daughter.*

Despite his shocked anger he hadn't missed the storm of fury and fear in Lilith's eyes as she faced him, but it didn't ease his resentment. What? Did she think he'd take the kid away from her or some shit? Lilith should know him better than that, for fuck's sake.

He had a right to get to know his daughter. *His daughter.*

Two words he never thought would be his. An image of the girl as she stood at the edge of the hall seared his gray matter, her green eyes, lighter than Lilith's dark jade, and wet with tears. An unexpected twinge of remorse caught him off guard.

Though maybe it shouldn't, considering he had spent some time with her in Pebble Creek and discovered he liked the girl. She and a couple of other kids, including Istaqa's son, had been rescued by Simon and Crane, who turned them over to Doc Mandy to watch over until their people could be contacted. Reaper had stopped by on the daily to offer what support he could to the traumatized kids.

Istaqa's son was a bundle of helpless rage, one of the girls was nearly catatonic, and Tabby had remained stubbornly mute. No one knew who Tabby belonged to until Charity showed up, and the little girl finally broke her silence. When Charity and Ruin left to hunt down the one responsible, Tabby decided, until her mother arrived, she would be Reaper's shadow.

At the time, he didn't fight it because as Lilith's daughter, Tabby was a high value target, so her safest place was at his side. His initial reaction to learning Lilith had a daughter careened between disbelief and resentment, but it eventually settled into an unusual need to protect. It didn't take Tabby long to worm her way under his skin.

He struggled with the idea of Lilith as a mother even as the prove of that fact tagged along. It didn't fit with the woman he knew, the woman who ran roughshod over everyone to secure a power seat. If asked, he would have laughed his ass off at the thought of Lilith having a single maternal bone in her curvy little body. Hell, the fact she managed to keep Tabby's existence quiet for years was a minor miracle. It was smart, because if it was known, it would leave Lilith exposed to her enemies.

It wasn't until Lilith showed up and the girl ran into her mother's arms, that the relationship hit home and put to rest any doubts he carried. He wasn't blind and clearly Tabby was a mini-Lilith. It was there in the tangle of reds, golds, and browns, that were a darker version of her mother's copper-edged red, and the up-tilted, lighter eyes.

*"You're simply a genetic donor."*

Damn Lilith for being right. He wrapped a hand around the back of his neck and squeezed. Nothing of him was reflected in that little girl. He dropped his hand and pressed the heel of his palm into the twinge in his chest.

Faced with the truth, his brain disagreed with her assessment and resurrected the rare instances of the kid's sneaky humor, or the familiar stubborn set of her chin when he tweaked her temper in an effort to distract her. Then there was the way she watched those around her, as if constantly calculating her options. That wary core of stubborn grit might be a result of surviving her time with the Raiders, but maybe it existed before they got their filthy hands on her. Either way, being at the mercy of the Raiders had hardened that core and taught her a callous lesson on surviving in the real world.

His thoughts wandered down the dark road of what-if's and it wasn't hard for him to imagine what Tabby endured to gain that painful knowledge. An unexpected desire to hunt down the bastards and make them pay—again took hold. To rein in his blood-drenched fantasies, he focused other, more subtle signs that pointed to his paternal position in Tabby's life. Like the way she rubbed her thumb over her finger knuckle when she was deep in thought. A quirk she shared not only with him, but her uncle, Math.

Thinking of his younger brother led to recalling how Math greeted Lilith tonight, and how, days ago, Math called Reaper out about leaving her all those years ago. Knowing what he knew now, it was obvious to Reaper that Math had known about Tabby for a long fucking time. Which made Reaper wonder what, exactly, was the relationship between the two? Before his brain could flesh out that thought, he slapped it back, pissed and mortified that he might be jealous.

Despite his knee-jerk taunt to Lilith on Tabby's parentage, Reaper knew better. Lilith was many things, but she wouldn't lie about this—not outright. Tabitha was his daughter. He found that accepting that fact was a hell of a lot easier than dealing with the rest of his argument with Lilith, like her denying him his daughter because she chased his ass out.

*How fucking fair was that?*

Had she told him she was pregnant all those years ago, he might have had second thoughts.

The snarky voice of his internal bastard who never cut his ass any slack piped up. *Would you really, asshole?*

Unflinching honesty made him pause and he winced. He admitted with brutal clarity—if only to himself—that no, it wouldn't have stopped him from leaving.

Not then. The blood was too fresh, the betrayal too bitter.

Long locked away, unforgiving memories took his private admission as permission and broke free, providing stark reminders of how one defining moment rocked his world and validated Lilith decision.

He braced his elbows on the top railing, bent his head, and dragged a hand through his damp hair as he stared unseeingly at his feet. Between one breath and the next, the memories surged, drowning out the present and he was back in the carnage-choked streets of Lost Angels during the last few vicious weeks of the Border Wars.

COATED IN DUST AND BLOOD, Havoc crouched next to him, his face grim.

Reaper coughed and tried to recapture enough air to talk. "Any breathin'?"

"Not a one." Havoc curled an arm around his waist and hauled him to his feet.

"Goddammit!" Sick fury filled Reaper and edged aside the guilt that bit at his soul. He and Havoc hobbled to the dubious protection of a crumbling storefront. "What the fuck happened to my backup?" His question ended on a pain-filled hiss as Havoc maneuvered him to the ground and exerted pressure on the wound in Reaper's thigh.

Havoc dumped the med-pack next to Reaper. "Dunno." He set their AK-15s, an old Russian Special Forces weapon, to the side, and put his knife to Reaper's pants, exposing the wound. "Dammit, Reaper."

*Yeah, those buried boomers always managed to do serious damage.*

Reaper's response was limited to a grunt since it was the only thing that could escape his locked jaw.

Havoc cleaned what he could and assessed Reaper's mangled thigh.

Sporadic explosions and gunfire sounded nearby and almost drowned out the screams still ringing in Reaper's ears.

Havoc grabbed Reaper's hand and shoved it against the crimson-stained field bandage. "Hold this." He waited for Reaper to do as instructed, and then dug through the med-pack. "Got to stop the bleeding before you join them."

*Wish to god I had.*

Reaper couldn't stop the thought or the guilt that pierced his rage. Even though the bodies of his once tight-knit unit were blocks away, the brutal images of their last moments haunted him. He dropped his head against the pitted brick he and Havoc were currently crouched behind. As protection it sucked ass, but it was better than nothing.

Pain seared up his thigh and he throttled back a pained

roar as black ate at his vision. He blinked, bringing the world back into focus. Havoc's grim face was aimed at Reaper's thigh now dusted with—*what the hell was that?* His voice was hoarse when he asked his friend, "What is that shit?"

Havoc slapped the bandage back in place and quickly wrapped it tight. "Black pepper."

"Don't need seasoning, brother, not dead yet."

Medical supplied filled Havoc's hands and they stilled above the med-pack, as he leveled a hard stare at Reaper. "Smartass."

"Better than a dumbass." The familiar retort fell flat and didn't even earn a lip twitch.

"It'll stop the bleeding."

"Should've just cauterized it, would've hurt less." Better to keep bitching about shit they had no control over, otherwise Reaper's questionable hold on his rage might slip.

"Stop being a baby."

If he didn't hurt so much, Reaper would've flipped him off.

A sudden burst of nearby gunfire chased an explosion that rained dust and pieces of brick over them. They froze with an anticipatory stillness and every sense went on alert. Shouts drifted through the heavy summer air and twisted through the ravaged streets of Lost Angels.

Havoc and Reaper shared a silent look. In the next moment, Havoc slung the med-pack in place, reached for their weapons, passed one to Reaper, and then scanned their surroundings

Reaper clutched his gun, set his teeth and used the wall to get to his feet, as a cold sweat broke out. His balance was fuckin' shot, but there was no way in hell he was sticking around and risking Havoc's life. Reaper had enough blood on his hands.

Once upright and ready to move out, he tapped Havoc on

the shoulder. Together, they slipped out of their small refuge, stuck close to the walls, and used the late afternoon shadows to disguise their movements. They cleared the first block and made their way down a narrow back alley before running into trouble.

Indistinct shapes moved in the haze ahead left by untended fires, their movements easily recognizable—a standard search pattern.

*Shit! They needed a way out of this rat maze.*

Havoc was clearly thinking the same thing because he stepped back and forced Reaper to do the same. Reaper put his back to Havoc's and watched their six, searching for an exit. They worked their way backwards until Reaper found what they needed.

A gap in the building's stone wall, half hidden by the surrounding rubble. It was tight, but wounded and seriously outnumbered, neither he nor Havoc had a burning desire to become a guest of the Cartel forces, so tight worked.

They moved as fast as they dared and squeezed through the opening. After leaving some skin behind to mark their passage, they used the decimated interior to slip away.

Once clear, they headed back out to the streets, and used the haze and cover where possible. It wasn't easy, but Havoc took point and trusted Reaper to follow. By the time they circled around their pursuers, the only thing that kept Reaper upright and moving was the furious strength of his will and the vow he made to return and exact retribution.

His men had trusted him to see them through hell and now their blood stained the ground. He wanted answers, answers that might dull the bitter edge of his guilt and soothe the vicious doubts he harbored for the last few months. The possibility that he had trusted the wrong man sank its lethal fangs deep. Two days ago, he sent word to Michael for backup.

The return response indicated it was en route and would be in place when needed.

Then things went to shit.

The promised backup was a fucking ghost. Despite the skill of his unit, each man had fallen, one by one, under the merciless barrage of Cartel forces.

As he and Havoc stumbled through the streets, Reaper's driving need for answers grew, and his rage deepened. He swore he would find the answers—one way or the other.

THE SOUND of the door sliding open behind him brought Reaper out of the past. He stiffened but didn't turn as a familiar presence crossed the deck and took up a position next to him. A breeze kicked up and sent a chill over his bare chest. A small, involuntary shiver escaped.

"Catch."

Reaper's head turned as Havoc tossed a bundle of material his way. He caught it before it hit his face. He shook out the long sleeve shirt and pulled it on. As his head popped out of the collar, he pulled his hair free, shoved the sleeves above his wrists, and finally met Havoc's eerie sea-green gaze. He took in Havoc's position  hip braced against the railing, thick arms crossed over his chest—and knew a come-to-Jesus moment loomed.

Sure enough, Havoc asked, "What now?"

Reaper grimaced. "You heard?"

Havoc raised an eyebrow, the one bisected by a small, curved scar. "Hard to miss." A hint of sarcasm colored his deep voice. "Every time the two of you share breathing space, smart people know to duck for cover."

Havoc had been with Reaper and Lilith since day one, and had played witness, sometimes referee, for many of their arguments. He turned back to stare into the night and muttered, "This is so fucked."

Havoc shifted until he mimicked Reaper's position. "So what else is new?"

"Well, I have a daughter," Reaper shot back in a dry voice. "Figure that should be more than enough."

"Congrats and all that shit."

Reaper snorted at Havoc's deadpanned delivery and rubbed his hands over his face.

But his friend wasn't done sharing his wisdom. "Going to do anything about it?"

*Was he? Hell, if he knew.* "Like?"

"Like being a part of her life?"

Leave it to Havoc to cut to the heart of this mess. It was strange to think of being a father, especially since he didn't have a clue how to go about it. Reaper dropped his hands and stared at the roadmap of scars and nicks that lined his skin. He spent his life using his hands to bring about vengeance and justice. How did that work when it came to a child? If all he had to do was protect her, he was set, but he knew damn good and well there was more to being a father than that. What did he know about being a dad? Wasn't like he had any sterling examples to pull from.

When Reaper didn't say anything, Havoc pressed. "You planning on walking away?"

*Fuck, no!*

His reaction hit hard and immediate, revealing something he never acknowledged—a hunger for a family of his own. Of course, wanting shit wasn't the same as doing the right thing.

The thing was, if he chose to stick around, his priorities would have to change and therein lay the real issue.

The kid deserved better than a patchwork father figure.

Even knowing that didn't ease his resentment triggered by everyone's judgement lately. Not that they weren't justified. For years his whole focus was centered on bringing Michael to his knees. Something he couldn't exactly walk away from now. "Got a few things going on."

Havoc gave a disbelieving snort. "More important than getting to know your kid?" He didn't wait for Reaper to respond, probably because Havoc knew better. Instead, he kept picking. "Know you, brother. Know exactly what you want, what you've wanted for years, but got to ask—you succeed with this, what's next?"

Havoc's question cold-cocked him, because it wasn't one Reaper had ever considered. "Haven't thought that far," he admitted.

Havoc sucked in a quiet breath at his brutally honest response. "Maybe you should."

Decidedly uncomfortable with the conversation, Reaper snapped, "Maybe I'll end up dead." As soon as the words left his mouth, he regretted them. "Shit, sorry."

Silence stretched between them, and he looked out over the yard. Normally Havoc's taciturn approach worked for Reaper. Tonight, not so much. Knowing his friend wouldn't let this go, Reaper muttered, "Pretty sure I'm not going to win father of the year any time soon."

Plus, his one and only example of fatherhood spent most of his time beating on his ma and whoring around. Well, until someone shoved a knife in his gut outside some bar.

Once he was out of the picture, Reaper and his ma skipped town and set up in New Seattle. Then Ma met Math's dad, lost Math's dad, and then got sick and died, which left a fifteen-year-old Reaper in charge of a thirteen-year-old Math. Not ready for the daddy role then, he handed Math over to a female friend of Ma's, then Reaper hit the road.

*"And look how well that turned out,"* his inner asshole pointed out.

So, yeah, being a father—probably not in his skillset. On the other hand, taking Michael out definitely fell within his expertise.

Havoc's voice was thoughtful as he kept his attention on the woods. "Maybe not, but think as young as she is, she might take what she can get."

Havoc was forgetting one very important hurdle—Tabby's mother. Reaper shook his head and bitterness laced his voice. "Pretty sure Lilith would run interference if I tried to step up."

Havoc straightened. "Maybe, maybe not. Won't know 'til you try." He tapped the railing twice with his knuckles until Reaper looked at him. "Question is, you willing to try?"

Was he? Hell, better question might be, should he? Reaper didn't have an answer, but he refused to lie to the man who was more of a brother to him than Math. "Don't know if I can."

As expected, Havoc didn't let Reaper wiggle off his moral hook. "Why?"

Reaper gave him the easiest answer. "Not sure Lilith will let me."

"Like that ever stopped you before."

*True.* Reaper raked a hand through his hair and considered his options. If he gave in to Lilith's temper, he could kiss any chance he had at being a part of Tabby's life goodbye. If he pushed this, it meant he was taking on Lilith, their shared past, and a daughter. What that entailed tripped through his mind, and left his heart torn between a strange hope and a resentful denial. Yet he couldn't dodge the biggest challenge of the whole situation.

"Honestly, I don't think I can live in her world." His

admission was reluctant, and he was uncomfortable with all its implications.

Havoc rubbed his chin, the rasp of his goatee over skin audible. "Maybe her world isn't what you think."

"Talking about Lilith?" Math stepped soundlessly out to the deck, his feet bare under the dark pants. His equally dark shirt was unbuttoned, but his hands gripped the ends of the towel draped over his shoulders. He stood there for a moment, the light behind him masking his expression in shadows. He moved closer and replaced the mask with a carefully schooled expression set among the faint bruises from his last go around with Reaper's fists.

Something about that look bothered Reaper, much like having his fur ruffled in the wrong direction and left him irritated. *Fuckin' great, just what he needed, his little brother joining the kick-Reaper-in-the-nuts party.* "Eavesdropping?"

Math took Reaper's bad-tempered question in stride. "I'm a spy. It's what I do."

"You're an assassin," Reaper snapped.

Math flashed Reaper a cocky grin. "That too." He tilted his head and rubbed the towel over his hair. "Something to remember if you're going to toss them away again."

Despite Math's casual tone, his warning was unmistakable and hit with uncomfortable accuracy, leaving Reaper disgruntled. "Don't start."

Undaunted, Math stopped with his hair drying routine and shrugged. "Just stating a fact."

Reminded once again that Math and Lilith shared something he couldn't touch, Reaper endured the annoying bite of jealousy. It sucked that he couldn't sink his fist into Math's face, at least not without Vex riding his ass. Instead, he flipped his brother off. "What's the deal with you and Lilith?" As soon as he asked the question, he wished he could call it back.

Math's grin was both arrogant and sly, and he wasted no time pouncing on what Reaper exposed. "Jealous?"

*Un-fucking-fortunately, yeah.* Not that he'd admit it to the smirking little shit. Instead, he decided to go with the easier response of anger. "No, trying to figure out how long you knew I had a daughter and didn't fucking share."

## six

**B**ehind Reaper Havoc heaved a heavy sigh, but kept his mouth shut. Whatever humor Math felt was wiped from his face by Reaper's deliberate provocation until what was left behind was the ruthless assassin forged in years and experience.

A twisted spark of pride lit deep in Reaper's chest at the lethal proof of what his brother had become. Not that he'd ever admit it. He couldn't, not with the way things were between them. There was a shit-ton of issues between them and most of the time, they managed to limit it to verbal parrying, but occasionally it required an exchange of fists.

This time Math stuck with verbal hits. "You want that story, ask Lilith."

Blood or not, Reaper didn't take anyone's shit. He faced his brother, folded his arms over his chest, lifted his chin, he held Math's gaze, and bit out, "I'm asking you."

Math wasn't the least bit cowed and repeated, "You want to know, go to Lilith."

Disgusted with Math's cagey response, Reaper let out a frustrated growl. "Your cryptic shit is annoying as hell."

The ruthless assassin disappeared under a shit-eating grin

as Math moved to Reaper's other side. "Ain't it." His grin faded and his gaze drifted to Havoc, then came back to Reaper, all signs of teasing gone. "I'm going to have to agree with Havoc."

Reaper wasn't following Math's topic switch and wasn't sure he wanted to, still he asked, "About?"

"Lilith." Math leaned against the railing and idly scratched his chest. "You might be too blind to see it, but Tabby's kidnapping might have her rethinking her options."

"Right." Reaper didn't tone down the extra-large portion of sarcasm.

No way in hell would Lilith give up everything she spent years fighting for. If anything, he would bet good money that what happened to Tabby only reinforced Lilith's determination to reign her world with a ruthless grip. On one level, he got it, but he wasn't in a hurry to repeat past mistakes and hang his ass out there just so she could kick it as she walked right the fuck over it. Again. "There's something you both seem to be forgetting."

Havoc muttered something Reaper couldn't catch and shared a look with Math. Before Reaper could pick it apart, Math arched a brow and said, "Oh please, enlighten us."

Reaper narrowed his eyes, looked between his best friend and younger brother, and felt like he was missing something important. Cautiously he explained the obvious. "Nothing and no one will ever cause Lilith to walk away from what she's worked years to get. She's got a death grip on that position because it's more important than everything and everyone. Which is why I left when I did."

"Calling bullshit." The surprisingly harsh announcement came from Havoc.

Reaper jerked his chin up and with clear condescension said, "Alright, smartass, share your wisdom."

Havoc studied Reaper as the second ticked by, his

thoughts hidden. Finally, he came to some internal decision and met Reaper's gaze. "Sure you can handle it?"

A ball of dread lodged in Reaper's gut at the unmistakable weight of Havoc's question, but he sucked it up and made a bring-it-on motion with his fingers.

Havoc didn't pull any punches. "She was right about one thing, you were determined to leave."

Out of the corner of his eye, Reaper caught Math's silent nod of agreement and gritted his teeth.

"Kind of like a bear with a sore paw," Havoc continued in a pitiless voice. "Made you deaf to everyone."

"Don't remember hearing you." Reaper's defensive retort couldn't erase the guilt caused by Havoc's comment.

Havoc took the hit without blinking and kept relentlessly pushing. "Only proves my point." He grimaced. "Do you know she came to me?" He read Reaper's stunned expression and shook his head. "You kept brushing her off, I think she finally got desperate. Asked me to talk to you." He turned back to the dark yard. "God knows I tried. Hell, I lost track of how many times I tried talking your ass off the ledge, but you were determined to jump. I finally gave up. Figured the only way to keep you alive was to stay at your side and remind you why you were still breathing."

Reaper opened his mouth to defend himself but stopped as what Havoc said penetrated. Memories rose, the edges blurred with bitter anger, but after eleven years, it wasn't quite so close or blinding. Without that shield, Reaper couldn't escape the fact that Havoc was right.

At the time, haunted by those he lost and driven by the craving for vengeance, he shoved everything and everyone away. He hadn't cared if he made it out alive or not. Every time he slipped too far into the darkness, only Havoc's stubborn grip had hauled Reaper's ass back.

But, looking back now, he could pinpoint the moment his

blind anger started to ease—it was when they hauled Vex and Ruin out of the streets of Portland. Being in charge of the teenage twins, who dragged some serious demons in their wake, gave Reaper a focus outside of his own needs because he hadn't been able to stand aside as they struggled.

Slowly, the Vultures came together and eased the ache of his lost unit, until he stopped taunting death on a regular basis, but even they couldn't shake his hold on his plans for that back-stabbing bastard, Michael.

Nope, that honor could now be claimed by Lilith, who made the first dent by telling him they shared a daughter. The ramifications of that started the hairline fractures that threaded his revenge-focused determination and left him questioning what he really wanted.

"The question now is," Havoc's quietly serious voice broke into Reaper's light bulb moment. "What do you want more? Michael's head or your daughter?"

Caught between his warring desires Reaper couldn't stop his equally soft question. "Does it have to be one or the other?"

He wasn't surprised when the men standing at his side remained ominously silent.

Lilith closed Tabby's door for the second time that night, her heart ragged, and rested her head against the door. Safe from her daughter's accusing eyes, she let out a shuddering breath. This part of motherhood sucked. Her explanation of Reaper to Tabby had left her heart-sore and mentally exhausted. Throw in her volatile relationship with Reaper, and the combination left her numb which was probably for the best considering she was about to walk into another argument.

She lifted her head as a shadow at the mouth of the hall moved.

"You okay?"

"Nope." Lilith pushed off the door, crossed to Charity's side and was startled when the younger woman gave her a quick squeeze. She returned it awkwardly.

As sad as it was Charity was the closest thing she had to a friend, but for a woman in Lilith's position, friends were a lethal liability. At least as Lilith's master spy, Charity could take care of herself. Not only was it a critical skill for a

'Hound, it was a huge plus in Lilith's book because Tabby would always have a protector in the lethal blonde.

They headed towards the living room and Lilith asked, "Where's your partner in crime?"

Charity flashed a smug grin. "Upstairs, making bets with Vex and Mercy."

"Dare I ask?" She didn't really need to since there was no way anyone in this house had missed the rather loud exchange between her and Reaper. Having an argument within hearing range of a bunch of assassins, spies, and mercenaries was like waving a red flag in front of a bull—you were just asking to get reamed.

Charity shook her head. "I wouldn't."

Lilith sighed, "That bad?" When Charity gave her a look filled with sly humor, Lilith shook her head. "Right."

They hit the living room and found it empty. The glass doors leading to the deck stood open spilling light into the night. Havoc faced the house and was leaning against the railing, his arms folded over his chest. He caught sight of them but didn't stop talking to Reaper who was next to him, back to the cabin, arms braced on the railing. Math stood on Reaper's other side, and as soon as he spotted Lilith and Charity, he turned on his heel and headed their way.

Lilith stopped and Charity halted next to her. Together they waited for Math to approach. Lilith watched Math cross the room and it was like she stepped back in time. He was a younger version of Reaper, before Michael poisoned him. That image arrowed through Lilith's heart and pierced the veil of numbness with a bittersweet regret.

Math stopped in front of her as sympathy lurked in his steel blue eyes. "Tabby?"

"Sleeping."

"Good." He searched her face. "She'll be okay, Lilith."

She didn't answer but clenched her jaw.

He reminded her, "She'd have to find out sooner or later, you know that."

As much as it sucked, he was right. He had warned her for years to give Tabby the truth of who her father was, but Lilith refused. First, she justified her decision with Tabby's age, but as the years passed, she continued to put it off because she couldn't find the right way to approach the whole messy situation. In the end it hadn't mattered because the decision was made for her. "I would have rather it been later."

*Or maybe even, never, but what she wanted never seemed to count for shit.*

Math got close, wrapped an arm around her shoulders, and dragged her against his chest. She didn't fight his hold and let him pull her in until her forehead rested against his chest. She closed her eyes and took a single moment to relish his silent support.

Years ago, when Tabby was barely a toddler, Math had shown up on the run from Greer, with a warning about a hit on Lilith. The minute she saw him she knew he had to be connected to Reaper. The similarities between the two men were unmistakable. Then he proceeded to watch Lilith's back until they could remove the threat.

During that time, Math connected the dots on who Tabby, and by extension Lilith, belonged to. When he confronted her, she responded by holding a blade to his throat. His answer was a bitter smile before he shared his own story of loss and betrayal a la Reaper. In the end, the events from that horrendous three-day stretch bound them tighter than blood.

She drew in a deep breath, lifted her head, and pulled back.

Math read her unspoken signal, dropped his arm, and gave her space. "You'll be okay, Lil."

She gave him a small smile she didn't feel. Her gaze slipped past him to see Havoc squeeze Reaper's shoulder, push off the railing, and head inside. Her fingers curled into fists. "Don't have much of a choice."

Math turned his head as Havoc stepped inside, surrounded by an air of determination and his attention on Lilith, and warned, "Brace, darlin'."

Lilith pulled her emotions close, locked them down, and waited for Reaper's closest friend to take his shot. *Some things never changed.*

Just like years earlier, she wasn't sure how she felt about Havoc. Part of her was grateful to him for keeping Reaper breathing all these years, but the other part wanted to rage and rail at the fact Reaper obviously held Havoc's opinion higher than anyone else's, including hers. Still, he wasn't someone to underestimate. She barely noticed when Math and Charity left, granting privacy to the two of them.

"Lilith." His deep voice hadn't changed.

"Havoc." Her gaze drifted beyond him to Reaper who still had his back to them. She couldn't help but ask, "Is he okay?"

Havoc's intimidating features softened. "Better question, you okay?"

She was startled by his unexpected question and jerked her attention back to him. "What?"

The normally taciturn man shook his head with a small lip twitch. "You still can't hide it worth shit."

Her heart gave a hard thump, her mouth turned dry, but she still managed to say, "Hide what?"

His eyes warmed. "Babe, you've loved that stubborn ass from the get-go. Never did listen to my warnings."

She kept silent since she couldn't deny it. What was there to say? Love didn't solve shit, it only created more problems.

He studied her with an uncomfortable perceptiveness and suddenly switched topics. "You remember that safe house?"

His question tipped her off balance and unlocked the

memories that pressed for attention tonight. "Of course," she murmured as the past swept the cabin away.

*She opened the door to the safe house and her heart clenched as she came face-to-face with two familiar, bloodstained, grim-faced men. She stepped aside, not bothering to ask what happened—easy enough to see things had not gone according to Reaper's plan.*

*Havoc lifted his chin in silent thanks as he maneuvered a stumbling Reaper through the door. As soon as they cleared the entry, she stuck her head out to scan the street. Nothing but drifting smoke and early evening sun and shadows. She stepped back, then threw the door closed and set the locks.*

*She turned and crossed the small room to help Havoc get Reaper down to the water-stained mattress. "Tell me."*

*"Ambush."*

*Havoc's one-word answer triggered a slew of silent curses and snuffed out the sliver of hope that betrayal wasn't going to blindside Reaper.*

*Dammit to hell.*

*For the last couple of weeks, she warned Reaper to watch his back, but he brushed her off and her temper turned her warnings into arguments. She hadn't wanted to be proven right. Not like this.*

Back in the present, as if he shared her trip down memory lane, Havoc gritted out, "You wanted to get him out of Michael's reach. He didn't listen."

His blunt reminder triggered old defenses, and she snapped, "I was there, I remember."

"Get it now, why you let him leave." There was a strange intensity to Havoc's gaze.

She kept her mouth shut and fought her urge to squirm.

Havoc didn't miss a thing and a spark of understanding infused his face. "You knew then, didn't you?"

She couldn't hold his gaze and looked away. The day she

learned she carried Tabby had been the best and worst of her life. The joy of knowing she was pregnant had slowly been snuffed out by the reality of the situation with the man she loved.

Reaper was obsessed with Michael, to the point that nothing else penetrated. The risks he took scared even her. When she realized that she wouldn't be able to keep her baby and Reaper safe, something in her soul tore, but she made her choice and watched Reaper walk away.

Havoc leaned in, his voice low and filled with something close to compassion. "Know I don't have the right to ask, but woman, fight for him one more time, yeah?"

He didn't wait for her answer, not that she had one, and headed upstairs.

Havoc's request echoed in her head and held her in place as a million and one questions swirled. Finally, she did a whole-body shake, like a dog settling his wet fur, and forced her feet to move.

When it came to Reaper, she wasn't sure she was ready to fight for anything, but for Tabby's sake, she could at least try to have a civil conversation.

*You share a child with the man, be the reasonable one.*

Right, because one of them had to be the adult.

She heaved a sigh, snagged the blanket puddled on the floor near the door and wrapped it around her shoulders as she stepped out onto the deck. Reaper's back tightened as she crossed the cool planks, settled into one of the padded chairs, and tucked her bare feet under her. Then she waited.

Finally, he turned, his face half hidden by the night, and leaned back against the rail. It was a painfully familiar posture reminiscent of when things weren't broken between them—arms folded, sleeves shoved up to reveal the dark ink scrolling over his forearms, jean-clad legs crossed at the ankles, feet bare. As the wash of memories swept over her, she steeled herself against the heartache and met his dark gaze.

He spoke first. "How is she?"

"Sleeping." She matched his cautious tone.

Reaper's chin dipped in acknowledgement, and he dropped his attention to his feet. "She's a good kid."

His unexpected compliment indicated she wasn't the only one trying to be an adult about this. Maybe they'd get through this relatively unscathed. "Thanks."

Reaper lifted his head, uncrossed his arms, and gripped the railing. "What do we do now?"

*"Oh, there's a 'we' now, is there?"* Lilith strangled the cynical internal voice with a stern reminder to be civil, for Tabby's sake. When his jaw flexed as he waited for her to answer, she figured she hadn't succeeded in keeping her burst of inner bitchiness hidden. She fought and found a neutral response that wouldn't aggravate things. "That depends on you."

Reaper grimaced. "Seems to be tonight's theme."

She gripped her blanket tighter and choked back a storm of accusations that would get her nowhere and blow the being the adult thing to dust. "That's not an answer."

*There, that was adult enough, right?*

Reaper shifted out of the shadows and studied her.

Unfortunately, she was out of practice and couldn't read his expression.

His gaze moved beyond her, to the house, and returned. "I'm shitty father material." His declaration was flat.

She bit her lip and kept her agreement silent.

His gaze narrowed, and a thread of determination ran through what he said next. "But I want a chance to know her."

It was Lilith's turn to look away as she struggled with the bitter sting of his demand. Why did hearing that hurt so much? She wanted to deny him but knew that reaction stemmed from their shared past. This wasn't about her, or what they once shared, this was about Tabby. Her baby deserves to know her father. And as much as she bitched about the man, she couldn't deny he deserved a chance to get to know her—no, their—daughter.

She tried to find her way through the maze of emotions created by a mother's protective need and a woman's disillusioned heart, and it wasn't easy. When she tore herself free, the emotional aftermath left her voice rough. "Why?"

Reaper's forehead furrowed, his brows lowered, and an edge of frustration bled through his answer. "She's my daughter." He made the statement as if it addressed everything.

The thing was, it did, and it didn't. With obviously strained patience, Lilith agreed. "Yes, she is, but she's also mine." She held up her hand in warning when he opened his mouth to argue. "I meant what I said. I won't let you hurt her."

A war raged in the depths of his indigo eyes, but it was locked away from his voice. "I get that."

She arched a brow even as she ached to bend, just a little. Unfortunately, that was a slippery slope to certain heartbreak. "Do you?"

Reaper pushed away from the railing and curled a hand around the back of his neck as he paced in front of her. "What do you want from me, Lilith?" He spun on his heel and dropped his hands to his hips. "I'm not planning on hurting the kid. You want me to promise to never leave her?" He gave a short, violent shake of his head. "That's never going to happen."

Lilith couldn't stop her bitter-choked laugh at his denial because it seemed they were right back where they started— her hoping he would stand at her side and him searching for the nearest exit. "Oh, I know that better than you, Reaper."

Anger swirled through her, and she couldn't sit still, but she was afraid if she got up, she wouldn't hesitate to get in his face and that would not end well. Lilith's breath hitched at the thought of Tabby suffering even a hint of the heartache her mother had already endured.

Always too observant, Reaper didn't miss her reaction. He took a couple of steps towards her, then stopped and searched her face. His voice was low, careful, as if treading over fragile ground. "You really ready to revisit this argument, now?"

"No." She shoved to her feet and left the blanket behind. "And not just no, but hell no." She spun away from temptation, stalked to the railing, curled her palms against the night-cooled wood, and held on tight. "The time to hash out that argument is long gone."

She heard the revealing harshness in her voice and took a deep breath, focusing on the wildness in front of her as she regathered her composure. Then she reminded both of them, "This is about Tabby, and only Tabby."

"So, I'll ask again." Reaper's tone softened, and he moved to stand next to her, not touching, but close enough to set the tension between them to a low burn. "What do you want from me?"

A minute ticked by before she turned her head and met his gaze, her voice hard. "What I want is for you to go away, but since that's not happening, I want you to be careful with her. She's been through hell and she's looking for safety." She refused to acknowledge his wince and didn't back down. It killed her to expose what his presence was doing to her, but this had shit-all to do with what she was feeling, this was about keeping her daughter's heart unbroken. "She's curious about you. Answer her questions, but don't lead her on. If you do, when you leave, she'll believe it was her fault." She didn't look away as she admitted, "I might suck at keeping her safe, but in this, I won't fail her."

Reaper studied her with an uncomfortable intensity, but she refused to look away. "Her kidnapping wasn't your fault."

"Wasn't it?" She knew her smile was as bitter, but it wasn't as if he wasn't thinking the same thing. He made no bones how he felt about her and her choices. When it came to Tabby, he deserved honesty because she was too important not to be truthful. "Me being me, made my daughter a target. You acknowledge her as yours, and more than Michael will be hunting her." Because what she would admit next hurt, she turned away. "I'm not sure I can keep her safe from everyone."

She was startled when Reaper brushed a finger under her chin to regain her attention. "She was taken because Michael's a dick of the highest order."

"That he is," she agreed because he so was, "but it doesn't change the facts. We can't charge in and take him out. The repercussions…" She trailed off as Reaper traced her jaw with an absentminded caress and fought back a shiver. His touch short circuited her brain and tripped her pulse. Her tongue darted out to wet her suddenly dry lips.

"Yeah," his gaze followed the telling movement and darkened, "the repercussions would be a bitch," he murmured his agreement and dropped his hand.

She retreated a single step, then stopped, unsure if she was relieved or disappointed at the loss of that soft touch. She took a couple of deep, unobtrusive breaths until the cool night air lulled the whisper of temptation quiet.

"We can keep her safe," he vowed.

God, it was dangerous how much she wanted to believe that, but she knew better so her response was soft, but undeniable. "There is no 'we'."

With implacable resolved, he said, "There can be."

# eight

Stunned by the unmistakable resolve in his voice, she was unprepared when he closed what little distance was between them and caged her between him and the railing, leaving her no escape. Instinctively, her hands went to his chest and pushed, as she tried to regain some space so she could make sense of his intentions. Her gaze lifted to his when he didn't budge. "But... you can't—"

"Give me a chance."

Shocked by his demand, she stared at him wordlessly as a fragile hope struggled for purchase.

His face twitched with an unnamed emotion before hardening with determination. "Give me a chance to be her father."

The ache in her chest deepened as that stupid, foolish, barely there promise withered. Grimly she hung on to the reminder that this was about Tabby. "You've got a bounty on your head. You won't be around."

In the navy depths of his eyes a fierce light burned, and he let go of the railing to grip her hips, holding her in place. "If I can take care of that, will you let me try?"

Advice from her long-gone father whispered through her mind. *"Don't forget, girl, everything in this life is a negotiation."*

Havoc's request chased after it. *"Fight for him one more time."*

Did she dare give him a chance? Was it worth the cost? She hadn't gotten as far as she had without taking a few risks. Granted this one was bigger than most, but with Tabby's future at stake... she made her choice and gave the first inch. Unconsciously, she gripped his shirt. "Answer something for me?"

Reaper's nod was slow in coming.

"If it meant keeping Tabby safe, would you walk away from Michael?"

Reaper's face went carefully blank, and his fingers dug into her hips before gentling.

Her heart sank.

He didn't break their stare when he asked, "Are you asking me to?"

There was nothing in his voice for her to work with, so she gave his question the consideration it deserved. *Was she?* She wasn't sure, but she needed to know who would win if he had to make the choice. It was a question she never dared to ask the first time, but this time she couldn't afford not to. "Yes."

Instead of answering her, he asked a question of his own. "Would you?"

To make sure she understood what he was asking, she clarified, "Would I leave Michael to it, walk away from everything, if it kept Tabby safe?"

Reaper dipped his chin in acknowledgement.

She wasn't surprised Reaper would turn the question around. Hell, she wrestled with it for years. Michael wasn't just a threat to Tabby, he was a threat to anyone west of the Mississippi. He spent years ruthlessly manipulating and scheming for every thread of power he could grasp, and he would never be happy until he was king in truth. Which meant anyone who stood in his way earned a top spot on his hit list.

As Lilith clawed her way to the top of the Rockies, she fought long and hard to keep those who looked to her safe, but over the last couple of years things changed and the price to protect those that were hers rose. Then came Tabby's kidnapping and Lilith was faced with the realization that she would trade everything and everyone to keep her girl safe.

*So, to answer Reaper's question...* she lifted her chin and met his eyes without flinching. "Yes."

Reaper's face went slack in stunned surprise as he released her hips before he quickly regained his composure. "Seriously?"

"In a fucking heartbeat." Lilith's voice was low and vicious. "Everything I've done, the deals I've made, the favors I've collected, none of that stopped Tabby from being taken and hurt." Her hands, still tangled in his shirt fisted, as the turmoil Tabby endured haunted her. "I can't change the past, but I can damn well ensure she's out of the line of fire from here on out."

His thick lashes dropped and rose in a slow blink as he gripped the railing, caging her in once more. "You'd really walk away from it all?"

"If it kept Tabby safe, yes." She let go of his shirt and shook her head, easily reading his doubt. It wasn't hard, she remembered it well since this topic generally led to their worst arguments. She went to push his arm away so she could leave, but he refused to move his hands and free her. With an irritated hiss, she gave him her back and curled her hands over the deck's rail. "You always thought it was about the power," she bit out. "I told you it wasn't, but you wouldn't listen."

He crowded close until the heat of him pressed along her

spine and his scent coiled around her. "Apparently, I didn't listen to anyone."

She looked over her shoulder, caught his frown, and was hit with a bittersweet pang. "I just wanted a chance to live my life on my terms." How sad was it that they were having this conversation now, when it was years too late to solve anything? She ignored the naïve thought and turned back to face the night. "You remember what I told you about my family?"

Some of Reaper's tension eased and he settled against her back, his hands on either side of hers on the railing. "They supplied weapons to most of the west coast."

She stared at his hands and absently noted he carried new ink and scars. "It was a lucrative business, and the family name was highly respected."

"And feared." His deep voice sounded close to her ear.

"And feared," she agreed softly. With her thoughts in the past, she let go of the rail and gave in to the temptation to touch him, covering his hand with hers. "When you're used to getting that kind of attention, you begin to believe your own hype. My father believed he was untouchable and made some questionable deals. When the markers were called in, he decided the best way to pay them back was to make sure no one was left to collect. It didn't take long before he pissed off the wrong people."

Memories pushed forward—hiding while masked figures burst in, bullets flying, her parents falling, her brother dragging her deeper into a hidden passageway as she stumbled along for what felt like forever, only to emerge into a night lit by the flames that devoured her home and into the arms of the three waiting men. "I watched my parents die as my brother dragged me away."

"Jake."

"Jake." She swallowed down the sudden, unexpected lump in her throat. Jake, and gave a small cough to clear the rasp in her throat. When she continued, her voice was stronger. "He was determined to pay blood back with blood."

*Just like Reaper with Michael.* Which was why she handled things between them the way she did. "We spent the next couple of years hunting down all those involved. I got tired of it."

It wasn't the killings that got to her, no, those were warranted so no regrets there. It was the sleepless nights, the endlessly looking over her shoulder, and never being able to settle that wore her down. "We had taken out all of our targets but one. Jake had a plan. I didn't agree, but he wouldn't listen. We argued. I refused to go with him, hoping he would rethink things." Even she could hear the self-recrimination in her voice. "It didn't."

Under her palm, Reaper turned his hand over until he could weave his fingers through hers. "His choice."

"Maybe, but he never got a chance to change his mind." Jake had been gone for three days before she started to retrace his steps only to find him and his target dead. She stood over the last of her family and swore it would be the last time. Then came Reaper. "So, no, it wasn't about power, it was about keeping those I loved safe."

His fingers squeezed hers. "You think walking away will keep you and Tabby safe."

Maybe, maybe not, but one thing was certain, something had to change. "I think, even if Michael's not around, who I am and what I hold guarantees me more enemies than I can afford. Definitely more than Tabby can."

"I'll give you that." He rubbed his chin against the top of her head in an absentminded gesture of comfort as he stood at her back.

She closed her eyes and tried not to reveal how much his closeness was affecting her.

"Hate to burst your bubble, babe, but as long as Michael's alive, no matter what you do, she won't be safe."

Lilith's lashes fluttered open, but she wasn't seeing the night in front of her but the deeply held fears that haunted her. "You won't give up Michael."

Reaper let go of her hand, shifted around her side, cupped her cheek, and added gentle pressure until she faced him. When he had her eyes, he softly said, "Not as long as he's a threat to our daughter."

There it was—the cruel heart of the matter. She knew Reaper was right. The whole reason she started finagling alliances with Fate's Vultures, Simon, and Istaqa was because of that truth. If Michael ceased to exist, so did his threat to Tabby. Not to mention it would make transitioning to her next role a hell of a lot easier.

With no recourse left, she gave into the inevitable. The mother stepped aside to let the Rocky Mountain Queen rule. "Do you have an actual plan to de-fang Michael?"

"Since I've been eating dust to get here, not yet." Reaper's tone was wry as he dropped his hand, finally stepped back, and set her free. "But got a meet tomorrow that might help."

She pushed off the railing and moved to his side. "With who?"

He walked to the door and flashed her an enigmatic smile. "Come with me and find out."

She stilled as she recognized the anticipatory light in his eyes from all the times she witnessed it, just before he did something stupid. She frowned. "Am I there as a partner or backup?"

His smile shifted to a full-fledged mischievous grin. "You were always good at multi-tasking, babe." He strolled inside and threw over his shoulder, "We'll leave after breakfast."

"Dammit, Reaper."

He ignored her and disappeared inside.

Since she couldn't trust him not to get dead, it seemed she was taking a field trip tomorrow. "Well, shit."

# nine

Someone was watching him. Reaper lifted the arm he used to block the morning sunlight and cracked open heavy lids only to come face-to-face with Tabby. She perched on the arm of the couch near his feet like some weird wild child gargoyle. He blinked a couple of times bringing her dark green eyes, in a strangely intense face, into focus and he found he couldn't look away from the questions that swam in her unsettling gaze. Their staring contest played out for a few tense moments before she broke it. "So, you're my dad."

*Right, guess they were having this conversation now.*

"Yep." Reaper stretched, dug his feet into the couch and pushed up until he sat against the other arm. A yawn stretched his jaw, and he rubbed a hand over his face, hoping his brain would kick into gear without the jumpstart of caffeine. He dropped a foot to the floor and twisted to nab the leather tie from the coffee table. He pulled his hair out of his face and tied it off.

Tabby slid down the couch's arm to the cushion, drew up her legs, and rested her folded arms on her knees, then set her chin on top. Throughout her entire move she watched him watch her. "We have matching points."

He aimed a puzzled look her way not quite following the kid's thought.

Reading him, she straightened and pulled back her sleep knotted hair, then indicated her widow's peak. "See?"

He grinned at the barely hidden pride and defiance in her tone and rubbed a finger over his V-shaped hairline. "Guess we do."

Tabby's gaze faltered and color rushed under her cheeks. She wrapped her arms around her legs and frowned at her knees, her finger rubbing her over her knuckle.

Reaper gently nudged her leg with his bare foot and regain her attention. When she looked up, he deliberately looked down to her hands and her nervous tell, then back up. "We share that too."

She looked to her hands and stilled her anxious movement. Her long dark lashes fluttered for a few seconds and a frown marred her forehead, but eventually she lifted her gaze to his. Her "Yeah," was soft as something big worked behind her eyes.

At her uncertain tone a dull ache settled in his chest. He didn't need to be a mind reader to guess at her thoughts. If their positions had been reversed, he'd have a shit ton of difficult questions with no idea where to start. He might be the adult now but even he wasn't sure how to navigate this, so he started with, "Tabby, if you want to know, just ask me."

The poor kid couldn't hide her emotions if she tried. Anger, hope, fear, it was all there in her face. He was unsurprised when determination finally won out and figured if she could find the courage to ask, he'd find the same to answer.

Her chin lifted, and her voice carried the typical weight of youthful doubt, as if she expected the adults around her to sugar coat things. "About anything?"

"Anything." He laid his arm along the back of the couch,

bent his one leg so his knee rested against the couch, and use his other foot to press against the floor until his spine settled into the corner. As comfortable as he could get considering the circumstances, he met her guarded gaze and tried to reassure her. "I promise I'll be as honest as I can."

His daughter—*would he ever get use to that?*—nibbled her lower lip as she studied the now open space between them and then took her time repositioning until she was sitting tailor fashion on the end of the couch, facing him. She mirrored her mother's backbone and took him at his word. "Mom said you didn't know."

Her statement carried a mix of accusation and pleading as if she didn't want to doubt her mom but couldn't help but do so. Since he hadn't had a chance to ask Lilith about her conversation with Tabby he was on shaky ground. He wondered how deep to take things only to remember Lilith's warning from last night about playing it straight. He could do that, so he locked down his reactions and kept his voice and face level and calm. "I didn't."

His admission earned him a nod, as if Tabby used it to confirm her mom was on the up and up. In her lap, her finger rubbed over her knuckle again, and she visibly took a big breath. "Are you mad?" It came out in a rush, and Reaper's confusion must have been obvious because she added, "That you have a kid?"

As hard as she tried, she couldn't conceal her anxiety and her simple question scraped over his battered heart. In that moment, it hit him hard that this conversation would be critical in how the two of them moved forward. "I wasn't mad, more like stunned." When she frowned, he was quick to clarify, "In a good way." Figuring their Q&A session should go both ways, he asked, "How about you?"

Confusion replaced the frown, and she angled her head. "What about me?"

Reaper pointed to himself with his thumb. "This what you expected for a dad?"

Her grin was small and so was the teasing glint in her eye, but she didn't balk at his question. "You're taller than I expected."

His chuckle was quiet.

Her amusement faded and was replaced by a hint of worry. "Actually, I thought—" Her eyes dropped to her lap and color once again flooded her cheeks.

Reaper did his best to lead her through what appeared to be treacherous territory. "Thought, what?"

She didn't look up as her finger went back and forth over her knuckle, her voice low and reluctant, her shoulders hunched. "I thought maybe Math was my dad or something."

Her admission stung like a bitch and reignited that green-eyed streak he was beginning to detest. He struggled to formulate a response that wouldn't make him sound like a self-centered punk when she proved a kid's mind was more convoluted than any adult's.

"Thing was, I knew Mom hadn't told my father," she snuck a look at him before correcting herself, "you, about me." She stopped again and bit her lip.

He stayed quiet, giving her a chance to say what she needed to say.

Her shoulder's straightened and she finally lifted her eyes to his. "Mom explained it was her choice, not yours, because she knew you were leaving. But she got this look whenever Math showed up, and he was always nice to me, like, I don't know, as if I mattered to him." Her shoulders rose and fell in an awkward shrug. "So, it made me wonder if it was Math. Then after..." Her voice broke and her hands fisted in her lap as the skin around her eyes tightened.

He was rocked by the sudden urge to gather her close, but he held back, knowing it wouldn't be accepted, not yet. It hurt, deep where the wounds would never show, to witness her struggle. He held her gaze, silently offering his support the only way she would allow as she fought her demons.

She swallowed hard and her voice was tight. "I met you, and you and Math look really alike." She gave another uncomfortable shrug. "Mom got all tense and weird whenever your name was said. Then watching you two at Pebble Creek, it made me wonder." She turned away and admitted, "I started kind of hoping it was you." She shot him another quick look from under her lashes and waited for his reaction.

*Okay, shit ton of things to unpack there.*

His mind spun, and he kept his face still, not wanting to give her an excuse to clam up on him while he worked through her revelations. The kid was scarily intuitive.

On some strange level he was pleased at Lilith's unsettled reaction around him. Especially since she managed to knock his ass off balance all the damn time. Then there was his reluctant gratefulness that Math had ensured this child knew she was important. He hated owing anyone anything, but in this, his younger brother had incurred a deep debt. Add in the curious melting sensation that Tabby's barely disguised hope in her last statement struck, and Reaper knew without a doubt that his life was forever tangled with this little girl.

The barrage of unfamiliar emotions left his throat tight. He coughed to clear it and his voice was gruff as he started to unravel what his daughter bravely shared. He decided it was easiest to start at the beginning. "Your mom and I met during the Border Wars. Do you know about those?"

Tabby nodded. "Yeah, we learned all about it last year."

He doubted school covered "all about" a years-long territorial dispute, but he was curious what it entailed. "Yeah?"

At his skeptical question she rolled her eyes and proceeded to elaborate. "The five Cartel families wanted to redraw the southern borders, but the Territories and Free People weren't down with that. After years of fighting, the Territories and the Free People came up with the Southland Agreement which granted Lost Angels, Phoenix, El Paso, and San Antonio to the Cartels. If anyone violates the Agreement, the Free People can deny them water rights."

Her bare bones recital was a simplified version of the messy shit that painted years in blood, but for this discussion, it worked. "Right." He rubbed his chin. "During the wars, your mom and I worked together and became friends, then more than friends."

Considering Tabby was alive and breathing, he figured that explanation was safe to use. Especially when she wrinkled her nose with the typical disdain of youth.

His momentary amusement faded, and he took them further into the weeds. "I led an infiltration unit."

"Like Mom's?" Her question proved she was far more aware of what was happening around her than most kids. Probably because she was Lilith's daughter.

"Close," he said. "Mine specialized in urban warfare, your mom's was in reconnaissance."

"Spying." There was a hint of pride in her voice.

It made his lips twitch. "Yeah, spying." Although he knew he had to address this next bit it was going to be a bitch. "Thing was, your mom found out about you right after I lost my unit."

Compassion softened Tabby's face. "All of them?"

Her quiet question snuck under his scars and Reaper could only nod.

"What happened?" she asked in a near whisper, as if afraid her saying it too loud would breathe life into the ghosts swirling around him.

Memories rushed him, shooting his vow to stay emotionally neutral to hell. He endured the painful surge of nightmares and bit out, "I trusted the wrong person."

"That sucks."

Her heartfelt sentiment hit Reaper deep and left his voice gruff. "Yeah, it does." He dragged in a big breath, then blew it out. "I was fuckin' pissed." Catching his verbal slip, he winced. "Sorry."

She waved it off with a roll of her eyes. "I've heard worse, trust me."

*Right, moving on then.* "I wasn't in a position where your mom felt she could share about you." He braced, met Tabby's gaze, and shared the harsh truth he learned last night. "She made the right decision."

Tears pooled in Tabby's eyes and seeing them made him feel like shit, but he promised not to lie to her, no matter how difficult. God knew he didn't want to admit this next part, but in this he was the adult. Time to reap what he sowed.

"Back then, I wasn't—I couldn't—" He dropped his head, rubbed hand over the back of his neck, and blew out a hard, frustrated breath, as he searched for the words that refused to come. He lifted his head, met her gaze, and difficult though it was, made the harsh admission, "Your mom was right not to say anything. I couldn't be a good dad, not then."

A tear spilled over and slid down her cheek as she looked away.

Unable to stop himself, he reached out, brushed the tear away, and dropped his hand to her knee. He gave her a gentle squeeze and waited until she looked at him. "Your mom loves you, and when she loves, she's very protective." It was truth he always understood, no matter what went down between him and Lilith.

Tabby fought back the tears and a mutinous look settled on her face. "What about you?"

Not understanding, he frowned and asked, "What about me?"

Her chin notched up and a combative glint lit her eyes. "Well, she had to love you to get me, right?"

*Out of the mouth of babes...*

He gave a slow blink at a question he never expected to field, and managed a hesitant nod, thinking that response couldn't get him into trouble.

"So, what about protecting you?"

Obviously, trouble was determined to find him. "Me?"

She nodded.

In that moment, confronted with his too perceptive child, he decided he would rather face down a strung-out Raider. Naked.

How to explain the emotional melee he shared with her mother? Especially when he rarely managed to navigate it unscathed? He thought how Lilith shared her reasons for choosing between him or her daughter and he carefully chose his answer. "Sometimes the best way to protect those you love, is to let them go."

She studied him, obviously thinking it over. Eventually her lip curled, and she gave a snort that was downright cute. "Is that like that saying, 'If you love something set it free, if it comes back, it's yours'?"

Taken aback, he wondered where the hell she picked that old saying up from. Before he could get sidetracked, he refocused. "Something like it, I guess."

"That's stupid," she muttered. "I mean," she waved a hand to emphasize her disgust, "if someone loves you, or you love someone, why would you leave?"

Despite her brave face, there was an underlying note of insecurity and blame in her comment. He consciously gentled his voice and shared, "Because sometimes love isn't enough."

Confusion clouded Tabby's eyes, and he decided it was too early to get into the complexities of that conversation, so he redirected their conversation. "What happened, happened. Can't change it."

She crossed her arms over her chest and a stubborn light bloomed worrying him that she was about to argue her point, but instead she gave a reluctant, "Fine." Her gaze narrowed and pinned him in place. "So, when whatever it is that's happening is done, are you going to leave?"

*God, she was a tough little bugger.*

Her questions echoed what he asked himself, but the problem was, he still didn't have an answer. At least not one that would give her the reassurance she was looking for. Instead, he gave her something else to hold him to. "How about you ask me again when we finish dealing with what's happening first?"

She worried her bottom lip and reluctantly accepted his offer. "Deal."

Since he didn't want to give her time to change her mind, he pushed out of the couch, turned, and held out a hand for her. "Okay, before you continue your interrogation, how about breakfast?"

Her nod was enthusiastic as she grabbed his hand and let him pull her up. Then he and his daughter hit the kitchen to scrounge up food.

# ten

Together Reaper and Tabby gathered and mixed the ingredients for pancakes. Tabby set up the griddle and when he took over cooking, she took a seat at the counter. For a minute or so, quiet reigned as he set the coffee to brew, then went back to the batter and flipped pancakes. When they were done, he set a small stack in front of her.

She pulled the plate close and reached for the dish holding the butter. "Reaper?"

"Yeah?"

"What's your favorite color?"

"Blue."

She grinned. "Mine too."

With that her curiosity floodgates opened, and Tabby peppered him with head spinning questions, whatever reticence she had taking a hike. He sipped his coffee and did his best to keep up.

*Could she call Math uncle now?* That's up to Math, so she should ask him.

*Where did he live?* No place in particular, mainly on the road.

*Could she go with him on one of his trips?* That's a question for your mom.

*Could she ride on his bike?* That one was easy—yes.

The questions kept coming until Charity and Mercy stumbled in and homed in on the coffee first, food second. By the time Lilith showed, Tabby had wound down and was sitting as close to Reaper as she could without being in his lap as they both finished up their breakfast.

Lilith stopped short in the entryway to the kitchen, her eyes widening, but she covered her shock fast, and moved forward, offering her daughter a smile. "Morning, baby."

"Mom!" Tabby jumped from her seat and hit Lilith hard enough to rock her.

With the kid's enthusiastic greeting, Reaper's concern about how things stood between mom and daughter eased. Lilith cupped her little girl's cheek, her witchy face softening under a depth of emotion he never thought he would witness. The image of the two and the emotion it invoked wrapped around his scarred heart and found purchase, leaving him unsettled.

When Lilith looked up, her familiar mask was firmly in place. Breakfast was had with sporadic conversations as people stumbled in, caffeinated, then left to get ready for the day.

Reaper was repacking his bag when he noticed Lilith pull Charity aside for a quiet conversation. From his spot by the couch, he couldn't hear what was said, but it was obvious when the conversation went wired.

Charity's normally relaxed movements took on an intense edge that did nothing to ruffle the merciless stillness that Lilith emanated. Curious about their exchange but not wanting to trigger an argument first thing in the morning, he kept his questions for later. And there would be a later, he promised himself, because something was definitely up.

It wasn't long before everyone filtered back into the

kitchen and dining room. Finished with his packing, Reaper went into the kitchen while Lilith sent Tabby off to her room to get dressed. After topping off his coffee, he turned to find Lilith waiting for her turn. He moved out of her way, faced the group at the table, and leaned back against the counter.

One end of the table was taken by Ruin and Charity, while Havoc and Mercy took the other. A bench provided seating between them on the far side. Currently, Vex was tucked between Math's legs, absently dancing a throwing blade through her fingers.

"Got a meeting in town that might net us a name behind the bounty." His announcement dropped into the murmur of side conversations and shut them down. He raised his cup, took a sip, and waited for the fallout.

"Might not be the name you're hoping for." Not surprisingly, Ruin spoke up first as he straddled a chair, popped the last piece of toast in his mouth, and chewed.

Actually, Reaper was damn sure it wouldn't be. "Probably not, but it'll give us a starting point."

"I'll be going with him," Lilith stated from beside him, her tone leaving no room for argument.

Ruin shared a look with Charity and then said, "No offense, but don't think the big man needs a shadow."

Lilith's lips quirked in a small, unamused curve, but she didn't turn her attention from refilling her cup. "He can't waltz in all by his lonesome." She finished her pour, then turned to Reaper with an arched brow. "Unless you're hoping to make someone easy money."

He refused to rise to her unspoken challenge and simply said, "Wasn't planning on announcing my arrival to all and sundry."

She made a soft hum as she stepped around him. She moved to one of the unoccupied chairs at the counter and sat down. She angled her seat so she could see both the group at the table and Reaper, her coffee cup cradled between her hands. "Correct me if I'm wrong, but isn't everyone but Charity on that bounty?"

Reaper waited until she lifted her gaze back to his. "And?"

"And," she drew the word out as she did a deliberate scan of the room's occupants. "You guys don't exactly blend. Not even a little bit."

Her observation irritated him, even if it was valid. Thing was, he couldn't just hide out, he needed to be out there, making his own moves. Sitting around wasn't his style. Something he was all too certain Lilith knew. Before he could decide which one of them was trying to start an argument—him or her, Charity chimed in. "We can fix that."

Lilith shot the other woman a narrow-eyed look.

Charity's expression remained unruffled. "We make a few changes, then split up, no one will be the wiser."

Lilith's knuckles whitened as her grip tightened on her cup. Her, "Split up?" warred with his, "What kind of changes?"

Charity shot a look at Ruin from under her lashes and got a slight nod in return indicating whatever she was about to suggest, she'd already discussed with Ruin. She turned back to Lilith and Reaper, and answered Reaper's question. "Nothing too major. You and Math are the most recognizable, so I say get rid of the beard and hair." She ran a critical eye over him. "Maybe wear something other than black."

He ran a hand over his shoulder length hair, and then the heavy growth on his chin, as he considered her suggestion. It was doable. On the road, opportunities for haircuts and shaves were few and far between. Not to mention how irritating it was when shit grew out. Hence the long hair and beard.

"I say keep the all black motif," Math drawled from his sprawled position at the table. He lifted a half-eaten piece of bacon towards his brother, his amusement evident. "He can be Lilith's bodyguard, and no one will think twice."

"Define splitting up, Charity." Lilith's demand cut through the back and forth.

Before the blonde could answer, Ruin cut in. "You aren't the only ones who need to make a run into town."

Charity put a hand on his arm but answered Lilith. "Ruin and I need to go in." She held Lilith's glare and added, "You wanted me to check on those two projects."

Lilith frowned. "Those can wait."

"No, they can't." Charity's tone didn't change, but there was no missing the infusion of steel or the tension that stretched between the two women.

For a moment it appeared as if Lilith might argue, but surprisingly she relented, and the strange tension dissipated. The unusual exchange made Reaper all the more curious about what, exactly, was involved with those projects.

Charity sat back in her chair and her shoulder brushed Ruin's. "Besides, there were a few things from our trip to New Seattle we needed to follow up on."

Not seeing the connection, Reaper looked to Ruin. "From here?"

"Yeah." All traces of Ruin's earlier laid-back attitude was gone. "Whatever is happening up there, it's got a long ass reach."

Reaper had sent Charity and Ruin to New Seattle to find out who was pulling the strings on the Raiders and the kidnapped kids. They made some progress and were getting close before shit went down with Greer that ended up with their faces on wanted posters. The timing of everything was worrying. When Lilith turned to him, he caught a reflection of his thoughts in her face.

*Yeah, this was a cluster fuck.*

He looked back to the couple. "You're certain it ties in?"

Ruin and Charity did another one of those silent conversation looks, before Charity turned back and grimaced. "Certain? No, but..."

"You've got a feeling," Lilith finished for her.

Charity gave her a nod. "Something tells me we're close."

As Lilith's Bloodhound, Charity trafficked in secrets and worked within the murky world of whispers. Her instincts were honed to an incredible edge and demanded respect.

A worried frown creased Lilith's forehead. "I need you with Tabby."

"Tabs will be in good hands," Vex cut in before Charity could say anything. "Promise."

Lilith shot the other woman a glare.

Undaunted, Vex continued to dance her blade through her fingers. "She wanted to work on her knife skills." With a quick twist of her wrist, the mesmerizing dance of metal stopped. "She's getting good." There was a glint of pride in her amber eyes as she shot Lilith a crazy ass grin and put the blade away. "Besides, Math and I wouldn't mind the break."

Reaper muffled his snort. Since Math and Vex managed to stir up a hornet's nest during their recent trip to the Hole they were better off staying out of sight. Their behavior had left the Hole's de facto leader, Trip, foaming at the mouth.

Math rolled one of Vex's beaded braids through his fingers. "We really wouldn't. Not to mention if Greer is the one behind this shit, she's got a hard-on for me that makes avoiding attention tough."

Even Lilith couldn't argue that one. "Fine." She aimed the next at Vex. "After blade practice, do me a favor and work on Tabby's hand to hand."

Vex drew a leg up and laid her arm over her knee. "Will do."

Reaper straightened and rounded the kitchen island until he stood close to Lilith. He met Math's gaze, knowing there was no one better at verifying intel than a Strix. "Might need access to your resources to confirm names."

Math waved a hand at Mercy. "Now that she's off the Cartels' radar, once we have them, she can reach out and get it."

"Plus, they like me better," the dark-haired assassin at Havoc's side added. "Since Math's got a price on his head, they won't expect him to show." She studied Lilith and Reaper. "I'm guessing you're heading out to get said names?"

Reaper nodded and looked to Havoc. "You going in with Mercy?"

Havoc's answer was to sit back in his chair and stretch an arm along Mercy's shoulders. "Once you're in the clear."

Amused at Havoc's protective behavior, considering Mercy was damn scary all by herself, Reaper couldn't help but grouse, "Can't be in two places at once."

"Nope," Havoc agreed. "But I can be close when you two pick up more trouble than you can handle."

Reaper hid a wince because he knew Havoc was spot on.

Ruin shook his head and muttered, "Would have to be a shit load of trouble if those two couldn't handle it."

Proving some things never changed, Lilith grimly echoed Reaper's thoughts with frightening accuracy. "Trust me, it generally is."

# eleven

Lilith rose from her seat as the other Vultures and their significant others wandered off to prepare for their various trips and tried to ignore the fact she and Reaper were alone. Tabby's excited voice drifted from the living room, and whatever Vex said triggered a rush of movement before the deck doors slid open, then close, leaving quiet behind.

The damnable attraction she shared with Reaper hadn't faded a bit over the intervening years and as it wove itself into the humming silence she turned away from Reaper's too perceptive gaze to head to the sink. The weight of his attention shouldn't make her nervous, but on a level she wasn't ready to acknowledge, it did.

She dumped the last dregs of her coffee, her skin pebbling when he invaded her personal space. His arm brushed hers as he drained his cup before setting it in the basin. As she rinsed the cups, she tried to focus on her task and not how his achingly familiar scent of musk mixed with the bite of spice burrowed under her emotional barriers.

He leaned in from behind her, trapping her between his

arms and the sink, his heat and strength blanketing her as he braced his palms on the counter. "Lilith."

His deep voice next to her ear made her breath catch, but she kept her gaze on the cup in her hands as she carefully let it out. "Hmm?"

"Could use your help."

She tried to suck in a steadying breath without being obvious about it and turned her head to find him inches away. "With?"

He angled his head so she could see his profile and rubbed a hand over his beard. "Getting rid of all this."

Although every survival instinct she owned screamed to escape, she held her ground, determined not to let a little thing like lust throw her off her game. She turned off the water and dried her hands on the towel at the counter. Despite the tight confines he allowed her, she turned, her curves brushing against his powerfully built form, until they were face-to-face. She set one hand flat against his chest and used her other to angle his chin as she studied him.

To Charity's point, if they shortened his hair and eliminated his beard, it might be enough to muddy the common perception of the infamous Vulture leader. His beard, the same blue-black as his shoulder length hair, was thick enough to blur the sharp edge of his jaw and added a menacing cast to his features. It was so... Reaper. She tried to recall if she'd ever seen him short haired or beardless but came up empty.

Caught in her memories, she didn't stop to think before she shifted her grip to brush a hand along his jaw. "You sure you want to ditch this?"

He gently pulled back as something flashed too fast to read in his eyes. "Yeah."

She turned away to hide the slicing hurt at his physical rejection of her touch, dropped her hand, and curled it into a fist at her side. *Right, message received—no touching.* "Okay then, grab a chair, take your shirt off, I'll be back." She pushed his arm out of her way and went to leave.

He caught her wrist and held her in place. "Hey."

She looked over her shoulder. "What?"

His gaze drifted over her face. "What was that?"

"What was what?" She twisted her wrist and broke his hold before he could answer and drag her into something she didn't want to address. "We need to get moving if you want to make your meet."

She turned away and left him there. In the bathroom, she indulged in a few mental head slaps as she searched through cabinets to see what she had on hand for an impromptu haircut.

*What was she thinking?* Just because last night's conversation offered a bit of hope that Reaper wouldn't bail as soon as he could, didn't mean he planned on sticking around for the long run. Nor would a single conversation with her baby change his long-held stance on fatherhood.

Granted, she wasn't harboring any happy ever after ideas because that would be beyond stupid, something she was too practical and too old to be. Not to mention her future was on the iffy side. Besides, her own future was on the iffy side. She was better served devising a way to deal with Tabby's emotional fallout when Reaper and his Vultures got safe and left.

She scrounged up towels, scissors, and a couple of razor blades, hoping it would be enough to get the job done. She returned to the kitchen only to be confronted with Reaper's naked chest and broody stare as he sat in a chair by the sink. The combination of the two created hormonal havoc she did her best to reel in.

She shook out and handed him one of the bigger towels to drape over his shoulders, and then set the scissors and razor blades on the counter. She ran the hand towel under the hot water and let it soak. With her back to Reaper, she took a few moments to steel herself, wrung out the towel, turned, and circled around Reaper to step in-between his legs.

The minute she moved into the intimate position, everything female in her ignored her earlier lectures on restraint and perked right the hell up, leaving her silently cursing. She avoided his navy-blue gaze, reigned in her libido, cautiously ran her fingers through his hair, and considered how best to approach his haircut.

Her concentration was shot to hell when he put his hands on her hips and his thumbs slipped under the edge of her t-shirt to brush the vulnerable skin below. The heat of his light touch roused a slow-burning hunger.

She went to step back, but his fingers tightened in silent refusal. Her breath caught, and her hands left his hair to grip his shoulders and she looked down and met his eyes, only to find an answering flare of want reflected in the navy depths.

When he arched a brow in a purely masculine taunt, she briefly considered the wisdom of entering such a dangerous game, but never one to back away from a dare, her lips curled into a bold, wicked smile as anticipation lit her veins.

*Challenge accepted, babe.*

She continued to hold his burning gaze as she leaned in to reach past him to grab the scissors and comb from the counter behind him. Her move meant her chest was pressed against his face, basically taunting him to resist what she offered. He didn't. He turned just that tiny bit until he could nuzzle her breast, and his hands at her waist tightened, tugging her closer.

The tantalizing tease of his warm exhale curled over her breast, leaving and ache behind. Her lashes drifted down for one interminable second as her breath stalled under the voracious hunger from that single, barely there, caress. She marshaled her endurance, clutched the cool metal of the scissors, and carefully straightened, praying the heat spiraling through her wasn't reflected on her face. She let her gaze roam over his face, taking in the rise of

He watched her, his skin colored by lust, and the tension between rose to an undeniable pitch.

She licked her lips, lifted her gaze back to his hair and sank her fingers into the thick strands as she swept it back from his face. "How short do you want it?" Her question was husky.

His answer was deeper, rougher around the edges, as his thumbs continued their slow slide over her skin. "Maybe buzz it?"

The desire pooled low and hot, and she could feel herself growing damp as decadent memories rose to taunt and tease. She continued to stroke his hair as she made an absent hum and considered his request. "Got a better idea."

"Yeah?"

"Let's do it a bit longer, maybe high and tight?" She trailed a finger along the curve of his ear.

He shifted in his chair and stretched his legs out as he settled deeper into the seat. "That works."

At his agreement, she got to work, and tried to ignore both his touch and the mental avenues they created. She might be able to get away with teasing him and taking things to the edge, but following that erotic path to its inevitable conclusion? No, not smart. It was best not to travel that path because other than easing an itch, it couldn't lead anywhere good.

Still, she got off on pushing both of their limits, which meant as she worked her way around him, her simple brushes skirted into seductive caresses and stoked the need between them higher and higher. Sounds from the others drifted into the electric quiet that filled the kitchen, but it did nothing to dispel the unspoken expectations coiling between them.

She was back at Reaper's front and made the last final cuts to his hair before lifting the scissors away. Most of his hair was gone, and what remained accentuated his masculine beauty, even with his beard. She brushed a clump of clippings from his beard, and he caught her hand and pulled it down. When he didn't let go, she met his gaze.

"If I kiss you," he broke the wired silence, "you going to stab me with those?" He titled his head to the scissors forgotten in her hand.

She stared into his achingly familiar features and recognized the hunger staring back. "Maybe."

A heartbeat passed as neither moved, then he said, "Fuckin' worth it."

He tugged her down and claimed her lips with his.

She didn't fight him because she wanted this just as badly as he obviously did. If she was being honest, she didn't give a damn if it was smart or not. Part of her needed to know if he still tasted the same, the other just wanted.

When he stroked his tongue over her lower lip and she opened, letting him in, she got her answer. Their tongues tangled, stroked, and fought. She couldn't stop her groan as the addictive taste she couldn't forget hit like a blowtorch and set her skin on fire even as it amplified their hunger.

She nipped at his lips and tugged against his hold until he let her hand go. The scissors and comb fell to the floor, their soft clatter barely penetrating the cresting wave of desire. She found a hold in his shortened strands to pull his head back so she could take their kiss deeper.

He gripped her hips and urged her closer as she swallowed down his dark rumble. She let him pull her in until she was straddling his lap, his arm curled around her back, and her knees on the edge of the chair.

The change in her position left her off balance, so she untangled her hands and gripped his shoulders, knocking off the towel. until nothing stood between his heated skin and her palms. She continued to kiss him as she ran her hands over his exposed chest. Under her, where she ached the most, she could feel his cock harden and lengthen until he pressed against her damp core. She lifted her head and fought for air, her chest heaving.

Undiscouraged, he wrapped her hair in one hand and tugged her head back until her spine arced. He nipped her chin and then trailed an intoxicating mix of open mouth kisses and small, painless bites down her throat.

Held in an erotic curve and driven by the urge to ride him until they were both lost, she ground down against his steel hard cock.

His hand left her hair to glide down her spine as his other drifted from her hip to cup her breast, his thumb tracing slowly tightening circles around her nipple.

Released from his hold, she cupped his face, angled it so she could take another kiss and muffle her groan. As they kept kissing, she settled over his hardness with a slow roll of hips and stroked down his neck to his chest as she mapped the lines of muscles and old scars. Her hands slipped lower and lower, until she dipped below the edge of his jeans and delved into the erotic warmth held within.

A low growl escaped Reaper as he shifted his grip, his fingers biting into her ass as he jerked her close and thrust his hips, grinding his cock against her damp center.

She couldn't stop her slow, answering roll if she tried. Her hunger as voracious as the fire raging inside her. It had been too damn long since she had a man, much less this man, and her orgasm hovered just out of reach.

A feminine shriek of outrage quickly followed by a burst of male laughter brought a sliver of sanity into Lilith's sensual storm. *What the hell was she doing letting Reaper all but fuck her in the kitchen?* She ripped her mouth from his, swallowed back a moan as he bucked under her, and somehow found the strength to get out, "Reaper, we have to stop."

The grip on her ass tightened and he nipped at the base of

her throat in punishment before dropping his forehead against her sternum, his shoulders rising and falling with his harsh breaths. "Dammit, Lilith."

Her breathing wasn't any better. In fact, it took everything ounce of discipline she had not to squirm against his cock that was right *fucking there*. She wrapped her arms around his shoulders and held him close, her fingers gently stroking the back of his neck. With a shaky laugh she bent her head over his and laid her cheek against the top of his head. "You started it."

They sat there for a long moment, their breaths heavy, as they tried to get their bodies back in control. When she thought she could move without shattering, she loosened her hold and leaned back.

Reaper sighed and let her go.

She carefully got to her feet and wasn't surprised to find her balance shaky as she stood in-between his legs. She braced one hand on his shoulder and brushed his heavy beard with the other. "You still need to get rid of this."

He covered her hand with his, pressing her palm against the surprisingly soft bristle, his eyes dark with lust and color still staining his skin. "Probably best if I do it myself."

She nodded as he pulled her hand away and held it. She curled her fingers around his, squeezed once, then let him go.

She stepped back and took him in—bare chested, sprawled in the chair, his cock obvious despite his pants, his face flushed with need—at the promise of decadence he offered, she wished she could be anyone else so they could finish what they started. But she wasn't.

His gaze to where he traced a finger along the slope of her breast to the beaded nipple that the t-shirt couldn't hide. "Thinking we're going to end up finishing this." He looked up at her through his lashes.

It almost hurt to let him and the temptation he offered go, but she did. "That's not a good idea, Reaper."

He pushed up in his chair, wincing as he adjusted himself. "Probably not, but it's inevitable."

She watched him get up and considered how much she itched to strip him down and fuck him until neither one of them could move, knowing he was probably right.

*What would it hurt, really?*

They were both adults, and neither one held any expectations. Granted, the fact she was seriously considering it, pointed to the fact that it had been too damn long since she'd gotten laid. Still, there was one, tiny factor to consider… "You don't even like me."

He gave a snort and ran a hand over his short hair. "Hell, you can't stand me." He folded his arms over his chest and aimed a wickedly decadent grin her way. "Besides, don't have to like you to fuck you, woman."

"Nice," she snapped, her temper burning as much as her pussy.

Reaper chuckled, but his humor didn't last long. "Never said I didn't like you. It was your choices I didn't like."

She lifted her chin in silent challenge. "If you didn't like them then, you're going to like them even less now."

"Why?" He closed in and tucked a stray strand of her hair behind her ear. He didn't stop there but traced the edge of her ear before his gaze met hers. "You going to turn me over to Michael and collect the bounty?"

She met his gaze and lied through her pearly whites. "You piss me off enough, I just might."

He curled a hand around the back of her neck, his thumb brushing along her hairline behind her ear. "Now who's not being nice, babe?"

"You started it." Her response was breathy, instead of the bitchy she was aiming for, but damn he was so close. Her hands went to his stomach—to bring him closer or push him away, she wasn't sure, but her nails bit in just a tiny bit.

The smoldering fire in his gaze leapt and raged, but he leaned in and put his lips near her ear. "I dare you, Lilly-belle."

Hearing the nickname only he ever used, set off unseen tremors. She fought to keep her footing as he kept shifting the ground under her feet. It would be dumb to give in, but just this once she wanted something just for her. She gave him, and her, one more out. "You sure you want to go there?"

Their gazes locked as he rested his forehead against hers and his hand at her neck held her captive as surely as a chain. "Yeah."

She swallowed and touched her bottom lip with her tongue in a nervous tell she couldn't hide.

He watched her do it and closed his eyes for a moment before reopening them. "Not like either of us is expecting more than to scratch an itch, right?"

If it was just about her, she wouldn't' hesitate to take him to the floor and show him her answer, but there was someone much more important at risk. "What about Tabby?"

The hold on her neck slid away as he let her go. "Tabby's not part of this." He brushed his knuckles along her jaw before he lifted his head. "No matter what happens with us, what goes down between me and her, stays between me and her.'

The part of her brain not hazed with lust knew there were all sorts of wrong with that, but she couldn't stop her soft, "Promise?"

The harsh lines of his face softened, just for a second, then returned with determination. "Swear on all that's holy, Lilith. I won't hurt her."

She studied him, knowing she might regret it, but unable to deny she wanted this chance with him. "It's stupid."

That earned her a small smile. "Yeah, it is, but we won't be able to fight it for too long. You know that. Besides, when has stupid ever stop me?"

She knew he was right, on both counts. "It's just sex." Maybe if she said it enough, her body would listen.

"Just sex," he agreed, swiping his thumb in a slow brush over her lower lip.

In an unconscious move, her tongue came out to chase it. The blue of his eyes deepened to indigo and he lowered his head to take her mouth with a stunning gentleness. She wrapped her arms around his waist and got lost in the kiss.

When he lifted his head, he asked, "Deal?"

She stood in his arms and knew, this time, she could do this. She knew how it would end—he'd leave, just like before. But this time, it would be her turn to walk away first. She knew it was petty and childish, but dammit, the idea of being the one to leave offset some of the old heartache she carried. Besides, sex would be a great stress reliever as they dealt with the shitstorm bearing down on them.

She might be full of shit and lying to herself, but even if her rationale was skewed, she understood the reality. Some things were inevitable—like ending up in bed with Reaper. Better she do this on her terms and keep her heart free and clear, and maybe, just maybe, she wouldn't repeat her previous mistake or forget the lesson he taught her years ago.

Decision made, her voice was steady when she answered, "Deal."

# twelve

A few hours later after a cold shower, Reaper followed Lilith's ass up a set of rickety metal stairs to the second floor of a red brick building as he tried and failed to get his mind out of the deviant gutter it currently occupied. That damn kiss in the kitchen left a mark, and he wasn't sure if he was thrilled or pissed at Lilith's agreement to keep it to sex.

A burst of drunken laughter was followed by the sound of glass shattering and snapped him out of his frustrated thoughts. His fingers tightened on the sun-warmed metal railing as a breeze drifted through the narrow confines and stirred up the stench of soured alcohol and rotted food.

He peered into the alley below where the Pearl Street bars were doing brisk business and saw two figures stumble into a pile of empty crates, sending them crashing over the pitted mix of gravel and asphalt. The taller one landed face down with a muffled groan, while a high pitch giggled escaped the shorter one as he managed a couple more steps before landing on his ass.

A quiet snort from above turned Reaper's attention back to Lilith who had one leg thrown over the inside ledge of an open window. With her face shadowed by a tattered cap that covered the bandana hiding her hair and the shapeless clothes that masked her curves and weapons, she looked nothing like the Rocky Mountain Queen.

When she met his gaze, she rolled her eyes and disappeared inside.

Reaper shook his head and didn't waste time following her in.

It wasn't smart to hang around in this area, not even at midday. Pearl Street once spanned thirty-five blocks and reigned supreme in downtown Boulder as a thriving street mall. Now it occupied roughly half that and mostly housed bars and other seedy establishments.

He swung his leg over the window ledge and ducked inside. He closed the window behind him, shutting out the noxious odors and the noise of the two bickering idiots below. When he turned around, he found Lilith wandering the room, her expression bemused.

He couldn't blame her.

A light scent of something exotic tinted the air. Lush fabrics that showed a bit of wear draped the bed that took up the majority of the room's space. A wooden screen stretched along one side and was decorated with a mishmash of various colored clothing that blocked off what was obviously a dressing area. On the bed's other side was a small table with a beaded lamp, the top drawer partially open. Lilith tugged it out and poked around inside, her smile quirking at its contents.

Since they were early, Reaper nudged a pile of lingerie out of the stuffed chair near the window and took a seat.

Lilith lifted a tangle of leather straps attached to an overly optimistic dildo from the drawer and met his gaze with an arched brow. "Interesting meeting place."

Reaper grinned. "What? Not your kind of place?"

A soft snort escaped as she dropped the toy back into the drawer, then wandered over to the cluttered vanity. She lifted a crop from the mess and ran it through her hands. She slid a look his way and said, "I wouldn't say that."

Her implication hit him right in the dick, and his mind resumed its earlier path, with a few intriguing additions. Something in his face must have given him away because Lilith's husky laugh ran over his nerve endings like a torch.

She sashayed over and set the edge of the crop under his chin, forcing his gaze up. "Down boy." It came out in a near purr.

Reaper let his hunger shine. "If you insist."

Color bloomed under her skin, but she tapped his chin with the crop and chided, "No time for that." She turned and tossed the crop back on the vanity.

"There's always time for that."

She shot him a look over her shoulder as she crossed in front of him and kept moving through the room. "Says the man." She peeked behind the screen. "How long are we hanging around?"

"We're early." Not done teasing her, he added, "Don't worry, he's coming."

His lame pun got a startled laugh from Lilith. She turned to face him and propped her shoulder against the edge of the window. "I bet they all do."

Reaper just grinned.

In the hall something slammed against the far wall and rattled the door. He and Lilith stilled and exchanged a look, their shared humor wiped away. She tilted her head to the screen, and he gave her a nod. She slipped behind it, light glinting off the blades in her fists.

He stayed in the chair as it was positioned so anyone coming in wouldn't see him until they closed the door. He pulled his knife free and kept it concealed along his thigh.

When a decidedly feminine moan filtered through the wall, he met Lilith's rolling eyes as her lips twitched and she shook her head.

Between the live audio track outside the door and their earlier conversation, Reaper's dick perked up. He forced his rebellious body under control as the low rumble of a male voice responded, just before something landed against the door again, shaking it in its frame. He watched the knob turn and the door slowly open to reveal the lean back of his contact —Dog, the leader of the mercenary group Dogs of War.

Dressed in faded jeans, weathered vest, and t-shirt, Dog kept his back to the room and gave Reaper his profile. He kept one hand on the door and one on the doorframe, his inked arm blocking the entry. "I owe you, Nessa."

Reaper's only visual of Nessa from his position was her feminine hands. Tipped in vibrant blues one cupped Dog's dick over his jeans while the other curled around his neck, and tugged him forward. "Yes, you do."

Dog managed to maintain his hold on the door, even as he leaned forward to give Nessa the kiss she obviously demanded. He finally pulled back. "You know I'm good for it."

"You will be." With that husky warning, Nessa gave him one last rub before her hand disappeared, freeing Dog.

Dog stood in the doorway for a long moment, obviously watching her leave. When he stepped back, he shoved the door closed and turned to survey the room in a quick sweep. His gaze found Reaper and Dog grinned. "Been waitin' long?"

"Why? Need a bit more time?"

"Nah, I'm all good." Instead of moving further into the room, Dog leaned back against the door and rubbed his silver-streaked goatee. His cocky grin didn't reach his dark eyes and twisted the thin scar that ran from temple to chin. "Thought you were comin' in solo?"

Lilith took the not-so-subtle hint and stepped out from

behind the screen, her hands now empty. Without saying a word, she positioned just to the side of the window, effectively putting Dog between her and Reaper.

Recognition flashed across Dog's face as he folded his arms over his chest and shifted his weight. "Well, now," he murmured. "That's somethin'."

Reaper clocked the nearly imperceptible change in Dog's position which gave the mercenary easier access to the blades Reaper knew were tucked away. He decided it was best to redirect Dog's attention. "Not exactly a smart move, considering."

"True," Dog agreed without taking his eyes off Lilith or moving his hands. "You being here, lady, makes me think the whispers are true."

With the cap shadowing her eyes and her head tilted just enough to keep it that way, the only thing either man could see was the grim little smile that played around her mouth. "Guess it depends on which whispers you heard."

Dog scratched an ear. "That maybe you aren't always where you're supposed to be."

Lilith's smile grew teeth. "I'm always right where I need to be, never doubt it."

Dog gave a bark of laughter and shook his head. "Ain't that a bitch?" He pushed off the door and with an ingrained swagger sauntered to the bed. He shoved the pillow against the headboard in-between the dangling restraints, threw himself to the mattress and settled in. He folded his hands behind his head and crossed his ankles, his heavy boots dangling off the edge. "Probably a good thing, though, considerin'."

Reaper sat back in his chair and some of his wary tension eased, now that Dog was lying down. "Considering what?"

A small frown darkened Dog's face as he switched his attention to Reaper. "That bounty, brother, ain't good news. Payment's comin' out of the Sandpit."

At that piece of news unease curled in Reaper's gut. There was only one reason a payment would be offered out of Phoenix. "The Cartels' financing it?"

Somber lines erased any hint of Dog's normal devil-may-care attitude. "It's what it looks like."

Something in Dog's voice gave Reaper pause, and he wasn't the only one because it was Lilith who asked, "But you don't think so?"

"Honestly? Don't know what to think," Dog replied. "Did manage to get a name—Digger."

"He the go-to for payment?" Reaper shifted the pieces around but too many were still missing to make them fit.

Dog nodded. "Thing is, Digger ain't picky about who he brokers for, so..." He shrugged. "Could be Cartels, could be anyone."

To Dog's point there were good reasons for the Cartels to want payback from Vultures. First, but not least, was the fact that Reaper and Havoc's reputations from the Border Wars meant either of their deaths would be considered a massive coup. Second, was the whole dust up with Mercy. The little assassin had stumbled across Havoc's path after she was wrongfully accused of taking out the youngest son of the Suárez family. Eventually, she was able to turn the real killer over to the oldest Suárez, but not before she stopped the Cartels' plans to take over the critical dams from the Free People. All in all, it made Mercy far from their favorite person.

Unfortunately, there was one thing Mercy hadn't been able to discover, who the Cartels were in bed with to control the most critical resource of the Southwest. Mercy and Math thought it was Greer, Michael's right hand bitch. After discovering that Greer was pulling Doc Mandy's strings and gunning for the Vultures, Reaper was beginning to believe the same thing. He just couldn't let go of the fact that her leash could easily be held by Michael's hands.

Dog broke into Reaper's musing. "Everyone's on edge right now. The Cartels are antsy as fuck. Michael's not much better. And his bitch, Greer?" Dog puckered his lips and blew out a puff of air. "Gone like the wind."

Reaper wasn't sure if that was good or bad news. Generally, if you were carrying a gut full of lead it would keep a person from causing trouble, but with the way things were going, he wouldn't count Greer out until he saw the damn body. He rubbed the back of his neck, leaned forward, and rested his elbows on his knees. "You think she's dead?"

Dog shook his head. "Don't know, but she's not honing in on shit like normal."

And he would know. The Dogs of War's notoriety might be just shy of the Vultures, but their fingers dipped into a ton of dirty pots, a few much dirtier than the Vultures liked.

"Her ass lickers?" Dog continued. "They're sticking close to home. Maybe cuz lately New Seattle's shakier than Mt. St. Helen's. Everyone's waiting for shit to blow sky high." He dropped his hands and used the heel of his boot to shove his body up until he sat upright. He aimed a considering look at Reaper. "Normally, this would make me happier than a pig in shit."

Yeah, Reaper could see why. Without the delay of dealing with Michael's forces, the Dogs of War could up their runs of black-market weapons, food, and medicine. "But?"

"But it's making my skin crawl." Dog rubbed his jaw. "Hell, even the Raiders have backed off." He grimaced. "Not by choice though."

That sounded ominous and concerning. Upheaval, like what Dog was describing, made for prime pickings for Raiders. Anytime things were thrown into disarray, it wasn't long before the Raiders crawled out of the bones of Las Vegas and scurried around like the roaches they were, making shit a hundred times worse as they took advantage of humanity's worst aspects. They were fucking masters at it. Something the Vultures re-learned when they took over the protection of the Central Territory supply lines.

Reaper tilted his head and narrowed his eyes. "What do you mean, not by choice?"

Dog sighed. "I can tell you that someone's got a lethal hard-on for those rats, just can't give you the who yet, but got someone working on it." He scratched his chest. "A few weeks back, the boys and I took on a job. We were asked to reclaim a shipment of firearms the Raiders managed to snag. By the time we ran them down, all that was left was bits and pieces— of them, and the weapons. We found one of the bastards bleeding out but breathing. He claimed the boxes were booby trapped."

A memory triggered at Dog's explanation and Reaper recalled a conversation with Lilith from years ago when they discussed tactics to stop the blitz attacks on weapons being shuttled between posts. Lilith's mind was sneaky as shit, not to mention creative and vindictive. A flash of Lilith talking with Charity this morning joined in, and his gaze slid to Lilith.

She stared back with cool arrogance even as a savage light danced in her eyes.

*Well, shit, guess his woman managed to find a way to pay back the assholes for taking Tabby.* Battling his amused pride down so he didn't give her away, he murmured, "Is that so?"

Oblivious to the undercurrents, Dog kept going. "Yeah. Might mean good news for you."

Not following his logic, Reaper asked, "How do you figure?"

"Bounty on you, it's high." Dog flashed a cocky grin. "Raiders are too busy tucking tail to snatch it up. The rest of us..." He shrugged. "Tempting as it is, most of us think twice about taking it."

Reaper arched a brow. "Most, but not all?"

Dog looked like the proverbial cat with the canary and drawled, "Think you and yours can handle the dumb and arrogant." His amused grin faded away and exposed the ruthless mercenary underneath. "Truth?"

Reaper hitched a shoulder and said, "Always welcomed."

Dog took him at his word and unflinchingly laid it out. "Payment may be out of Phoenix, but this bounty on you—it's personal. No way to miss that. That number is fucking high. Maybe too high. That's why most are steering clear. Besides, those who ride the roads, we do it because we don't do so well with rules. Live and let live, yeah?"

Reaper nodded.

Dog continued. "Doesn't mean we don't have them. Some are ones you just don't break. Like, not fucking with one of ours." He caught Reaper's gaze. "Know why I choose the roads?"

There was an unmistakable intensity in Dog's voice, one Reaper understood. He slowly shook his head.

Dog's voice lowered but his gaze remained rock steady. "Served in the Border Wars, and when it was winding down, realized the opportunities inventive trading could offer me. Worked with some hard ass fuckers who taught me plenty. Heard stories of what went down on the lines during the war. Some were padded with bullshit, but there was one that hit home—yours."

Tension crawled through Reaper's veins, but he didn't move as Dog's voice invoked memories best left buried.

"Not just for me, but most of us," Dog went on. "Because we'd been there, one way or the other." In the depths of Dog's eyes, raged an unholy mix of bitter betrayal and fierce pride, bound together by an indomitable determination. "Like you, I found putting my life on the line for someone else's profit was bullshit."

The mercenary was far from done and his voice was rough.

"Crews, like yours, like mine, we're the last line of defense for those who don't want to live under someone else's fist. We're their last chance at justice, at making things right. We don't have to play nice to make it happen either. Most of them out there can't risk it, too much at stake—families, livelihoods, things like that. Those of us that ride the road, none of us have ties that can hang us, but we can see what's coming. We're just waiting to see which direction we need to take it."

Sitting across from a man he'd known for years in a whorehouse with a bounty on his head and the one woman guaranteed to test his resolve at his side, it hit Reaper like a fist to his gut—this whole situation involved much more than his personal vendetta against Michael.

Hell, Lilith had been right all along. When he finally managed to take out Michael, the impact would reach far and wide, and the power vacuum would be daunting. Something he needed to seriously consider because feeding his need for vengeance might bring about a worse future for his daughter, and the world she lived in.

He had a responsibility, hell, they all did, to make sure that the future wasn't a nightmare for those who managed to carve out a new way of life. Dog managed to remind him, for the first time in a long time, of what bound groups like Fate's Vultures and Dogs of War together. It wasn't about getting their own back, or taking out the assholes of the day, it was a hell of a lot bigger.

It was about holding those determined to destroy the last bits of humanity accountable, and ensuring justice was served —one way or another.

# thirteen

Lilith dropped from the questionable stability of the fire escape and moved quickly out of the way as Reaper followed. Since they were trying to keep a low profile, using the same entry route as their exit made the most sense. The drunken duo from earlier was gone, and all that remained was a couple of broken crates and scattered shards of glass.

Lilith stilled in the lengthening shadows of the late afternoon sun as a slight breeze brought a nose full of sweat and dust. She scanned the faces that rushed along the street as voices, animals, and makeshift vehicles created a hum of noise. It wasn't the heavy flood typical of quitting time, but there was enough happening she and Reaper could easily blend in.

Reaper came up to her and she corrected her last thought. She could blend, but Reaper? Not so much. Between his coiled stillness and his calculating gaze that sifted through the crowd with merciless intent, there was no way to downplay his predatory nature.

"You ready?"

He switched his attention from the street to her. "You in a rush?"

"Kind of, yeah."

He frowned. "Why's that? Havoc's not expecting us for another couple of hours."

"Good to know." She studied the ebb and flow of the street. "Should give me just enough time."

When she said nothing more, he pushed, "For?"

She stifled her sigh at the biting edge of his tone. *Great, someone was getting grumpy.* Instead of answering him, she asked a question of her own. "You plan on heading into Phoenix?"

He crowded her and braced a hand on the wall's edge above her head, the heat of him covering her back. "There a reason for me not to?"

Since she wasn't looking to start an argument, she kept her voice bland. "Nope, but if we're making a trip, I need to take care of a few things before we head out."

A horse drawn trailer stuffed with a vocal collection of poultry trundle closer. The cumbersome transportation forced the foot traffic on their side of the street to give way.

"Don't remember inviting you." His growl rumbled next to her ear.

She angled her head just enough to meet his eyes. "Really? Because considering your options, I figured I didn't need an invite."

She didn't wait for his response, but grabbed his wrist, and pulled him along behind her as the hen express started to pass by. They paced the trailer until the road widened at the next intersection. She let go of Reaper's wrist as they slipped into the stream of pedestrians and wound their way down the street.

Reaper stayed at her back since she left him with little choice but to follow. She kept an eye on the passing traffic, needing a ride like... she spotted the perfect solution, grabbed Reaper's hand, and picked up the pace. "Come on."

Dragging a six foot plus male in her wake made weaving through others a bit of a challenge, but she made it to her goal —a flatbed wagon that lumbered its way down the street. She let go of Reaper, closed the distance between her and the driver, and waving a arm, issued a sharp whistle to gain the driver's attention.

The steel-haired woman twitched the reins of a pair of swayed back horses, and the flatbed's slow pace became a crawl. "Help you?"

Lilith noted the woman's not too subtle move as her hand disappeared down the side of the bench, indicating she was likely armed. "Maybe." She offered a friendly smile as she walked alongside the wagon. "Considering your load, my man and I, we're hoping we might hitch a ride to Pigeon Jim's."

The older woman's eyes narrowed in her sun-worn face as the wagon continued its slow roll forward. She twisted in her seat to check out Reaper and kept a loose hold on the reins. Her shift in weight didn't even register with the horses as they kept plodding forward. She took her time thinking over Lilith's question, rolling the thin, half smoked cigar from one side to the other. Finally, she jerked her chin up. "Ay' right, hop on."

"Thanks much." Lilith dropped back, grabbed the rough edge at the back, and hauled her ass up to the wagon's boards. Reaper was right behind her. Once their weight settled, the woman clicked at the horses and resumed her previous pace.

Lilith squirmed around until her back was against the wagon's side, propped one foot against the floor, and dangled her other leg off the back. Across from her Reaper tried to get comfortable despite the plethora of wire cages filled with beady eyed pigeons that dominated the wagon's bed.

Oldest domesticated birds or not, they were freaking creepy as far as she was concerned. She caught Reaper's lip curl as he eyed the cage and thought she wasn't alone on that opinion. Or maybe it was just the smell.

He turned back to her, all sorts of unhappiness in his face. "How long?"

It wasn't easy, but she managed to ignore their avian audience. "Fifteen, maybe twenty minutes."

He glared at her for a moment before shaking his head and turning back to watch the street.

She could tell Reaper had a few things to say to her, but luckily her ride choice meant she didn't have to deal with his inevitable questions. Not only would any conversation have to be loud enough to be heard over the creak and groans of the wagon, which meant their driver would get an earful, but the curious pigeons were cooing their little hearts out.

By the time they arrived, chances were high that not only would her head be aching, but her butt would definitely be numb. She leaned back, tugged her brim down, and studied the man across from her.

A muscle in his jaw jumped and in a familiar tell and he was rubbing his thumb over his knuckle. She figured he was probably still struggling with Dog's take on his past. Although why he would was beyond her, because Reaper and his doomed unit were practically legend.

For a man like Reaper, losing his unit had been a crippling blow. He took his position as their leader deep and it showed in the unmistakable bonds they shared. Bonds that became blatantly obvious the longer the Border Wars dragged on. Especially when Reaper and his men had no issue questioning the orders they were given.

Lilith often wondered if that, not the ultimate betrayal, hadn't been the start of the end for Reaper and Michael's relationship.

Lilith first met Michael during the Border Wars. At the time, the Territories were working together with enough crossover cooperation that certain names started to set themselves apart. Reaper was generally at the top of that list and Michael was the rising star in the Northwest. Crane was the established hand for the Central, and Jacob held the Rocky Mountains with Lilith as his right hand. She couldn't pinpoint when Michael's attitude changed, but by the time the wars were coming to an end it was obvious Michael was not content with being second in anything.

And when Reaper was involved, second was all Michael could get.

It didn't help things that Reaper tended to generate a level of loyalty Michael craved. Unfortunately, Reaper never quite grasped his importance to those around him. He was one of those innate leaders who served those he led and his reaction to Dog's revelation made her wonder if Reaper realized he had replaced his lost unit with Fate's Vultures. He gathered both warrior and survivor types like bees to honey, probably because they shared the unbreakable core of strength that ran through his stubborn soul. He might bitch about his responsibilities, but he never shirked them.

The wagon hit a hole, and her shoulder cracked against the side. She shifted, rubbing the sting away, and caught Reaper watching her. His implacable mask slipped and revealed a heady mix of frustration, hunger and want.

She held his gaze even as her body reacted to his scrutiny with an answering craving, proving the passage of time hadn't changed a damn thing. Maybe agreeing to sleep with him wasn't her smartest move, but in the end, it wouldn't matter because she was a glutton for punishment. No way was she turning down prime naked time with him. A woman deserved to indulge occasionally.

Another sharp crack and a shout broke their staring contest. They both turned to watch a street rat hurdle a display and disappear. An angry man gave chase, shoving his way through bystanders even though his prey was long gone.

As they left the Pearl District behind the crowds thinned. They rode into the remains of what once housed one those planned neighborhoods, every house exactly the same on the exact same size piece of land. Reclaimed by a living green cloak of Mother Nature, the once similar structures were made unique by the creative vegetative growth. Some sported blackened bones in silent testimony that once upon a time this neighborhood had been ravaged by the riots.

Lilith couldn't tell if anyone had claimed the homes tucked further back, but it wouldn't surprise her if they had. Scarcity of materials necessitated the creativity of recycling shelters. Case in point, one of the two-story homes now doubled as a tree house thanks to the spreading branches sprouting through the hollow eyes of glassless windows. Untamed patches of wildflowers and bushes devoured yards and abandoned vehicles until this little 'hood was far from boring.

Lilith resettled against the rough siding and resumed brooding.

Sex wasn't all she craved from Reaper. If she was brutally honest, it was the intimacy of being with him—as a partner and a lover. Before it fell apart, he had been one of the few she could trust without question. Afterwards, as she rose in power, that was an indulgence she couldn't afford. Which is what made her rash decision to reignite things with him so dangerous.

It would be too damn easy to slip back into what they shared before, which meant grappling with the same unresolved problems, and repeating old mistakes was asking for a world of hurt.

Reaper said he didn't want to be part of her world—but he already was. When Crane sent out his SOS, Reaper wasn't obligated to answer. Even after he did, he could've walked away from the entire mess, and not one person would have blamed him. Not even her.

Hell, the only reason she was involved in this was because Tabby had been taken. That horrifically eye-opening experience had slammed home the importance of keeping her daughter safe at any cost. Otherwise, she would've stayed the hell out of it. Risking the stability, she managed up to that point was not worth taking on Michael.

But after the threat to Tabby? Yeah, she'd risk it all for her baby. The alliances she was pushing weren't for the greater good. They were to ensure she had enough people on her side so others would think more than twice about going after her or her daughter.

For her this wasn't about politics, but self-preservation.

But not Reaper.

Whether he wanted to admit it or not, he chose to stand and fight, not for Crane and despite what he said, not for Simon, but for those who called Pebble Creek home. It made him a hell of a better leader than she could ever be. People loved him, they just feared her. Yet, she couldn't see him walking away from it all just because it was too fucking hard.

The wagon made a turn and headed down a tree-lined tunnel. Knowing they were closing in on their destination, she straightened her back and stretched her arms above her head in an attempt to alleviate the stiff muscles.

Across from her, Reaper shifted and craned his head to see where they were headed. When he turned back to her, she told him, "Almost there."

The wagon slowed and the soft coos of the pigeons picked up volume. They pulled in front of a crumbling apartment building. Once it stood four stories, but now parts of the end sections were gnawed down to three, sometimes two floors. Signs of life were reflected in the bright blooms hanging off rusted railings. At the tallest point, the flat roof was lined with pigeons.

Their driver brought the wagon up to the base of graffiti-covered stairs and hopped down from the bench seat with a spryness at odds with her apparent age. "Jim! Delivery!" She flipped the reins over the metal railing as Lilith and Reaper jump down from the back. "And visitors!"

"Keep your panties on, Mildred. I'm coming!" A booming voice drifted from above.

Lilith and Reaper moved to the foot of the stairs, each of them picking a side as Mildred puttered around with the pigeons.

"You're running late, woman." A white-haired, barrel-chested man in stained jeans and a faded tie-dyed t-shirt ambled down the stairs.

At the head of the last set of stairs, he caught sight of Lilith and recognition flared. He didn't manage to stifle his grimace before he ducked his head and gave it a small shake as he came down the rest of the stairs. He brushed between her and Reaper without a word and joined Mildred at the back of the wagon.

"Here, let me do this," he muttered. A sharp smack sounded, and Jim jerked back, shaking his hand and frowning. "Dammit, woman, what was that for?"

Mildred didn't stop what she was doing. "Told you a hundred times, I can do it myself." She got the cage door open and stepped back as the pigeons did a mass exodus.

Most headed for the roof, but a couple landed on Jim. One settled on his shoulder, and another perched on his head. Something he appeared not to notice as he folded his muscled arms over his chest and glowered at the unimpressed woman. "I was just trying to help."

"Don't," Mildred snapped. She waited until the last bird left the cage before securing the door. Then she leaned in deeper and dragged out a bag. "Here." She shoved it at Jim, who barely managed to catch it when she let it go. "Supplies." She moved around him, her intent to leave obvious.

Jim shifted the bag to his free shoulder and caught Mildred's arm, holding her still for a moment. "Got to get your payment. Dinner tomorrow."

A sweet smile broke over Mildred's face, easing the worn lines and revealing a graceful beauty. She reached up and cupped Jim's face. "Dinner, tomorrow," she agreed. "Don't make me wait."

Jim lifted her hand and brushed an old-fashioned kiss over her knuckles before letting her go. "Never."

Then they all watched Mildred drive away.

# fourteen

The pigeon wrangler slowly turned and finally acknowledged them as the tail end of the wagon disappeared. "What, pray tell, brings me the pleasure of your company?"

Lilith braced her arms on the railing and gave Jim a grin. "Just making a quick stop, my friend."

Jim, unimpressed by her friendliness, made a rude noise in the back of his throat and walked between her and Reaper, heading back to the stairs. The pigeon perched on Jim's wild mane of gray uttered soft cooing's as it rotated to keep Lilith pinned with its's creepy serial killer stare. Difficult though it was, she managed not to engage in a stare down with the flying rat.

With one foot on the bottom step, Jim glared back over his shoulder and grunted. Correctly interpreting his unspoken, "Follow or leave, I don't care", she and Reaper followed the old man up the steps.

Lilith was halfway up the second flight when an ominous creak sounded. A warm hand palmed her ass as she clutched the railing. She looked back at Reaper and narrowed her eyes.

He was all mock-innocence when he asked, "What? Didn't want you to fall."

"Uh-huh," she muttered, then turned back around and resumed her climb.

She paid closer attention to the boards under her feet because if she fell through the stairs, she had no doubt that Reaper would use it as an excuse to leave her ass behind. On the third flight she skipped a couple of the more questionable steps and started up the last set when ahead of her, Jim nimbly maneuvered up the ladder that leaned from the fourth floor to the roof.

Since the ladder looked as rickety as the stairs, Lilith waited until Jim disappeared over the roof's edge before following. Heights sucked. She pulled in a quiet breath and grabbed the edge of the ladder until her knuckles showed white. She detested meeting here, but if she wanted to get her messages out, she had to follow Jim to the roof because the old man and his flying rat brigade wouldn't come to her. Wrapped tight in her phobia, she didn't sense Reaper coming in close.

"I've got you." His arms came around her and he gripped the ladder's edges just below her hands.

Her shaky flutter of nerves calmed under his reassurance and the fact that he remembered her qualms settled deep. She gave him a small nod, bit her lower lip, and with his heat at her back climbed up to the roof.

She stepped onto the surprisingly solid surface and inched to the side so Reaper had room to join her on the rooftop. There was a negligent ledge, maybe a foot and a half tall that ran along the edge of the wall. Not much of a deterrent, but it might stop someone from taking an unexpected fall. Say, someone like her.

She moved towards the center of the roof and not being able to see how far from the ground they were meant her breathing dropped from a pant into a more normal pattern.

Shed-like enclosures lined the four sides and coop had a set of double doors wrapped in chicken wire. Currently they were wide open, so it was easy to see the rows of open-ended boxes topped by inverted V style perches, many occupied by Jim's feathered minions. The design of it left enough space for a couple of humans to meander around inside.

Lilith eyed the layer upon layer of bird shit covering the floor and decided to stay out the roof where only one layer spotted the tiles.

Reaper, his attention on the birds, stopped at her side. "What's with the colored bands?"

"They use an internal GPS." It was Jim who answered, his pigeon crown bailing to join a group gathered near the corner. "The colors identify who belongs where." He waved a hand at a blue banded grey one that stood on the edge of the doorframe. "That fellow's coming from the Healing Gardens up in the mountains." He pivoted and revealed a white bird on his wrist, a silver-streaked, green band wrapped around its leg. "This one is out of the Tri-City area." He undid the small tube and lifted the bird until it fluttered to a roost.

Reaper eyed the birds and then shifted his attention back to Jim. "I'm guessing this is some kind of flying postal service?"

"Pretty much," Lilith said. "If you need to get a message to someone who's nowhere near one of the few existing land lands, or doesn't have access to the bootleg web, this—" she motioned toward the pigeon collection, "—is your best bet."

Reaper stepped around her and made his way to the long table where pencil filled rusted cans, colored baskets, and stacks of paper strips, were scattered among the rainbow of bands and metal tubes. "And we're here why?"

Jim flicked the top off the tube in his hand and pulled out a rolled-up piece of paper. "That would be my question."

Lilith left the relative safety of her spot and headed over to the message table. "I need to send a couple of messages, maybe catch up with anything new and interesting."

Jim looked up, his gaze shifting to Reaper before quickly returning to Lilith, his expression bland. "Depends on what you consider interesting."

She leaned against the table, folded her arms, and settled in. "Heard any rumblings recently? Maybe from down south or up north?"

He tapped the rolled-up paper against his whisker-covered chin and narrowed his gaze in thought. "Got a few enterprising souls in the more questionable markets down south in a dither."

*Hmm, that counted as interesting.* "About?"

Under the gray whiskers, Jim's jaw worked, a sure sign he was contemplating which bits and pieces to share. "Rumors are flying that a couple of Cartel bigwigs have been spotted skulking around Phoenix. They're making people nervous."

"That's it?" That wasn't really news because the Cartels' leaders tended to stick to their territories down south, which left their enforcers to roam through the dust-choked streets of Lost Angels and Phoenix.

"What more you need?" Jim waved off the approach of a plump flier. "Jumpy sellers make for a shaky market, and right now sellers are tap dancing their way through deals trying to steer clear."

Not exactly the news she was hoping for, but... "I'm guessing everyone's ducking for cover."

"Pretty much." Jim grimaced. "Though not sure there's much cover to be found down there. Got to wonder why the bastards fought so damn hard to take that dust bowl."

"Control of the Colorado waterways." Reaper absently twisted a purple band around his finger, his voice hard as he shot Jim a wolfish grin. "Unfortunately, they forgot about the Free People."

Speculation was clear in Jim's gaze, but he echoed Reaper's grin. "Yeah, and it sucks to be them." He started towards the table, unrolled the message between his fingers, and once it was open, scanned it. A dark frown wiped away any lingering amusement and when Jim lifted his gaze to them, it was hard. "Seems it sucks to be you too."

Lilith, without appearing to rush, quickly moved between the two men and intercepted Jim's attention. She motioned to the message he held. "Let me guess. Bounty notice?"

Jim eyed her carefully as the lines bracketing his mouth carved deeper into his craggy skin. "Guessing there's more to this story?"

"Much." Reaper stepped up behind her, his voice an intimidating rumble.

She leaned back just that little bit until his chest met her spine and basically restrained him with her body. "Too much to share, actually."

A long, tense minute passed as Jim considered them. Finally, he blew out a noisy breath. "You know I can't keep this from Gil."

Some of Lilith's tension eased. "I know."

"Who's Gil?" asked Reaper.

Lilith tilted her head back and shared. "Gil manages the incoming bounties around here when he's not busy printing up the local paper. He's got his fingers in a lot of different pies, some of which are less than admirable." She turned to Jim. "All I'm asking is a delay before you share."

Jim held her stare, his expression unrelenting.

She aimed for the man's one soft spot. "How about you give me until after you enjoy your dinner with Mildred?"

Jim looked at Reaper then back to Lilith, before reluctantly saying, "A day. No more, Lilith."

"Thank you." Anything was better than nothing.

Jim crossed to the far edge of the table and dropped the bounty message into one of the color-coded baskets. "You said you needed to send a message?"

Lilith rounded Reaper, went to the table, and nabbed a pencil and a couple of strips of paper. "One to Silas and Arabelle, both in Denver." She quickly wrote out a few coded directions.

"Got a well-rested bird," Jim told her. "I can send him out when you're ready." He left her and Reaper to head over to the coop to get his errand bird.

Reaper came up to her side as she was finishing up her note, and she turned her head to find him watching her.

"Who's Silas and Arabelle?" He kept his voice low so Jim wouldn't hear.

She followed his example and answered equally quiet. "They're my advisers, for lack of a better term."

"Advisers?" A thread of disbelief wove through his voice.

She rolled up the first note, picked up a second strip of paper, and started writing. "Uh, yeah."

"You have two advisers?" he repeated.

"No," she corrected. "I have three." When he arched a brow in silent question, she heaved a sigh. "Silas, Arabelle, and Everett."

Reaper flattened his palm on the table and rubbed the back of his neck. "Why the hell don't I recognize those names?"

Since he asked the question out loud, she figured he wasn't just asking to ask. She made a final notation on the paper and started to roll it up. "Maybe because it's not something we advertise. Not smart to give your enemies clearly defined targets." She set aside the rolled notes and feeling his stare, turned to meet his gaze. There was something on his face she didn't understand, but she propped a hand on a hip and asked, "Did you think I ran this entire territory by myself?"

Exasperation edged out whatever he was thinking, and he frowned. "I know it takes more than one person to run something this size." He studied her and this time she had no problem reading his expression because it was one he had aimed at her a time or two before. "How well do you know them?"

His suspicion was all well and good, if it was deserved, but as far as she was concerned, her advisers had more than proven their loyalty. "If I didn't trust them completely, they wouldn't be in their position." *Hell, they wouldn't be breathing.*

His mouth tightened at the edge in her voice indicating he was slipping along thin ice. "Dog said you weren't where you're supposed to be. Want to explain?"

*Did she?*

She wasn't sure because no matter how much it felt like they were stepping back into familiar roles, they were still worlds apart in a great many areas. Enough so, that sharing with him to that extent would put her at risk and she definitely wasn't ready to take that leap of faith yet. She turned, took another piece of paper, and jotted a few things down. Without looking at him, she asked, "Why all the questions?"

"Just answer me, Lilith."

Her pencil paused, then started up again. To get him to back down she would have to give him, maybe not everything, but something. "Fine. I'm due in Denver tomorrow to help Silas and Belle broker some shipments coming up from Bayou country."

"Instead, you're here. With me." The last was said with a hint of a bite.

"No," she denied, her voice sharp as she set the pencil aside and rolled up the third note. "Instead, I'm here with my daughter. Belle and Silas can handle it all by themselves. It's called delegation." His questioning of her judgement did not give her warm fuzzies. "Kind of like what you and your troupe of merry pranksters are currently doing."

Undeterred by her attitude, he folded his arm and glared. "And if something happens to you?"

*Was he worried? About her?* The thought was so unexpected she could only blink. "Charity will make sure Everett, Silas, and Belle have everything they need to keep things moving."

"And Tabby?" he pressed.

It clicked then and some of her puzzlement disappeared. To ease his worry about a role he may not want, she said, "Vex and Charity have her covered." Unable to pass up a chance to poke at him, she cocked her head and batted her eyelashes. "Are you worried about me?"

Completely unamused by her antics, he growled, "I'm worried about taking you into a situation where everyone's gunning for me. They don't give a shit about who gets caught in the crossfire. If it happened to be you, they would consider it an unexpected bonus."

His serious response held enough sincerity to leave her off balance. Not sure how to take it, she stopped baiting him and went with honesty. "I'm going with you, Reaper. Remember the whole allies' thing? That's kind of how it works."

Frustration lit his eyes as he straightened, putting a couple inches between them. "I don't like it."

She stepped in until their bodies brushed, tilted her head back to maintain eye contact and studied him. A mix of frustration and temper did a piss poor job at hiding his worry, and her heart turned over. She patted his chest in mock sympathy. "Now maybe you'll understand how I feel about you facing down Michael all by your lonesome."

Reaper's jaw locked and his lips thinned as red, from anger or frustration, or both, spread under his face.

*Yeah, someone didn't like looking into a mirror. What a shocker.*

Their semi-silent argument was interrupted when Jim cleared his throat loudly and dropped more messages into various baskets. When he spotted the third rolled note Lilith left on the table, he asked, "That need to be delivered too?"

Lilith stepped back, picked it up, and handed it to Jim. "Need it to go to Everett."

"Isn't he in town?"

"Yep." She didn't elaborate and waited to see if he'd ask because sometimes Jim's curiosity got the best of him. Since he continued sorting the incoming messages, she figured this wasn't one of those times. Good thing, because the explanation on why she couldn't be spotted in town would take too damn long.

"You asked for news." Jim returned to their previous conversation.

Lilith made a noncommittal hum.

"Did you hear that someone's been hunting down Raiders?" Jim rattled on. "Guess they pissed off one too many people, because they're dropping like flies."

"Bound to happen when you shit on everyone," she murmured.

"True," the old man agreed.

She touched Jim's arm and when he looked at her, she nodded to the notes and said, "Thank you."

"Welcome." Within seconds he had the rolled messages safely encased and had gathered up three bands. "Anything else?" His tone implied he hoped not.

"We're good." She preferred not to stick around with the flying rats. Besides, she and Reaper needed to head back in time to meet with Havoc.

Jim gave a sharp nod and started to turn away.

She called his name, and when he turned back, she held his gaze and warned with lethal hardness, "No Gil."

At her implied threat, Jim swallowed hard, and wariness flared in his eyes. "Twenty-four hours," he stated.

Confident she'd get those hours, she dismissed him and turned to Reaper. "Time to go."

# fifteen

Reaper and Lilith worked their way through the Pearl District to meet up with the others as evening knocked on the door. The afternoon heat had been replaced by the incoming night's cooler breeze, and they stuck as close to the lengthening shadows as possible, not tempting fate with anyone watching, and there was no doubt that someone would be watching. Jim might not share the bounty notice with Gil, but as Dog pointed out, word traveled fast.

Some of the shops and street stalls were closing down, while others were just getting busy. The hum of corn-fed engines joined the mix of hooves and wheels, and the noisy chorus played counterpoint to conversations punctuated by bursts of laughter that spilled from the openings of eateries and bars.

Reaper stayed at Lilith's back and constantly scanned the passing faces for possible threats as he stewed over her earlier comments. Her taunt that he was worried about her was mostly true, and frustration simmered at her insistence at coming with him to the Sandpit. Not that she couldn't take care of herself, but should something happen to her, guess who'd get blamed? And he had enough shit on his plate without having the entire Rocky Mountain territory hounding his ass. Not to mention what it would do to Tabby to lose her mom.

But if he was completely honest, that wasn't the real problem.

No, the real problem was how much hell Lilith's presence played with his control and his emotions. Having her at his side woke not only his protective nature but other feelings he was better off without. Bad enough the Vultures and Math were sucked into this damn mess, but having Lilith, his daughter's mother, in the crosshairs of the brutal maniacs currently hunting him? That went against every instinct he owned.

They moved down a particularly busy section of the street and a rowdy group gathered around a gambling hall entrance forced Lilith out of the shadows. Reaper smoothly moved to her side, curled an arm around her waist, and put himself between her and the street.

"My hero." Her soft sarcastic drawl barely reached him.

He dropped his gaze and caught the small smile that played over her lips just as the hair on the back of his neck rose to attention.

Lilith's gaze drifted past his shoulder and her smile went sharp. "Incoming."

He edged her closer to the buildings and kept the stalls and crowds between them and the threat closing in. "How many?"

"Two."

Which meant more were probably lying in wait. He slowed their pace and let his gaze skim over the street ahead. Sure enough, in the street ahead, two more figures stepped out from a bar.

He pulled Lilith close and lowered his head, giving the impression they were just another couple on a stroll. With his mouth near her ear, he murmured, "Twelve o'clock."

She played along, turning deeper into him, and bunching his t-shirt in her free hand. She angled her head, the rim of the hat leaving her face shadowed as they kept moving. "Guess you're just too famous for a simple makeover."

Maybe, or maybe ol' Jim hadn't kept his word.

Not that it mattered, but if got the chance, he'd get an answer from the arrogant pricks trying to collect.

The two behind them closed in and Reaper's spine twitched. Ahead the other duo started down the sidewalk. Reaper was about to pull Lilith into the street when a boisterous group burst out of a nearby doorway with a raucous spat of laughter.

Reaper wasted no time using the unexpected cover and thrust Lilith ahead of him with a hand on her spine. "Go!"

He stayed at her back and followed her through the still open door into the shop's confines. The shift from evening sunlight to the even dimmer interior lighting left him momentarily blind. Smoke hit his nose and by the time his eyes adjusted, he and Lilith were halfway through the haze-filled room.

They wove their way through low-slung couches that surrounded small tables where occupants puffed away on hookahs and barely batted an eyelash at their passage. He followed Lilith through a beaded curtain and into a dark hallway where he almost missed the faint edges of a door on their left.

He snagged the back of her shirt and pulled her to a stop. "Hold up."

She spun around, a frown on her face. Her mouth opened, probably to bitch, but when she noted the door, it snapped close. Smoke wafted back on a shift of air and her gaze darted behind him. "Hurry up," she hissed.

Light glinted off the top corner of the doorframe and he reached up to silence the bell as he twisted the knob and inched the door open. Fresh air slipped through the narrow opening. He pushed it just wide enough for Lilith to squeeze through. "Go."

She ducked under his arm and darted out. He pivoted and followed, holding on to the bell as long as possible before carefully letting it go and shutting the door.

"Here." Lilith handed him a thick board.

He propped it under the door handle and then spotted a rusted-out bike engine nestled under a tarp among the garbage bins. "Grab that!"

She shoved the bins apart and started dragging the engine over. Once she was within reach, he helped her get it into place.

With the door blocked, it was time to get the hell out of dodge.

Normally the narrow alley they found themselves in would mean easy street access, but not this time thanks to the metal fence that blocked the entrance. The back wasn't much better—a brick wall decorated in street tags, topped by metal rods, and tipped with spikes guarded the exit.

Lilith disappeared into the heavier shadows at the far end and her soft grunt was followed by the screech of metal. He joined her where she was crouched over a metal screen that barred a basement well. She straightened, her face grim. "Welded shut."

"Shit," he muttered. They were boxed in.

The metal fence at the end rattled.

He and Lilith inched back into the shadows as two of their pursuers tried the fence again. Something heavy slammed into the hookah shop's door and the engine scraped across the pitted ground with an ear-splitting screech. It would only take a couple more hits before they broke through, and the others would make short work of the damn fence.

That left him and Lilith with left only one option. Up.

He caught Lilith's wrist and drew her towards the back wall. "Come on." He knelt at the base and cupped his hands. "Ready?"

Lilith grimaced and groused, "Seriously?" Then she gripped his shoulders and put her foot in his hand.

"You're welcome to stay and entertain our guests." He didn't wait for a response before he straightened and propelled her up.

The slap of her hands hitting the metal posts was drowned out by another hard hit on the door. He waited until Lilith had pulled herself up and carefully maneuvered over the spikes before he stepped back. He had no choice but to risk being spotted because he needed the distance.

Sure enough, a shout went up behind him and the metal fence at the end groaned.

Reaper didn't bother to look but rushed the wall and leapt. His chest slammed against the brick just as the door behind him cracked and gave way. His hands locked on the metal posts and his muscles burned as he used his arms to pull himself up the wall. He managed to find a couple of precarious toeholds to help his ascent.

He caught a flash of light off metal out of the corner of his eye, but it was quickly followed by a pained grunt from below.

Lilith leaned over the wall's edge. "Unless you like playing dartboard, I suggest you move it."

He swung his leg up, ignoring the burning slice of the rough edge scraping through his jeans along his calf, and made it to the top of the wall. With Lilith's help he avoided the worst of the spikes and dropped on the other side. He got to his feet and studied the roof. It was fairly flat with a couple of old, broken vent housing units.

Good enough. Even better, no witnesses.

He looked back down to see the three men rushing the wall. "You've got to be kidding me." Did they not get that all he had to do was pick them off as they hit the wall?

"Reaper, dear." At Lilith's call, he turned his head. She motioned with a knife to the roof on the left. "Looks like they invited their friends."

Two more figures were heading in fast. He pulled a knife from his boot, then shot Lilith a grin. "Ready to play?"

Lilith flexed her wrists and brought her blades up. "You really know how to show a girl a good time, Reaper."

"Only the best for you, darling."

She shook her head. "Go entertain our wall crawlers, I'll take care of our party crashers."

A familiar anticipation curled through his veins and adrenaline sharpened every sense as he turned back to the incoming threat, leaving her to it. He danced out of the way of a vicious knife swipe, slammed his boot on the wrist holding the blade and trapped it against the roof.

His would-be attacker gave a pained yelp and tried to pull himself up. When his head popped over the roof's edge, Reaper pivoted, and the idiot's wrist snapped under Reaper's boot. He followed up with a deadly kick and nailed his toe into dumbass's temple. The idiot's dead weight yanked his wrist from under Reaper's foot and the body hit the ground below with a dull thud.

Unfortunately, Reaper's meet and greet allowed the other two enough time to scramble up and over, and they now hemmed him on both sides. Reaper jerked back, barely dodging a wicked gut slice from the one on his left, as he blocked the thrust aimed at his kidneys from the other side.

Reaper drew his two assailants deeper onto the roof and

away from the edge, giving himself more room to move as he did a quick threat assessment.

The attacker to his right kept his blade in close and his focus on Reaper's chest, demonstrating experience. The one on the left, waved an overly large blade from side to side with what Reaper figured was supposed to be a frightening smile. That one would the easier target. Young, dumb, and easily provoked.

To test his theory, he matched the kid's steps and held his blade still. "Careful there, you might cut off something important."

The kid's grin went manic. "Kind of the plan, asshole."

Reaper kept moving and forced the kid to unintentionally block his partner. "Didn't your buddy ever tell you bigger isn't always better?"

"If it gets me the bounty on your ass, bigger is fuckin' better, my man."

A sharp curse erupted from where Lilith was currently entertaining her guests.

Young and Dumb rushed Reaper.

Reaper stepped into the attack and blocked the incoming thrust with his arm, the hit reverberating down into his shoulder. Nose to nose with the kid, Reaper gritted out, "How much?"

The kid, face red, puffed out, "Half a mil in credits."

"Not enough." Reaper sank his blade into the idiot's gut, sliced up, ran the knife along the kid's ribs, then twisted his wrist as he yanked the blade free. He spun, dragging the dying kid around and shoved him at his incoming partner.

The older man pushed the stumbling kid away as Reaper closed in. Reaper knew it was dangerous to drag this out, so he went low as the man swung out, his knife kissing a line of fire over Reaper's shoulder and arm. Before the silent man could follow through and inflict more damage, Reaper whipped his blade across both femoral arteries.

It didn't stop the man from scoring another line of fire along Reaper's back. Reaper rolled away and came up on his knees just in time to block a vicious kick. He caught the man's leg in a ruthless grip, trapping it against his chest. Then he dropped to his back and forced the man off balance.

In a futile attempt to escape, the man twisted and landed on his stomach next to Reaper.

Reaper rolled to his knees and sank his blade into the man's kidney.

The dying man yowled and swung back trying to get Reaper. He missed.

Reaper didn't. He yanked out his knife, sank it into the base of the man's skull, and pulled it free.

*Better safe than sorry.*

He wiped the blade on the dead man's shirt and lifted his head to find Lilith standing over her last opponent.

She had one hand in his hair and the other was etching a grisly red line across his throat. She shoved his head forward and followed it with a vicious kick to the spine. The body dropped face first to the roof. She stood there, hat gone, knife in one hand, the disappearing sun adding an edge of fire to her wild tangle of hair, and it hit him in all its glory—an image of fierce beauty and undeniable temptation.

Reaper got to his feet, sheathed his knife, and stalked toward her. When he got close, he wrapped a hand around the back of her neck and dragged her against him.

Her free hand went to his chest, but not to push him away. Instead, she grabbed his t-shirt and pulled him closer, her face flushed with a savage light.

Taking it for the invitation it was, he ravaged her mouth with his as adrenaline and brutal hunger crashed through him, and she met his hunger with her own white-hot need.

Her taste hit his bloodstream like a fireball and shot straight to his dick.

Keeping his hand at her neck, he curled his other arm around her waist and pulled her tight against him, grinding his aching length against her scorching softness.

Their tongues dueled as her hips met his demand and then she made a few of her own. She tore her mouth away and sucked in air.

He tightened his hold in her hair and tugged her head back, arching her neck. He left the heated pleasure of her lips to nip her chin and lay a line of open mouth kisses along her neck.

She made a sound suspiciously close to a purr and shifted her hand to his bent head. Her change in position rubbed her tits against his chest and sparked a cascade of sensation. She got a grip on his short strands and tugged. "Reaper." His name came out husky.

With a strong suck, he left a strawberry at the base of her throat before letting her lift his head. "What?"

Her kiss-swollen lips curved into a wicked smile, and the same hunger that crawled under his skin darkened her green eyes. "We're going to be late."

"Fuck 'em." He dipped his head determined to return to his previous business, but she kept a painful grip on his hair. He growled.

"I'd rather you fuck me," she managed, laughter clear in her voice. "Just not where everyone can watch."

Since he'd rather be fucking her as well, he pressed a quick, hard kiss to her lips. "Fine." He reluctantly let her go and stepped back so she could sheath her knife. He looked around at the bodies. "We leaving them here?"

She scanned the roof and then pointed to the vent housings. "Let's use those. If anyone's looking for them, might take them a bit to find them."

"Unless they come up and see that." He motioned to the blood that smeared the pitted surface.

She shrugged. "It is what it is."

Since he couldn't argue, he helped her stash the bodies. Instead of retracing their steps back to the hookah shop, they decided to use the roofs lining the street to make their way further down. About a block out, they found a different route back to the street, and once on the ground, they beat feet to where they were to meet the others.

<h1 style="text-align:right">sixteen</h1>

Night settled in as they headed a block or so north and left the light and bustle of Pearl District behind. The streets were quieter and darker, even at this short distance, which made it easier for them to pass unnoticed.

The designated meeting place had once been a house of worship, complete with peaked roofs and a statuesque turret, but now its patrons were more concerned with the earthly delights of wine, food, and flesh. Lights danced through stained glass and rained colorful illumination over the cracked, tree-lined sidewalk.

Reaper followed Lilith up the three stone steps, and then caught the edge of the wooden door she pulled open. She ducked under his arm to slip through, and he followed her inside where ornate benches lined the main hall and heavy wooden tables with high back chairs filled the main space. The din of laughter and conversation competed with the smells of food.

Lilith aimed for the back of the hall, winding her way around busy servers and eclectic patrons, leaving Reaper to trail in her wake. She made her way to a tall, gray-haired man who resembled a scarecrow and stood sentry before a set of doors.

He watched them approach, his lined features expressionless, and his faded blue eyes sharp as he opened the door. "Good evening, madam."

"Thank you, Yuri." Lilith gave the man a polite smile and stepped through the doorway only to turn back and ask, "My guests?"

Yuri's thin lips barely curved, and Reaper wondered if a full-on smile would break something. "Have already arrived." The sentry eyed Reaper and addressed Lilith. "Will you need anything else?"

Lilith shook her head, seemingly undeterred by his dour demeanor. "No, thanks. However, should anyone ask..."

Amusement glinted in the old man's eyes. "You were never here."

Lilith patted his arm and turned away. Reaper followed Lilith into a short hall shrouded in hushed quiet and behind them, Yuri closed the door and locked them inside.

As they walked side-by-side down the lighted hall and passed closed doors, Reaper shot Lilith a look. "Tell me that's not our only exit."

"Relax." She stopped in front of a door near the end of the hall and rapped her knuckles against it twice. She didn't wait for a response but turned the knob and pushed it open to reveal a comfortably furnished room.

Familiar voices drifted out—Havoc's rough tones and Mercy's lighter ones—along with the smell of food, and Reaper's stomach rumbled as they crossed jewel tone rugs that littered the stone floor of the main sitting area. "Please tell me you left us something to eat."

"Help yourself," said Havoc without moving from his position on the couch where Mercy was perched on the couch's back, working his shoulders. "Charity and Ruin are already heading back to the cabin."

Lilith followed Reaper into the kitchen that was to the right of a squat hall with two closed doors—presumably bedrooms, and they got busy piling plates high with food. He finished first and returned to claim one of the two easy chairs that bookended the couch. "What did they find out?" He took a bite of fried chicken.

"Not much," Mercy answered as she dug an elbow in Havoc's shoulder and earned a muffled groan from the big man. "No sightings of Michael in New Seattle, so consensus is he isn't there."

"And Greer?" Lilith asked as she set a plate filled with fruit on the coffee table and took a seat on the floor.

"Not a damn thing," Havoc said.

Mercy shook her head and grimaced. "Actually, there was something, just not sure how solid it was."

"Share," Lilith demanded.

"You know how tight Greer holds her position as Michael's right hand?" Mercy waited for Lilith's nod. "Seems during the last half year or so, she's encountered a bit of competition."

The strawberry Lilith was dragging through peanut butter stilled. "From?"

Mercy shrugged. "It's not real clear, but I get the impression it's one of her men."

Reaper frowned because that didn't make sense. From what he knew of Greer, she wasn't one to put up with unnecessary shit, especially from someone who had the balls to question her. "Why wouldn't she just get rid of him?"

"Good question," Mercy said. "Problem is, I don't have an answer. Whatever's happening, it's not widely known which makes getting details a challenge."

Yet, the little spy still managed to ferret out the fact and share, proving a Strix never lost their touch. It might be nothing or it could be something, but either way until they understood how it played into the overall picture, it was best to tuck that information away.

Reaper eyed Mercy's hands as they worked Havoc's shoulder and asked, "What happened?"

Havoc winced as Mercy's lips twitched, but she gleefully shared. "His trip from the cabin was rough."

"Damn bike's a piece of shit, Lilith," Havoc grumbled.

Lilith's hand paused halfway to her mouth. "Tell me you didn't total it."

Mercy snickered and a hint of color worked its way under Havoc's cheeks. "Frame's bent."

Lilith glared at him.

"I'll fix it," he grumbled.

"Damn right you will," she snapped back before taking a bite of her apple slice.

Mercy gently pushed Havoc forward so she could swing her leg around him and slide down next to him. "We got your stash. Should be enough to get you to Phoenix."

Since that request was a recent addition to his to-do list, Reaper arched a brow. "Guessing you ran into Dog?"

Havoc nodded. "He filled us in. Didn't take much to figure out your next step would be a visit to the Sandpit. Thought you could use a little extra support."

Reaper's fork full of beans paused halfway to his mouth. "You talking about you or the weapons?"

Havoc met his gaze. "Both."

"Guess you're riding with Reaper then," Lilith said. "Because I'm not riding bitch all the way into Phoenix."

Mercy laughed. "No worries, got us some sand bikes."

Reaper was impressed because those were hard to find up here in the mountains. "Did you now?"

The dark-haired woman flashed a knowing grin. "It's all

about connections, my man." She pushed off the couch and sauntered out of the room to collect what they brought back.

Lilith called out behind her, "What else did your connections share?"

"Think there's a meeting going down." Mercy yelled and then returned with an oversized duffle bag she dropped on the floor next to the coffee table. "Figured we should bring our own party favors." She crouched, undid the zipper, and pulled out a well-taken care of M40. "A long range with scope." She set it on the floor, reached back in, and brought out three old style Gloch 19s. "A couple of semi's." They joined the rifle before she went back in. "Filtration masks, a couple of boomers, and—" she brandished a long roll of paper and started to unroll it on the table, "—this."

"What is that?" Curious, Reaper set aside his food and sat forward on the edge of his chair, duly impressed with Mercy's connections.

"This is the layout of Castille Duna, our most likely target."

"How'd you figure?" Once upon a time Phoenix was home to millions and sprawled over two thousand square miles. Like much of the major metropolises, survivors gathered in clusters, shrinking its reach, and leaving most of it abandoned or buried in sand. Castille Duna was an old rehabbed casino development that had belonged to the Free People before the Cartels claimed Phoenix. He'd been there during the Border Wars and his memory was good, but not good enough to try an infiltrate all these years later.

Mercy frowned and glanced at him. "Dog."

"Funny, he didn't have much on details when we ran into him." Not that Reaper didn't believe her, but if Dog had known this, why hadn't he shared when they talked earlier?

"Didn't when we saw him before, either," Havoc elaborated. "But Lash just got back from down south and mentioned increased activity on the east roads, complete with armed escorts."

"Add in the fact the Cartel prefer to stay where they're familiar with—" Mercy set a heavy glass on the corner of the plans and Lilith held the one closest to her, "—and you get this."

Considering the time Mercy spent spying on the Cartels, Reaper couldn't discount her opinion. "Works for me."

She shot him a mischievous grin. "See, I knew I'd eventually win you over."

He couldn't stop his lip twitch at her quip. Truth be told, he actually did like the assassin, if for no other reason than her unquestionable devotion to Havoc and how she lightened the shadows that haunted his best friend.

"You got any guesses as to where in this place a meet would happen?" He eyed the plans, noting just how big the old casino was, and based off the drawing, it was also outdated. He pointed out the long eastern wing. "This section is either buried or blown to shit, so we can cross it off."

"Yeah," Havoc agreed as he leaned in from the couch, his arms on his knees and studied the plans. "The other side is somewhat habitable." He motioned to the other section. "Or at least it was a couple years back. Most of the back side of this is unreachable now that the dunes have settled over it."

"That leaves us with here." Lilith circled an area that included the bottom floor and an entrance set within a curved wall. "If we can find a way in through whatever is standing on the west side, we might get lucky and find a ringside seat to this shindig."

Reaper knew breaching Castille wasn't the issue, not with the numerous access points created by the decades of abandonment. It was finding a passable route to access the few remaining areas that could be secured. Most of which would leave whoever dared to try bruised and bloodied.

For the next twenty minutes or so they pored over the plans and brainstormed options. When everyone was finally satisfied that they covered what they could, Mercy pushed to her feet and stretched. "Since we need to hit the road early, I'm calling it a night." She offered her hand to Havoc, who took it and rose from the couch.

Lilith stood and began collecting the empty glasses and bottles. "Those sand bikes have lights?"

"Yeah." Havoc wrapped an arm around Mercy's waist and pulled her close.

Lilith took her collection to the kitchen. "Then I suggest we head out before dawn. We're looking at, at least thirteen hours on the road."

"Sounds good." Reaper leaned back in his chair, rested his head against the back, stretched his legs out, and rested his bare feet on the table. "If we time it right, we might be able to outrun any late afternoon dust storms or monsoon rains."

Havoc and Mercy murmured their agreement before bidding Lilith and Reaper goodnight and heading towards the bedrooms.

Reaper let his eyes close and enjoyed the momentary respite. He drifted while the soft sounds of Lilith setting the empties in the bins, then puttering around the kitchen punctuated the quiet. He didn't know how much time passed before something cool and wet pressed against his arm. He opened his eyes to find most of the lights had been turned off, leaving the room dimly lit.

Lilith stood next to him with a fresh bottle. She lifted it from his arm and waggled it in silent question.

He took it and held it loosely between his fingers. "Thanks." He took a swig, and then set it on the side table.

She took a seat on the chair's arm, hitched one leg on the padded armrest, and braced the other one against the floor. "You falling asleep?"

"Thinking about it." His lashes drifted down and enjoyed the quiet they shared. It hit him then, how much he missed this, spending time with her. Funny how the last few, angry weeks of their relationship had dominated the affection and compassion of the previous months.

"You do that, you'll be stiff as hell tomorrow." Her fingers drifted through his hair, and brushed through the short strands with slow, mesmerizing strokes.

He groaned as the sensation wandered down his neck and carved a path of heat that curled deep in his gut. It left his skin highly sensitized and reignited his earlier edgy hunger. He hadn't forgotten her agreement to sleep with him. Hell, the anticipation lurked at the edges of his mind all damn day, just waiting for a chance to pounce.

She shifted and he barely lifted his lashes as her scent filled his lungs. He swallowed a groan when he realized her newest position put her tempting breasts within nuzzling distance. Predictably, other parts of him stirred in hopeful interest.

"Think you can make it to the bedroom?" The husky rasp of her voice invoked sultry images and his dick went from hopeful to painful in a matter of seconds.

He raised his gaze to find her watching him with a mysterious feminine grin. "You're an evil woman, Lilith."

His comment earned another one of those X-rated laughs. "Considering your current position, I'm thinking your earlier promises were a tad over enthusiastic, and for tonight I'm safe from your lecherous intentions." She pressed a kiss against the top of his head.

*Like hell!*

He wrapped an arm around her before she could draw

back and dragged her into his lap, her laughter soft and knowing. He cut it off with a quick kiss as he slipped his other hand
behind her knees. "Don't be so sure."

He took her lips in another hungry kiss, shoved to his feet,
and headed to the bedroom determined to prove her wrong.

# seventeen

As Reaper carried her to the bedroom Lilith curled her arms around his neck and lost herself in the heat of his kiss. The past had collided with the present when she came back from the kitchen and found him sprawled out in the chair. It was so reminiscent of better times that it taunted her with an unrelenting promise only Reaper could keep or break.

The lingering adrenaline rush of their shared kiss after the fight joined in with the poignant hunger and sparked a fierce craving she could no longer starve out of existence. Besides, if things played out as expected, this would be their best opportunity to feed it before he changed his mind. She consoled herself with the reminder that they agreed to keep it to just sex.

If he was any other man, she wouldn't hesitate to simply take what she wanted without apologies and call it good. But this was Reaper, the one man who touched her on levels no one else came close to so she went for a sneaky play of questioning his ability to follow through on his promise. Just like the first time, it worked because he couldn't resist a challenge, and considering where she currently found herself, she considered her plan a success.

The taste of him hit her system like a fireball and burned through her shaky rationalizations. His tongue danced with hers, stoking her rising need higher and eroding her typical restraint. Her hunger matched his and she was determined to make every moment tonight count.

He lifted his head and held her gaze, locking them in a maelstrom of voracious need, as he bumped open the bedroom door with his shoulder.

Her restraint was in tatters, and she decided it was only fair to destroy his, so she drew her nails lightly over the back of his neck and nibbled along his shadowed jaw. Trusting him not to drop her, she turned deeper into him, a soft groan escaping when her move crushed her breasts against him. She didn't stop with her kisses, her mouth working down his neck to his throat as she petted over his broad shoulders and down the hard planes of his chest as he froze in the doorway, his back to the door.

His hold on her tightened and threatened to leave marks, but his head fell back and hit the door with a thump even as he gave her more to taste and tease. "Fuck me, Lilith."

His words were a deep groan that vibrated against her lips and further down as it rumbled in his chest. A cascade of electrifying sparks swept through her, coiling through every erogenous zone she had until she ached.

She sucked hard where his neck curved into his shoulder and made sure to leave her mark before she lifted her head. Noting the deep color seeping under his cheeks and the dangerous glitter in his eyes, she purred in feminine satisfaction. She licked her lips and found her voice. "That's the plan."

He pushed off the door with a feral growl, kicked it closed, and lowered his head to reclaim her mouth with a destructive skill not lost in the intervening years. The intimate dance of lips and tongues was interwoven with small, erotic nips that added fuel to the turbulent inferno.

Memories crested and broke against the searing pleasure of Lilith's reality, and for a heart-stopping moment, everything in her stilled under the stunning force of what raged between them because hidden deep, where she tried not to see, warning bells triggered.

Reaper nipped her lower lip, and the sensuous sting shook her free of her momentary immobility. She went to soothe the ache with her tongue only to find him there already, gently swiping it away. The ferocious edge of his kiss gentled, and she willingly sank under the carnal wave. She curled her hands into his shoulders and pulled him closer, matching the intensity of his provocative assault.

Under her palms his muscles coiled, and she lost her grip when she suddenly found herself weightless. She blinked as her ass hit the padded mattress. Reaper crowded in before she could catch her breath, forced her legs wide to accommodate him, and tore his t-shirt over his head to reveal an erotic expanse of muscled skin.

She scrambled to her knees not wanting to miss her opportunity and swept her hands over him, taking in as much as she could in greedy passes. Under her touch his history lay in the collection of scars, some familiar, others not, that marred the lines of defined muscle and left his skin an intriguing map of rough and soft.

Her gaze followed her hands as they moved to his shoulders, and only then did she note the angry looking cut that disappeared down his back. The nasty mark chilled her lust-filled haze and shifted her touch from seductive to determined. She tugged him around and found another slice on his upper back that spanned the space between his shoulders. She let out a hiss of displeasure. "Dammit, Reaper. We need to clean you up."

"Later." Reaper broke her hold with a determined twist and caught her wrists, drawing her hands away. His head lowered, his intent to get back to where they were clear.

Although her body was in ferment agreement with his plan she tugged against his grip until he reluctantly let her go. She couldn't not touch him, so she brushed her hand along his stomach and slid it around his ribs as she slipped out from under him and off the bed. "First aid now, sexy, fun times after."

He heaved a put-upon sigh and rolled to his back. "It's a fucking scratch, woman."

*Stubborn, bullheaded ass.* She grabbed his wrist, intending to lead him to the bathroom, and shot him a dark look. "Your scratch might need stitches."

When he opened his mouth to argue, she shifted her grip, leaned over him, pressed a hard, quick kiss against his lips, and then drew back just enough to meet his eyes. "Be good and maybe I'll kiss it better."

His free arm wrapped around her waist, holding her so close she couldn't miss the long, hard length of him between them. "In that case, I have an injury you haven't seen yet." Every move of his lips brushed hers.

She released his wrist, leaned back enough to get her hand between them, and then glided her fingers over the clenching muscles of his stomach until she could stroke along his rigid shaft. "Patience is a virtue."

"Patience is overrated," he muttered as he buried a hand in her hair and pulled her down so he could press a series of heated kisses along her neck.

The feel of his lips and the teasing edge of his teeth left her shuddering and her nipples rising to aching peaks. In a desperate attempt to alleviate the aching fullness of her breasts, she arched her back, forcing them against his chest, the nails of one hand digging into his shoulder, her other tightening on his impressive girth.

His startled hiss and quick twitch of his shoulder jerked her unruly libido back in line and served as a reminder of his wounds. She sucked in a deep breath and pushed up until she could get to her feet. "Bathroom. Now." She followed her order with a gentle tug on his wrists.

He let her pull him up from the bed and to his feet. He trailed his finger down her neck, along her collarbone, and down over the swell of her breast, his indigo eyes dark and hungry.

Mesmerized by the combination of his heated stare and his touch that left a line of fire in its wake, she held her breath as he drew closer to the aching tip of her breath. But wicked man that he was, he dropped his hand just shy of its goal. She couldn't stop her small whimper of wordless protest from escaping. His lips curved with masculine satisfaction as he retreated to the bathroom.

Following him to the confines of the bathroom, she accused, "Tease."

"Oh, I have every intention of following through, babe," he promised as he backed away so she could crouch in front of the sink and rummage in the cabinet. "You're the one insisting on tending my boo-boos."

Their close proximity sent awareness prickling over her skin. The flimsy cabinet door was the only real barrier between them, and it wouldn't take much press the advantage of her current position without coming close to those cuts.

*Patience.*

The reminder did little to ease the cravings eroding her control. She shook her head, dug out a basket filled with medical supplies, and rose to set it on the counter. "Let me make sure it really is a scratch, tough guy." She grabbed a washcloth, turned on the tap, and bossed, "Turn around."

The hunger in his eyes deepened, but thankfully, he did what she asked, and gave her his back as he braced his forearms on the shower rod. Any other time, in any other situation, his position would inspire all sorts of carnal delights, but her need to make sure he truly was okay won out.

*Dangerous, he was so dangerous.*

She wrung out the washcloth and noted the fine tremor of her hands. She took a deep breath, grimly steadied her hands, and then focused on cleaning his cuts. Once she got rid of the dried blood and dirt, she discovered they weren't as deep as they first appeared. Medical tape was needed to keep a couple of spots closed, but the majority just needed ointment. "Doesn't look like we'll need stitches."

"Told you."

Behind his back, she rolled her and finished treating his cuts, gently taping the edges and spreading the ointment in a thin layer. Considering where the night was headed, she figured it was best to give him some protection and added a layer of gauze to the few serious ones. She tossed the last of the supplies on the counter behind her and brushed a long stroke along his spine. "There, all done."

The muscles of his back jumped under her touch, and he rolled his broad shoulders like a great cat urging another stroke as he held his position.

She took his silent invitation to heart and stepped in close, her thighs brushing the back of his as her fingers traced the elaborate tattoo curling along his spine. Once upon a time, those curving lines were an addiction she happily followed for hours. Etched in shades of black, the stylized raven wrapped its wings from shoulder to shoulder, the edges of the feathers curling over his biceps, its beak just below the base of Reaper's neck.

Time hadn't lessened her craving and now that she could indulge, she dipped her head to his heated skin and followed the captivating pattern with mouth and tongue. She traced her fingertips along his ribs in a slow path to his front, where she flattened her palms against his stomach. The heat of him seared her palms as she explored the rise and fall of his washboard stomach and her hands slipped under the waistband of his jeans, trailing along the defined lines.

His breath shuddered out on a low groan.

It was all the encouragement she needed. She slipped the button open and slid his zipper down, carefully releasing his hard cock. Her breath quickened as she used her hands to spread open the material and her pulse skyrocketed as his hot, hard length filled her palms.

*Got to love a man who went commando.*

She curled her hands around his thickness, and he jerked at her initial touch. But when she began to stroke him with deliberate, wicked purpose, he rolled his hips, deepening her strokes. She pressed against his back, her heart racing, the ache between her legs growing, and ground against him seeking ease.

Her mouth moved over his heated skin with greedy hunger as she kept up her devastating caress. His heavy breaths matched hers as the air heated and filled with the musky scent of their combined need. She slid her thumb over his blunt tip on her next stroke and smeared his arousal over silken skin.

"Enough." He covered her hand with his and enforced his gritty demand with a squeeze, forcing her to stop.

"No." Her denial was hoarse, and a shuddering breath escaped as she dropped her forehead against his spine and fought to regain her balance in the raging sensual storm. "More." Entreaty edged her voice, but she didn't give the first damn if it sounded like begging because the desire tearing through her left her aching on such a deep level it was almost painful.

His grip on her hand tightened and nearly crushed her

fingers against his dick. Afraid of hurting what she most wanted, she let him go. He kept his fingers locked with hers as he turned around, pulled her close, and trapped his hardened length between them. He tangled his other hand in her hair and tugged her head back to ravage her mouth.

She surrendered all her doubts and worries to the carnal storm he created and let them drown in the tempest of unrestrained hunger. Want, need, hunger, it all boiled together to create a fast and furious storm that swept her away.

When he freed her hand, she realized he was backing her out of the bathroom. With nothing to hold her back, she swept her hands over his chest, taking all that he was in through touch. She softly flicked his nipples in a tease before coasting down his ribs to trace the tantalizing muscled paths to where his jeans hung on his lean hips. Her thumb brushed his blunt tip, and she trailed her fingers along the edges of his hard length as he lay against her stomach.

He continued to ravage her mouth with destructive purpose, holding her head between his hands. When he finally let her come up for air, he shifted his grip to her hips and lifted. "Up."

She clutched his shoulders in automatic obedience and hopped up as he cradled her ass. She curled her legs over his hips and settled against him, their groans coming simultaneously as her damp, heated core rode his rigid cock. Despite the barrier of her pants, she swore she could feel his heartbeat pulsing in his shaft as it pressed against her aching bundle of nerves. Like a junkie in search of a necessary fix, she began a slow, evocative glide. Somehow, he managed to keep moving, and with every step his dick bumped her clit, detonating tiny bombs of sensation until by the time they hit the bed, she teetered on the edge of coming.

He dropped her to her back on the mattress, settled his weight against her, and braced his arms on either side of her head. When he pushed up, the shift in his position lifted him from her chest but drove his groin deeper into her.

She clutched his shoulders and used the mindless lift of her hips to hold him in place. "No." A sharp smack to the outside of her thigh cleared her lust-filled haze and loosened her legs from his hips. Sprawled wantonly before him, she snapped, "What the hell, Reaper?"

He pulled back, his dark eyes glittered with lust, and the echo of the hunger crawling through her veins lined his face. He ran his knuckles down the center of her chest to the edge of her shirt, and then tugged it up. "Want you naked, woman."

Totally on board with his plan, she ripped her shirt off as he straightened and shoved his jeans down. She was working on her bra, when Reaper's busy hands went to her waist and undid her pants. Her fingers fumbled at her back as he dipped his head and nuzzled her belly before shoving her pants and undies down her legs.

His soft, erotic bite on the curve of her belly got her fingers working again. She tossed her bra aside and wiggled her feet to kick free of her jeans. Free from her clothes, she sank her hands into his hair, and held on as he continued to tease and taunt. His tongue dipped below her belly button and left a scorching damp trail to her heated core. Her breath caught in anticipation, and her legs shifted restlessly, giving him room.

He didn't make her wait long. His wicked mouth settled over her as his tongue swiped through her cream and curled around her clit in an erotic kiss. Pleasure slammed through her, and escaped on an airless scream. He continued his devastating assault until she was a boneless bundle of sensation, trying to relearn to breathe. He gave her one last, long, luxurious lick and she shuddered in dark delight.

*Damn, it had been too long.*

He rested his chin against the top of her mound and rubbed it across her in an absent caress. The rasp of his heavy shadow against her sensitive flesh caused her recently sated hunger to rouse. When she was able to focus, he asked, "Better?"

"Mm-hmm." It was the best she could do considering he'd just blown her mind. A sharp nip on her hip had her lifting lashes she hadn't realized had drifted close. "Hey!"

"Don't fall asleep on me," he demanded as he crawled over her and trapped her in a cage of his body. "We're not done."

Oh, she liked the sound of that. She caught his hard length in her hands and stroked. "Obviously."

Reaper twisted his hips out of her reach. "Uh-huh."

"Not fair." She put her empty hands to his shoulders. "I want to touch."

He shifted his weight to his knees and caught her hands, locking them against the bed by her head. "Won't last long if you do."

She was about to remind him that was the point when he bent his head and sucked a nipple into his mouth, his tongue curling around the tip, lashing her with erotic fire. Her spine arched, and she fed her breast deeper into the heated cavern of his wicked mouth. He used his teeth and tongue with wicked skill until all she could do was squirm under his onslaught. His name came out on a wailed demand. "Reaper!"

He ignored her pleas and never let up. Every scorching kiss, every erotic bite, was designed to throw her deeper into the maelstrom of sensation that rippled through her body and left a storm of hunger in its wake. He was ruthless in his sensual assault, stretching out against her and giving her more of his weight as he kept her pinned to the bed, her fingers curled into fists.

His hard length lay against her thigh, far from where she ached the most. Determined to get what she wanted, she untangled her legs from his and spread them wide in blatant invitation, forcing him to settle between her thighs. Their groans sounded simultaneously when his cock slid through the heated wetness between her legs.

He ground down and she countered by lifting her hips. Then she curled one leg around his hip and dug her heel into his ass in a desperate attempt to hold him in place. "Again!"

This time he heeded her breathless demand and rolled his hips, tormenting them both with another long, devastating glide. "Patience." He growled against her lips as his grip on her wrist loosened.

She tugged her arms free, caught his face in her hands, and held his gaze with her. "Fuck patience," she whispered.

His grin made all sorts of decadent promises. "Thought you wanted to fuck me."

For a moment she was tempted to admit she wanted more, so fucking much more, but the past kept the words locked tight. Instead, she gave his chin a punishing nip before saying, "I do, you bastard."

Something flickered in the depths of his eyes, and for a moment she worried he saw more than she wanted, but before that worry could grow, he gave her a purely wicked grin and cupped her hips, tilting her so he could drag his cock along her aching center. "You say the sweetest things."

Done playing, she tugged him down and ravaged his mouth with hers.

The fingers on her hips tightened and held her restless movements still as he slowly gentled the kiss and lifted his head.

Her arms went around his shoulders as their eyes met. For a breathless moment she wondered if her gaze mirrored the same dazed hunger and aching emotion that stared down at her. Then he shifted his hips, and with one hard stroke, drove his cock through her tight depths.

She curled her fingers into his neck as her body bowed in blinding pleasure, but she couldn't escape his gaze, nor did she want to. Instead, she gloried in how he filled all the empty places inside her. When he drew back, she almost sobbed, her muscles clenching in a frantic attempt to keep him. "Don't!"

Something infinitely tender gentled the harsh lines of his face. "Don't worry, baby, I've got you."

He did another controlled move, slid back in, deeper than before, and stayed there. He dropped his face into her shoulder, and she barely caught his rough, "Missed this."

Then he began to move, not giving her a chance to respond.

He rode her wild and hard, the storm raging out of control, sucking them both into a world of heat and hunger with only one, inevitable escape. They flew higher and higher, until they skirted so close to the blazing inferno, there would be nothing left when she fell.

But she didn't care.

She needed this—his taste, his touch, the feel of him powering between her thighs—it spilled into the aching emptiness that haunted her since the day she watched him walk away and settled in like a missing piece. But it was more than the fierce dance of their bodies, it was the delicate emotion that locked them together, a bond that endured despite the intervening years.

As they chased each other over the edge and fell into a world that only ever existed between them, she held him close, part of her knowing if he walked away this time, she might not survive.

# eighteen

With one arm folded behind his head and the other wrapped around the woman curled on his chest, Reaper stared blindly at the shadowed ceiling and wondered what the hell he'd been thinking, fucking Lilith. Caught in the vortex of hunger, he had no problem believing he could fill the years' old hole she left behind with one go around without a damn thing changing.

*Good luck with that, dumbass!*

One time hadn't done shit but prime the pump. Hell, after the initial storm broke, he barely surfaced for air before diving back in and taking her under with him. At least they managed to remember the condom during the second go around.

Even now, with his body happily worn out, the hunger still crawled through him. No matter the self-recriminations that battered his brain, he didn't move away from the warm weight of her. Nope, because he was a sorry ass bastard, and like a junkie with his favorite fix, he refused to acknowledge the truth that stared into his dark soul—his need for Lilith had never gone away. And this little adventure not only confirmed that fact but proved his desire for her was so deep he wasn't sure he'd ever escape.

*Did you really want to?*

Not ready to answer, even in the safety of his head, he played with her thin, beaded braids in the moonlight that seeped through the partially opened curtains. He drew lazy patterns along the warm silk of her back, his fingers slipping under the sheet tangled at their waists to drift along the sweet rise of her ass and back up.

A hitch in her warm breath feathering over his chest ended in a delicate shiver that pressed those enticing curves closer. Guess he wasn't the only one awake. Not ready to break the delicate peace, he didn't stop caressing her, willing to let the quiet hold a little longer.

It was time to man the fuck up. Ten plus years was a hell of a long time to hold a grudge. Not to mention, it was fucking exhausting to maintain. Havoc and Math accused him of being willfully blind when it came to Lilith, and they weren't wrong.

What was that saying? Hindsight is twenty-twenty? Looking back, he could admit he'd been hell bent on taking Michael out, to the point he hadn't given the first damn about anything or anyone else. As far as he had been concerned, you either joined the Michael Hate Parade or you got the fuck out of his way, and that went double for his woman. When she refused to get on board, he left her, blaming her choice to put others before his vengeance.

There was no doubt it was a shitty thing to do, but damn it all, his unit had been wiped out in one vicious stroke and that brutal reality check left his imagination roaming through endless nightmares, until he finally made a decision.

Better for him to push the last few remaining important people in his life away, than lose them to someone's treachery.

Problem was, Havoc didn't let him get away with that shit

and stuck to his ass like a tick on a dog. But Lilith? She let him go without blinking.

*You didn't give her a choice, asshole.*

He winced. No, he hadn't, but a small part of him hoped she would fight back and when she didn't, it fuckin' hurt, and that hurt didn't take long to turn to anger and resentment. Despite that, part of him always believed he'd go back for her and make her listen.

*You're an arrogant shit!* His internal SOB was relentless.

Because he hadn't been thinking straight back then.

*And now?*

Now? Now he wanted a future with her and Tabby, because under that historical mess lay the truth—Lilith had fought for him and their unborn daughter, the only way she knew how. Despite all of it, he still loved Lilith—every frustrating, challenging, intriguing inch.

Unfortunately, after the monumental error of breaking Lilith's trust all those years ago claiming that future would be an iffy endeavor. Not that he realized the depth of his mistake until their conversation at the cabin, and that kind of damage did not have an easy fix.

Truth be told, sometimes it could never be fixed—his vendetta with Michael was proof of that.

All these years later, Michael's bullshit was still screwing with Reaper's life. Until he dealt with Michael and the bounty, Reaper didn't have a future to consider. Yet once that mess was done, then what? If the threat of Michael was eliminated, where would it leave him and the Vultures?

The Vultures had been born out of a need for impartial arbitrators who held the strength to follow through on their verdicts. They weren't the only ones out there, but their hard-earned reputation stretched far and wide. Despite their shared bond as Vultures, now that each of them—Ruin, Vex, and Havoc—had found a partner, their futures, and his, may not include riding the open roads. Eventually, the couples would want to settle down and Reaper couldn't begrudge them that desire, it wouldn't be fair.

But it left him standing alone at a crossroads.

Did he stay on the lonely road, or reach for Lilith and Tabby? He knew what he wanted but carving his place at Lilith's side was going to be challenging. At least on the whole territory thing. Asking her to walk away from her position wasn't an option and would be beyond stupid and selfish, no matter what Math and Havoc insinuated. So, he needed to figure that shit out, which meant a serious conversation with Lilith needed to happen soon.

As for the dad thing, well, the kid was easy to love so he was all over that. Besides, if he did the exact opposite of his sperm donor, he should be on the right track. Plus, he didn't have a doubt that Lilith would make damn sure he didn't fall down on the job.

He combed his fingers through her hair and enjoyed the way the wild curls wrapped around his fingers as if reluctant to let him go. Not that he wanted her to.

What would he have without her?

The answer was easy, not a hell of a lot, and if he dared to share his thoughts, what would she say?

His gut clenched because the sad truth was, he didn't know. Hell, if he was honest with himself, he was afraid she would shut his ass down, which was a very real possibility. She had him tied in knots, always had and probably always would, but since he relished jumping through her hoops, he didn't mind—much.

He bunched her hair in his fist and dropped a kiss to the top of her head. He prayed something of what she once felt for him still existed, because there was no walking away this time.

The soft stroke of Lilith's fingers as she traced his map of scars and ink stilled and brought him out of his spinning thoughts. She shifted in his hold until she could fold her arms on his chest. With her chin resting on her hands, she met his gaze.

Even in the dimness he couldn't miss the way her gaze searched his face or the way her body began to tighten against his. "What's wrong?" she asked.

He carefully untangled his hand from her hair and smoothed out the strands. Since he planned to start as he meant to go on there was no point in lying. "What isn't?"

Wariness flashed in her eyes, but her voice stayed level, all emotion squeezed out of it. "Having regrets already?"

*What the fuck?*

Why her question surprised him, he didn't know, but it did. Knowing actions spoke louder than words, he hauled her up his chest and took her mouth in an unforgiving kiss. When her nails dug into his chest and the need for air became critical, he lifted his head, cradling her face in his hands and glared at her. "Does that feel like I'm regretting shit?"

Her long lashes lifted and revealed dark jade depths. She cupped his jaw as her gaze drifted moodily over his face. "Tell me."

It didn't take much to fall back into old patterns. No matter how deep into his own head he got, talking things through with her always brought him clarity. Thing was, he wasn't sure he was ready to dive into the deeper end of things between them, so instead he focused on the most pressing issue. "Since Michael's not great about sharing, I'm trying to wrap my head around how the Cartels fit in. Why's he working with them?"

She brushed an absent caress against his lower lip with her thumb, but he could see her mind working. "You think the Cartels are part of this mess, because..."

"Bounty's out of Phoenix," he supplied as she trailed off.

When she simply raised a brow and stayed silent, he lowered his chin. "You don't agree?"

A small sigh escaped. "I don't have enough information to make that determination."

"Neither do I, but I've got to follow my gut." He tucked a strand behind her ear. "Play it out with me."

Her lips quirked, but she went along. "Fine, let's say that Michael made a deal with the Cartels—they give him what he wants, he'll ensure they get what they want."

Reaper wasn't so sure that was the right direction, but he asked, so now he followed. "No way Michael would give up territory."

"Who says he's the one giving anything up?" Her voice was edged with dry amusement, but she didn't wait for his response before adding, "What if he promised them territories held by others? Or maybe a clear shot to run the routes to the Northland border?"

Reaper failed to stifle his snort of disbelief.

She frowned. "What?"

"The Cartels aren't stupid, so if Michael was arrogant enough to promise a clean run for their drugs and flesh, no way in hell they'd believe it." He shook his head. "Promising the land, yeah, that I could see."

Her head tilted. "Why are you so certain the only thing the Cartels would demand from him is land?"

"It's been, what, twelve years since the Border Wars actually ended?" He blew out a breath. "That fucked up fiasco was all about territory. When the dust settled, the Cartels were far from satisfied with the concessions given."

"They weren't the only ones screwed over in the deal, you know." She worried her bottom lip and studied his face. When she braced, so did he. "Not to pick at a sore spot, but Michael isn't the only bastard out there."

"Not blind, babe." Obsessed with taking Michael down,

yeah, but not blind to the array of threats that roamed through the remnants of civilization. When he lost her gaze, he knew she was debating whether or not to let this line go. Not wanting to lose the slim chance he might still have with her, he met her halfway. "Lil." He waited until he got her attention. "Share what's bothering you." When she continued to watch him warily, he bent as much as he could. "Give me a chance."

She lifted her chin and set her jaw set as she took him at his word. "Have you considered what will happen if Michael's eliminated?"

His arms tightened before he could check the movement. When she stiffened in his arms, he knew she hadn't missed his defensive reaction.

Her voice was low and tight. "You and I both know how dangerous a power vacuum can be."

She had a point, but it did shit-all to stop old resentments from crowding in. He tried to temper his resentment and heed the logical point she made. "So what? We let him continue to get away with his shit?"

When poorly concealed ire flashed in her eyes, he figured he failed to check his reaction enough. "That's not what I meant, and you know it."

She pushed against his hold, but he didn't relent. If he let her sit up, no way would he be able to keep his mind on their conversation. It was hard enough keeping his mouth in check, much less other, more obviously obnoxious body parts.

She finally subsided but continued to pin him in place with her glare. "I'm all about shutting Michael down. I just want to ensure when it's all said and done, me and mine don't get buried in the blowback."

He knew who she was really worried about, so he had no problem making her a promise. One he had every intention of keeping since it was quickly becoming a key motivator. "We'll keep Tabby safe."

Deep in the jade depths a spark of relief lit, and her lashes swept down as her lips quirked with a gentle curve. Her spine softened as she met his gaze once more. "That mean you have a plan? Or are we hitting Phoenix, diving in, and hoping for the best?" She tapped his chest with a warning finger. "Because I've got to tell you, I don't think that's the best plan."

Her unexpected concession was laced with wry amusement and loosened the tight knot of old doubts. There was a measure of satisfaction in knowing this time when he faced Michael, it wouldn't be a solo endeavor. He traced her fading smile. "First thing, we need to find out whose pockets are behind the bounty."

Lines marred her forehead. "Not sure it really matters who's the money man. Either way, you're being hunted."

He touched the tip of her nose and then shifted his position to sit up against the wall. "True, but knowing who's paying for it, gives me something to work with."

She moved with him, sitting up, and thankfully bringing the sheet up to tuck it in place under her arms. "Why? You think you can make a deal with the Cartels?" Whatever she saw on his face replaced any lingering amusement with disbelief. "Are you insane? You can't trust them."

"And we can trust Michael or Greer?"

The hand not holding the sheet fisted in her lap. "Reaper—"

"Lilith." He waited in silent demand for her attention. When he got it, he continued, "I want this entire thing finished. One way or the other."

Her throat worked as she swallowed, and darkness invaded her eyes, leaving her face a carefully composed mask. "You still have a death wish."

"No, I don't." He bent his leg until his knee tented the

sheet, then braced one arm on it. He reached with the other and covered the fist in her lap, his thumb brushing over the white knuckles. "I want it done so I can have a future."

She searched his face, her mask firmly in place. "Why? What's changed?"

"Fucking everything." His hand tightened over hers. He needed her to hear what he was saying. To believe him. "You gave me a daughter, Lilith."

A barely there wince was followed by the flash of something painful as her gaze slid away and her chin dipped. "It can't be that simple. Not after everything." Her accusation was low and hard to hear, but he caught it.

His previous behavior warranted her wariness, especially since it was him who chose to walk away. No matter how many times or ways he said it, it would take time for her to believe in his sincerity. He caught her chin with the tip of his finger and nudged it up until her eyes met his. "It is, babe."

She pulled back with an angry jerk, and drew her legs up, adding a few more inches between them. "No, it's not."

He wrapped his hand around one sheet-covered ankle, not wanting her to pull further away. "Yeah, it is."

She nailed him with another glare and ran an agitated hand through her hair. "Say you manage to take out Michael, or whoever's behind this. You think you're being hunted now? What do you think will happen then?" She didn't wait for his response, but kept going, determined to lay it out in no uncertain terms. "For fuck's sake, Reaper!" Exasperation and worry made her voice sharp. "Michael commands a hell of a military force, with or without Greer, they'll be gunning for you. All of them." She pounded her knee with a fist. "Not to mention you take on one Cartel family, you provoke them all. How long do you think you can outrun them? You'll never be safe, no matter how many of us are on your side, we'll all be targets. With the position I hold, there's no way for me to avoid the fall out and they'll target Tabby to get to me."

For the first time he saw it, her bone deep fear, a mother's fear for her child, heard it when she asked, "How do I keep her safe?"

The depth of emotion fueling her agonized whisper hurt to hear. He couldn't not touch her, to reassure her in some way that she wasn't in this alone. Not now. He caught the back of her neck in a gentle hold and squeezed carefully, attempting to still her anxious movements. He held her gaze and let her see he meant what he said. "We do this smart, so that won't happen."

Her laugh was bitter. "We? There is no we."

Since arguing would get him nowhere he wanted to go, he decided to make sure his point got made. Using his hold, he dragged her close and nipped her lower lip in punishment.

A feminine hiss of fury escaped as she drew back and soothed the ache with her fingers. "What? Outside of fucking me, you want nothing to do with me."

With a frustrated growl he silenced her painful words in a kiss. They were skating too close to hurtful past truths, truths he wanted to dispel. Their tongues met in a wild clash as their volatile emotions added a rough edge to their shared hunger. Yet as her taste sank deep and he took her to her back, he knew his actions were just adding proof to her accusation.

What simmered between them went beyond lust, and he needed to convince her he wanted something deeper, something lasting. With that thought in mind, he forced his libido back from the edge they teetered on. He cradled her head between his hands and gentled his kiss. To get her to listen to him would require the unexpected.

He raised his head and stared into her flushed face, his thumbs brushing over her damp lips. "I was wrong."

Her fingers dug into his shoulders, and she gave him a long, slow blink. "What?"

His gut tightened and he gave her what he would never give another. "I was wrong."

Her restless movements stilled, and she studied him. Bit by bit she reassembled the familiar mask she wore to face the world. It hurt to see her do it, because he now understood, it was the mask she used to keep herself safe.

"I'll ask again." Her voice was carefully neutral. "What's changed? I'm still the Rocky Mountain Queen and you're still a Vulture."

It shouldn't surprise him that she would demand they tackle this sooner than he wanted. Now, more than ever, Lilith had a shit ton at stake. But then, so did he. Except this time, it was his turn to take the risk. "Nothing lasts forever, babe."

Trapped in his hold, she took her only option to avoid his eyes and dropped her gaze.

Not about to let her get away with that, he caught her chin and forced her to meet his gaze. "Tell me you're happy doing what you do."

Guilt shadowed her eyes.

He ruthlessly quashed a spark of fledgling hope and took another step to establish their connection. "Only going to ask once, and, Lilith—" he waited until he had her focus, "—I'm fucking begging you, be honest, yeah?" He held his breath as he waited for her slow nod. Once it came, he asked, "If you could, would you walk away?"

He gave her credit, she didn't baulk, but her tongue peeked out to nervously touch her bottom lip. "It's not that simple." Her voice was strained and husky as her mask crumbled. "I have to think about Tabby, and what will keep her safe."

Now that she was really listening to him, he needed her to hear his question, really hear it and believe that Tabby's safety was just as important to him as it was to her. "If walking away meant our girl would be safe, would you leave it all behind?" He waited for her answer, tension coiling through him.

"In a heartbeat."

With three, simple, heartfelt words she blew his years of assumptions to pieces and left him struggling with an unfamiliar sense of elation. He dropped his forehead to hers but couldn't miss the mixture of defiance and guilt coloring her face. God only knew the cost of her admission. As he had no intention of making her regret sharing the truth with him, he took another leap, knowing what it would reveal. "Could you be happy living like that?"

They were so close his lips brushed hers and all he could see were her eyes, and the struggle she fought was reflected in their depths. He swore his heart stopped when she finally gave a slow nod.

He closed his eyes as something tight loosened in his chest and the last of the dread unknotted in his gut. Beyond words, he gave her a chaste kiss, his emotions spilling into the gentle touch. He carefully released his hold and rolled to his back to lie next to her. Unexpected pressure built behind his eyes and stung his nose as the impact of her gift hit. He threw a hand over his eyes and breathed through the realization she'd given him the one thing he could hold onto as he fought for the future he wanted to share with her, hope.

The mattress rocked, and then Lilith's weight settled on his chest. "What about you?"

Not quite ready to endure her all-too perceptive gaze, he curled his free arm around her waist and held her close. "What about me?"

A warm puff of air emerged on her soft sigh. "If you had to, could you walk away from the Vultures and be happy?"

Insecurity lurked under her question, and because she deserved the same bravery she gave him, he lifted his arm to face her. A thin braid half hidden by a thick curl that trailed down her face and tickled his chest caught his attention. He tucked the soft strand behind her ear. "Nothing lasts forever." He met her gaze. "In case you haven't noticed, things are changing. The others, they're all finding their place. However this plays out, things will never be as they were."

She frowned. "That's not an answer."

Yeah, he remembered this too. Her stubborn refusal to accept vague answers. His lips quirked. "It's the best I can give you right now. Once things are finished, ask me again."

She narrowed her eyes. "You going to be there to ask?"

He took that because she had the right to ask. "Yeah, babe, I'll be here."

For once she didn't snap back. He endured her study, wishing he knew what she was looking for, so he could give it to her. Unfortunately, he was going to have to dig deep for patience, because the only thing that would convince her he had no intention of bailing was to stick to her side. Eventually, she would have to admit he wasn't going anywhere.

*Right?*

No one answered.

nineteen

As massive haboob chased the four riders as they hit old
ravine of the Salt River and bypassed the casino.
Although the sandstorm loomed a good half hour out, dust
was already mixing with the heat turning the afternoon into a
hellish haze. Mercy led the way as they breached the old city
limits and navigated through half-buried rusted car skeletons
and toppled metal poles that once held traffic lights.

Their surroundings appeared deserted until they worked
their way further in. Finally, signs of life emerged`. Residents
hustled inside and pulled metal covers into place in prepara-
tion for the incoming sandstorm. Reaper played chicken with
those intent on finding shelter and narrowly avoided a mangy
looking mutt that darted across the street.

Their passage garnered a few head turns, but hidden under
head scarves, goggles, and filtration masks being identified
wasn't a worry, they were just another anonymous group
making their way through the late afternoon in Phoenix.

At one point they got stuck behind a lumbering caravan,
and it took a combination of luck and skill to skirt around the
bulky travelers without running anyone down. Finally, Mercy

turned into a cluster of sand-pitted buildings that sprawled along an old freeway in a layout that Reaper recognized as an old shopping mall.

They approached the oversized entrance where one half was already sealed by a thick, graffiti-covered metal door and slowed. A figure draped in typical desert dweller fashion of loose clothes and goggles stood on the other side, monitoring incoming traffic.

Mercy raised her hand and received a wave in return. She led the way inside and the rumble of their engines echoed in the cavernous entry and mixed with the surrounding din of chaos. They merged with the motley group of motorized rovers that peeled off to the left, leaving those on foot to continued further inside.

It took a few minutes to snag a protective spot for their bikes. Reaper pulled up next to Havoc under an old escalator, shut his engine down and took a moment to stretch his cramped muscles. He unsnapped his filtration mask and let it hang as he freed his water-filled canteen. He rinsed the layer of road from his mouth and then offered it to Lilith when she came up to his side.

"Thanks." Her voice was scratchy, and her wince was quick. She did a swish and swirl, followed by a delicate spit to the side, before actually taking a drink.

Mercy adjusted the straps of the bag slung crossways over her chest and joined them, her dust-covered clothes not doing much to hide her weapons. "Bikes should be safe for now." She tilted her head to indicate a doorless entry that led to what must have been a loading dock. "If we need to bail with bikes, that's our best bet."

Reaper scanned the comings and goings of those around them and was pleased to see no one paid their group the least bit of attention. "What's the travel time to the casino from here?"

Mercy kept her voice low as she did her own surveillance. "Thirty minutes by foot, less by bike." A shrill wail of wind sang above the din of the crowd and heralded the storm's imminent arrival. "Wouldn't advise trying it until the worst of the storm's passed," she warned.

Havoc slung an arm around Mercy's shoulders. "Thinking we've got about forty minutes to kill before we chance it."

"I say we get something to eat," Lilith offered, handing Reaper back his canteen.

Reaper's stomach agreed, so the four headed deeper into the indoor bazaar in search of food.

Understanding their forced confinement upped the risk factor of being identified, they shoved their goggles to the top of their heads and let their filtration masks hang down because wearing them inside would be too suspicious. Instead, they drew the extra material of their grit-covered head scarves over to cover the lower half of their faces.

They moved out to the main walkways and blended into the sweltering mass of humanity. It didn't take them long to find a little out of the way taco stand and get in line. Once their plates were piled with steaming corn tortillas, rice, and meat, they commandeered a rickety looking table in towards the back. They huddled over their lunch and ate with an economy of movement, their gazes constantly scanning nearby faces.

Lilith nudged Reaper's shoulder and he chased the last few pieces of Spanish rice with his tortilla. When he met her gaze, she tilted her head to the side in a subtle indication. He took his last bite, sat back, and shifted enough to put his arm around the back of her chair. His change of position gave him a better angle to watch what caught her attention. He refastened the tail end of his scarf with a deceptive casualness and covered everything from his nose down.

Three men at a nearby table did a piss poor job hiding the

fact that they were military. It was there in their regulation length haircuts that were revealed by their discarded headscarves. Not to mention when the one nearest their table reached for something across the table, his clothes shifted enough to reveal the gun strapped to his thigh. Guns weren't a preferred weapon for most since acquiring the bullets necessary to make them worthwhile took more effort than most wanted to spend. Hence the reason the majority of the population preferred edged weapons. They were easier to care for and readily available. Especially here in the Sandpit where dust and grit wreaked more havoc than man.

Reaper's pulse leapt, and then fell into a steady pattern. The soldiers' presence meant chances were good that Michael wouldn't be far behind, because a security force of that caliber indicated someone of importance was nearby. Reaper knew only one important player, Lilith, and since they weren't here for her, he'd bet his ass that Michael was in town.

On Reaper's other side, Havoc and Mercy's quiet conversation hiccuped. Reaper flicked Havoc a look and gave a barely there head shake in warning. Havoc's brows lowered, and he shifted a bit closer to Mercy as he resumed his conversation.

Reaper was too far away to hear what the soldiers were saying, but the kernel of concern he carried about coming here eased. At least they were on the right path.

Hidden behind the covering of his scarf, his fierce satisfaction escaped in a grin. Maybe, just maybe, he would finally get his chance to deal with Michael once and for all.

# twenty

L ilith stood in the shadows on the second level of the Castille's main floor and swore she could feel Reaper's need to pounce vibrating along her skin. It was so intense, it raised the hair on her arms, and to keep his ass in check since his wasn't the only one on the line, she issued a soft hiss of warning.

*Swear to god if the man made one wrong move...*

All four of them were in a precarious position and swinging in the wind on this little foray. The last thing any of them needed was a confrontation with the armed men gathered below.

Lilith, Reaper, Mercy, and Havoc had trailed the security detail through the bazaar undetected, and once the worst of the storm had passed and the doors opened, they continued to ghost the three-man team hoofing it into the night by using the lingering haze of dust-filled shadows to their advantage. When the returning trio paused to bullshit the guards on watch at Castille, the four trailing hunters found Havoc's alternate entrance by slipping deeper into rubble of the wrecked sections of the old casino.

Not an easy feat as the bleached architectural bones stretched high above the mounds of ruins and marked the structure's old hundred-foot height. What remained was now a tricky terrain of sand-covered disasters waiting to happen that left them exposed. Although the night stayed quiet as they worked their way in, Lilith's neck itched under the weight of unseen eyes during the entire nerve-shredding trek.

That itch didn't fade until they were safely inside, and Lilith came face-to-face with why this end of the building was unsecured. The forest of rebar and maze of half-collapsed walls were a daunting prospect, especially when their only light sources were their small, hand-held solar sticks.

As it was sharp broken ends snagged her clothing, some scraping away a layer of skin before she could get free. Footing was just as tricky because apparently solid ground would shift into ankle-twisting pits that slowed their progress to a near crawl. It took them roughly twenty minutes before they surfaced and if not for Havoc's memory and Mercy's blueprints, they would have never found their way through the debris-choked narrow passages.

It didn't help that the tight passages had created a serious case of claustrophobia and caused serious concerns for the two broad-shouldered men. In fact, they had been forced to stop a couple of times to bind Havoc and Reaper's more serious cuts so as not to leave a blood trail. Once nice thing about headscarves, they made damn good bandages. In the end, Lilith wasn't alone in sporting an impressive collection of stinging scratches and irritating bruises.

Once out of the worse of the ruins, they followed the rise and fall of muted conversation until they pinpointed the meeting place. Heightened security quickly became apparent as they dodged random patrols prowling the area. Staying undetected was a challenge, but the chosen spot sat in what was once a mixture of dining and gaming areas. The main floor lay wide open and was surrounded by an overhanging walkway interspersed with thick pillars that created a second level viewing area.

Despite the risk, the four agreed the viewing area was their best bet. The railings that once connected the columns were long gone, so they had to watch their step. Yet there were enough nooks and crannies not even the security detail could cover it all. It was a bitch for security and privacy, but great for their needs which made Lilith wonder whose bright idea it was to pick this place for a clandestine meeting.

They had split up—her and Reaper to one side and Havoc and Mercy the other. Once in place, the four settled in for the show. Now snippets of conversation drifted to where she and Reaper hid in a dark alcove half protected by a pillar, confirming the only thing that hadn't gone to shit around here was the acoustics. As long as they remained aware of the patrolling guards, listening in on the conversation would be easy.

Their hiding spots proved to be effective as they evaded the armed patrol's last walk through of the second level. Even as the guards took their final positions at strategic, stationary points along the second level, all four hunters remained undetected.

Lilith identified two distinct groups among the guards— one carried the notable rough edge of the Cartels, the other the rigidity indicative of military training. There were a total of sixteen men, evenly split between the two groups.

A lean, brown-haired man who issued clear orders in a level voice, led the military group. The speed with which his men jumped when he directed the majority into positions around the main floor lent weight to Lilith's assumption of his position as a security leader. He sent two of his men to the second level.

This meant Lilith and Reaper were forced to sneak

cursory looks from their hidden positions to take in what was happening below. Lilith wished for Charity's insight as the security leader continued to issue orders. No doubt her master spy would know who the hell the man was and what threat he represented. For now, Lilith was relegated to playing audience to the unfolding drama below, while praying Reaper's legendary control held steady.

And the stage was definitely set for drama. A ring of solar lights surrounded what looked to be two reclaimed leather chairs that sat in the floor's center and were divided by a small table. While the set up highlighted the meeting area, it left those guarding the perimeter in shadow.

Tension rode the air and strung Lilith's nerves tight, but she wasn't the only one. Done with his orders, the leader took up a position just inside the entrance, his attention on the Cartel men moving in to take up their positions in-between his security force. Hell, if someone dared to fire a shot, it would guarantee an old-fashioned shoot out with no survivors.

Xavier Suárez, the oldest, and last surviving son of the Suárez family, and second only to his father was sprawled in one of the leather chairs, and he did not look impressed. In fact, if Lilith were to hazard a guess based upon his stony countenance, she'd say Xavier was pissed. There was no sign of Greer or Michael, but her instincts whispered that wouldn't be the case for long.

A minute ticked by and the second counted down when Xavier finally broke the quiet. "Where is he?" The accented demand was directed to the security leader.

The response was clipped. "He'll be here shortly."

Xavier grunted and the strained silence resumed.

Lilith caught the measured cadence of an imminent approach at the same time things below went wired. She dared to peek around the crumbling edge of the pillar in time to watch the entrance of two men.

The first was dressed head to toe in familiar desert tan, their weapons clearly displayed. They cleared the entrance and unwound their head scarf to reveal a harsh angled profile under a buzz cut. The man's gaze swept through the room in a practiced surveillance as he exchanged a nod with the brown-haired man in charge of the military group. Lilith watched the newcomer's behavior and revised her earlier assumption. This new arrival was the true head of security.

Dressed in similar fashion and standing next to him, was another figure. When they shoved their head scarf back a head of dark hair was exposed. He moved forward and Lilith's breath caught at the familiar profile. Next to her, Reaper went solid, and a chill emanated from him.

Michael had arrived.

Xavier, his face an unreadable mask, maintained his casual position, even as he tracked Michael's approach.

Michael stopped near the chairs and held out his hand. "Xavier."

Tension crested as Xavier held his dismissive position for a breathless moment. Then, just as it threatened to snap, Xavier rose to his feet with an unhurried grace and shook Michael's hand. "Michael."

Greetings exchanged, Michael waved Xavier to resume his seat. Once Xavier settled, so did Michael. "I appreciate you making time to see me."

Xavier held his tongue and his gaze never strayed from Michael as he dipped his head in acknowledgement.

One of Michael's men stepped forward and set two amber-filled glasses on the small table. As the heavy cut glasses hit the wood, Xavier glanced at the drinks and then lifted one dark brow in mocking question.

Michael, correctly reading the other man's suspicion, reached for a drink, and raised it. "*Salud*."

Xavier leaned over, grasped his glass, and mimicked Michael. "*Salud*."

Lilith gave Xavier points for waiting until Michael took his sip before doing the same. She wasn't sure she'd be quite so daring.

Michael sat back and templed his fingers, his expression filled with a sincerity Lilith learned long ago didn't stretch beyond the surface.

On the second floor the two security personnel shifted into roaming mode which had Lilith and Reaper sliding deeper into their hiding spot. Forced to rely only on her ears, Lilith concentrated on analyzing the conversation.

Michael's voice floated up. "My condolences on your recent loss."

"Yes, my brother's death was deeply felt." There was a sibilant undertone to Xavier's response. "I had hoped to gain more insight into the situation from your second." Then came a pregnant pause. "However, I do not see her here."

It was no surprise that Xavier wanted to talk to Greer since she had partnered with Felix, a Suárez lieutenant, to undermine the Free People's hold on the all-important dam that supplied water to the Southwest. Unfortunately for Greer, Felix had decided to improvise on his own and took out Tavi, the youngest Suárez, after he questioned Felix's behavior. Felix would have gotten away with it if Mercy hadn't been an unintentional witness.

With the consummate smoothness, Michael said, "Unfortunately, Greer is currently resolving a rather pressing matter."

Lilith would bet that pressing matter was all about the Vultures.

"Yes, so I've heard." Xavier's reply was layered with nuances, and the Cartel heir apparent landed the first blow.

"While I understand such things must be addressed, due to the current situation and recent events, my father and I have serious concerns."

"I understand," Michael's voice was tight, "and I share those concerns, but please be assured, they are being addressed."

Lilith's memories filled in the visual blanks. Michael would be the picture of unconcern, complete with that damn cold, mocking smile he always wore to hide his disdain of dealing with those he considered beneath him. She didn't doubt that Michael felt he was far above Xavier and the Cartel families, but it wouldn't stop him from working with them to get what he wanted.

"Are they?" Xavier's question was filled with patent disbelief. "Explain to me, _señor_, why should I trust _la perra loca_ to take care of such things? Especially after her actions in Salt Lake? Or perhaps a better question—why should I trust you?"

Rustling noises were followed by Michael's unruffled reply. "How would you like me to answer that?"

Next to Lilith, Reaper's predatory vibe shifted to a disconcerting stillness. Being mindful to not draw unwanted attention, she carefully turned and shot him a questioning look. Since his attention was firmly focused on the meeting below, he missed it.

Yet the rigid set of his jaw and the dark frown that marred his face triggered her concern. Reaper had caught something, something she missed, and he was far from happy.

Unease curled in her gut like a heavy weight.

"Greer was simply correcting a problem," Michael continued, not waiting for Xavier's response. "Something I would think your family would be grateful for, as we delivered the one who betrayed you."

_What a crock!_ Lilith wondered how he managed to choke that lie out. Greer wanted to kill Felix, not turn him over to the Cartel. In the end, it was Mercy who tossed the traitor into Suárez's arms, not that he gave her much choice.

"You may have corrected one of your problems, but not all of them." Based upon the cold edge of Xavier's statement, Michael's manipulation missed its mark. Lilith wasn't surprised. Xavier was probably still pissed at almost being blown to kingdom come by Greer's crazy ass plan in Salt Lake.

"That is why we are here, correct?" Michael's voice lost some of its smooth and a tense moment passed before he continued. "Since our schedules are rather tight, shall we get to business?" The sounds of weight shifting and bodies moving indicated further positioning. When it settled, Michael began. "The concerns you and your father have—"

"Are many," Xavier cut in with a hard voice, clearly not buying Michael's bullshit.

"Are in the process of being solved." Michael's straining patience was evident in his sharp correction.

A humorless chuckle sounded. "And I am to believe you simply because you say so?" Xavier delivered his insult and continued down the same challenging path. "The last promise you made has not been kept. The dams still stand under the hands of the Free People, no?"

"That was most unexpected." Michael's curtness evidenced his fraying temper and made Lilith wonder how much longer before he snapped. Yet somehow the arrogant ass leveled out his tone. "While not ideal, there will be other opportunities." There was a creak of leather. "More importantly, we've managed to cause major disruptions on the routes between the borders, allowing your shipments to slip passed with ease."

"And yet our last shipment, the one guaranteed to further our interests north, did not arrive." Nothing in Xavier's tone indicated Michael's justifications were working.

"I did warn you and your father that Raiders are not the

best choice for such runs." Michael's derision was loud and clear.

"Funny—" Xavier's accent deepened as his patience waned, "—how those same Raiders inched closer to your territory when their shipment mysteriously blew sky high."

"Need I remind you, I lost a significant investment in that shipment as well?" Temper eroded civility in Michael's voice and left behind the lethal manipulator at the heart of the politician. "Prime condition, military grade firepower is not so easily salvaged. Yet, I am resupplying your father's order out of my own pocket as my indication of good faith."

"*Está bien.*" A humming silence fell and then Xavier broke it. "Let's hope, *señor*, such firepower does not find its way into hands lifted against *mis familias*. It would not bode well."

Michael addressed the unmistakable threat in an unforgiving tone. "I have no intention of reigniting the Border Wars, Xavier."

"No," the other man drawled. "You simply want to expand your territory."

"And yours." Michael was quick to shoot back. This time the quiet was longer. "The shipment will be replaced and back on the road within the next couple of weeks. A small delay, nothing serious."

Xavier grunted, wordlessly letting the discussion go. "And this situation Greer is taking care of?"

"A minor setback we expect to be rectified shortly." Back on more solid ground, Michael regained his earlier balance, his voice once again confident.

"Minor?" Xavier mocked. "I'm not so sure the Vultures, or this Crowe person, could be considered minor. Not even with the hefty size bounty you've issued."

"They're being dealt with." Michael's voice was tight, the back-and-forth animosity obviously playing hell with his control.

Undaunted, Xavier continued to swipe at Michael. "You seem to accumulate enemies like ticks on a cur."

"In a position like mine, enemies are to be expected." A sly note crept in. "It's not as if you and your father haven't garnered your share."

"*Es verdad*, but once they're put down, they tend to stay down."

Even Lilith couldn't miss Xavier's implication.

"So do mine." Michael took the verbal gloves off. "Enough with the bullshit posturing. You didn't come here to bust my balls for giggles. What do you really want?"

Xavier proved he was just as dangerous as the man across from him and laid it out. "What we want is reassurance that your current troubles will not impact our plans for the future."

"They won't." Michael's utter confidence worried Lilith.

Xavier, on the other hand, was unimpressed. "Prove it."

"How exactly do you want me to do that?" Exasperation and frustration leaked into Michael's voice.

In a clear demand, Xavier left no room for negotiations. "You have two weeks to clean your house and ensure no more problems raise their pesky heads."

"Two weeks?" There was no hint in his voice as to how Michael felt about Xavier's deadline.

"*Sí*," Xavier said. "Fail, and we are done."

At that, an edge of fury erupted and rode the air as Michael protested. "Reneging on our agreement would not bode well for your family, Xavier."

"Perhaps." Xavier didn't sound at all concerned. "But it bodes worse for you, *señor*." With that, the sharp scrape of chair being shoved back was followed by a barked command in Spanish, and the two Cartel guards on the second floor slipped away.

# twenty-one

As the sounds of departure drifted up from below, Lilith dared to peek around the pillar's edge, felt Reaper do the same next to her, and then they watched the backs of the two Cartel members disappear. She looked across the open space and caught sight of Havoc and Mercy barely visible in their chosen spot. Reaper's arm lifted and Havoc responded with a chin lift before he and Mercy faded into the shadows.

Before Lilith could move out, Reaper squeezed her shoulder, and whispered next to her ear, "Hold tight, babe."

She heeded his direction and eased back, understanding that now with no one on watch nearby, she and Reaper could observe the activity below without fear of detection. She crouched and carefully adjusted her position so she could see the happenings below. With Xavier now gone, Michael talked in low tones to the man who had accompanied him. Whatever Michael said had Buzzcut frowning in disapproval and shaking his head. Michael appeared no less thrilled and made a sharp movement with his hand.

Whatever their disagreement was, eventually Michael won because Buzzcut, with obvious reluctance, conceded. He half-turned from Michael and did a wind-up motion with his hand. The security force started to move out and file through the entrance. Buzzcut shot Michael one last hard look and followed, leaving the Northwest leader alone in the vast room.

The silence barely settled from the exodus when Michael twisted, picked up one of the half-filled glasses, and threw it across the room.

A shadow detached from the edge of the room as the echoes of shattering glass faded. "Feel better?"

Michael kept his back to the newcomer and dragged a hand through his hair. "Fucking Cartel roaches."

"A necessary evil." The shadow moved into the light and became an impeccably dressed, sandy-haired male.

Lilith studied him, knowing this was no military man. Not by a long shot. Nothing about his appearance stuck out, but there was something about him that made her think she had seen him before somewhere.

Before she could chase that thought, the out of place male went to Michael and clapped his shoulder with the ease of familiarity. "Still, that went better than expected."

Michael's laugh was harsh. "Guess so since we're both still breathing." He stalked away, his hand fisted at his side, and paced the floor with obvious agitation. "Fucking Greer! If she wasn't already dead, I'd be tempted to kill her myself."

At that, behind Michael's back, a dark wave of fury washed through Sandy's face.

Lilith snuck a glance up at Reaper and found an echo of her resigned relief at Michael's unintended bomb, in his face. It was nice to know they were down one worry considering it looked as if they'd just picked up another.

When she went back to the drama below, Sandy's earlier fury was gone, replaced by his previously bland expression as Michael faced him. His voice held a deceptively mild chiding note as he placated the clearly riled man. "She didn't fuck this up, Michael. Need I remind you, that blame falls on the inter-ference of the Vultures and that bastard, Math."

Michael closed what little distance existed between him and Sandy, stopping just shy of the other man. His lip was curled into a sneer and contempt dripped from his voice. "If she'd managed to do the job right the first time with the Strix, we wouldn't be dealing with either of the two now, would we?"

Lilith couldn't check her wince. *Guess Reaper was right about Michael.*

Not that she hadn't believed his assumptions about Michael on some level because hearing just how deep into this twisted shit Michael really was, barely rocked her. Part of her was glad that neither Math, nor Mercy, was within hearing distance, because Michael's accusation was spot on. If the massacre Greer led years ago had been successfully, neither Strix would have escaped to later interfere with Michael's play to take over the dam or take their shot to scrub Greer out of the picture. In fact, if Math or Mercy had heard that last little bit, Lilith knew Michael would never leave this room alive.

Sandy was unmoved by Michael's temper. "It doesn't matter now."

Michael snarled and turned away to stare off into the shadows.

Sandy locked his hands behind his back and watched Michael, his voice unruffled. "Once everything is in place, we'll gain control of the dams and the remaining Western Territories."

Michael's head dropped on a hard breath, then he turned back and folded his arms over his chest. "Yeah, we just have to give the fucking Cartels everything south of Salt Lake and Denver." There was an unmistakable bitterness in his voice.

Impatience flickered over Sandy's face. "We can't afford

another Border War." The statement carried a stern rebuke. "Not yet."

Michael's jaw worked but he held his tongue.

"When the time's right, we'll get it all back." A grim twist curved Sandy's lips. "It is, after all, a long game."

"And a long game requires patience," Michael snapped back. He held Sandy's gaze for a long moment, then looked away and dropped into the chair, his fingers drumming on the padded armrest. "Xavier's a smug ass bastard. He and his demented father think they have us over a barrel."

Sandy toed the other chair around and took a seat. "Until we eliminate the Vultures and weaken Lilith's hold, they do."

Michael shot him a look. "Two fucking weeks is cutting it close."

Sandy shrugged, clearly unconcerned. "Perhaps, but it is doable."

A nasty smile curved Michael mouth. "You just want blood for Greer."

Unmoved by the obvious dig, Sandy held his gaze. "Don't you?"

There was something in the unknown man's tone that raised the hair on Lilith's arms and warned her she needed to figure out who the hell he was and what game he was playing.

"Of course." Michael's smile sharpened and his tone picked up a merciless edge. "But she knew the risks. We all did."

The two conspirators maintained a silent war.

Strangely it was Michael who stepped back first and scrubbed his face with his hands. "Fuck, sorry, man." The words were muffled, but when he dropped his hands, sympathy had replaced his earlier fury. "That was uncalled for."

The seemingly heartfelt apology made little to no impression on Sandy, who continued to study Michael from behind a stone-cold mask. The only indication he heard Michael was the loosening of his fist on the armrest. "The last intel I received put the Vultures on the road heading south."

At the deliberate change in conversation, Michael winced and surprisingly didn't push the point. Instead, he asked, "You think they're running to Istaqa?"

"Maybe."

"Where else would they go?" When Sandy said nothing, Michael gave a disbelieving bark of laughter. "You think they'll go to Lilith's?"

His question earned another shrug from Sandy. "It is not such a stretch to consider."

"Isn't it?" Michael mocked. "For fuck's sake, did you forget what Greer told us?" He didn't wait for an answer. "Reaper can't stand that bitch, Lilith. No way in hell he'd go to her."

Sandy's calm eroded under Michael's constant derision and his voice was snide. "Need I remind you, you don't have to like someone to work with them." His implication was loud and clear.

Sandy's rebuke wiped away Michael's mockery and his response was granite. "I get that our options were limited. Especially since we couldn't find leverage to break Crane or Istaqa but using those crazy ass Raiders and the Cartels?" He shook his head. "Dangerous, my man, very dangerous."

As Lilith listened to the conversation below, she started to question Michael's sanity. It was one thing to end up in bed with the Cartels when the worst that could happen was to lose your tongue and acquire a new, grisly necklace. But getting down and dirty with the Raiders? There was no end to the nightmarish possibilities when the depraved nomads who called the desert-encrusted ruins of Vegas home found out you screwed them.

"Dangerous is sometimes necessary," Sandy said.

"I guess." Michael's response was grudgingly given, and he shot Sandy a look. "The Cartels may be dirtier than shit, but they're a hell of a lot more reliable than the nut jobs holed up in Vegas, you know that right?"

A humorless smile curved Sandy's mouth. "I dare you to call Tyke a nut job to his face."

Michael's dark chuckle was chilling. "I'm not suicidal, my friend." He raised the last glass high. "At least Greer convinced Tyke to take out Crane." He threw back the contents and slammed the glass back to the table.

"She was a genius when it came to finding the right motivation," Sandy agreed, unable to hide his admiration for Greer.

"Got to give Greer credit where it was due, she didn't just find motivation, she provided it," Michael murmured. "Too fucking bad she got tripped up by that damn do-good doctor."

Sandy's mask slipped and a bright, lethal fury broke through for a heart-stopping moment. "That wouldn't have been an issue if you hadn't put forth your bright idea to kidnap the kids first."

"You might not have agreed with my suggestion," Michael shot back, "but even you have to admit it got the job done."

The words detonated inside Lilith's skull with a lethal ferocity and the detrimental shrapnel tore through her carefully constructed control. As the blinding rage crashed into an unforgiving hunger for vengeance, a hard warmth covered her mouth and left her struggling to draw in air.

A band of steel wrapped around her and held her still as the barely whispered words broke through her rage. "Calm, Lil, calm."

She fought her way back to the here and now and struggled to bank her wrath. Reaper's hand loosened enough so she could breathe, but he didn't take it away. Instead, he continued to whisper against her ear, reiterating why they couldn't chance taking out the men below while the guards lingered outside. He promised her they would find a chance to make them pay. And it was this vow that helped her regain control.

When she finally nodded, he loosened his fingers one by one, and she concentrated on drawing air into her lungs. She used the repetitive pattern to strengthen the lock on her emotions. The arm at her waist eased its pressure, but she dug her nails into Reaper's arm to hold it in place. Better to keep it there in case she gave in and went her blades, or the gun strapped to her thigh as she continued to listen to the two soon-to-be-dead men below.

"Hell, even Greer was surprised how well it worked." Michael's satisfied voice drifted up, oblivious to the vengeance lurking above him. "Taking those brats rattled Istaqa and Lilith's world."

"Not long enough, considering they seem to regain their balance pretty damn quick," Sandy groused before continuing with an unmistakable warning. "Much like Suárez, they won't forget."

"That's the least of our worries now." There was no hint of concern in Michael's response. "We've got two weeks to put an end to the Vultures and anybody stupid enough to align with them. Time to apply some pressure."

"You'll be sending out a unit." Sandy wasn't asking a question.

"I'll get Walker on that," Michael confirmed. "He's been itching for action."

"Do that," Sandy murmured. "In the meantime, you might as well get some rest tonight. We need to head back in the morning."

The sound of the two men getting to their feet drifted up.

"Think you can find me something decent to eat in this

pit?" There was no missing the layer of contempt in Michael's voice. "Preferably not unidentified meat."

A door was pulled opened, orders were given to the waiting guards, and then there was silence.

As Lilith stood in Reaper's arms, she vowed neither man would leave Phoenix alive.

# twenty-two

As Reaper and Lilith made their way through the twists and turns of what was left of the second floor, Reaper didn't dare let go of Lilith. He could feel the tremors running under skin through the loose hold he kept on her wrist. He recognized her rage since the same baleful fire sat in his gut. In an echo of his roiling emotions a soft rumble of thunder drifted through the half-collapsed ceiling and was followed by a flash of light.

The casual way the men discussed the damage done to the young lives was beyond sickening. Even worse was the cruel callousness of using children in the first damn place. The only thing that held him back from dropping into that room and gutting both bastards was the knowledge that Lilith would be at his side. The problem wasn't eliminating the assholes, it was escaping the security force while still breathing. Since Havoc and Mercy left to follow the Cartel party, he and Lilith were left to face off against an unknown amount of security, and that did not make for great survival odds.

Neither did his growing sense of unease. He couldn't exactly pinpoint the cause, but it lay somewhere in the exchange between Michael and that ass that slithered out of the shadows when Xavier left.

Maybe it was Michael's demeanor, or something he said, but the longer Reaper listened to the two, the more his certainty grew that Michael was not the arrogant, self-entitled, cunning bastard Reaper knew and hated. That sliver of doubt dug in like an itch he couldn't scratch and before he made both assholes pay, he needed to yank that sliver out.

Despite the knots in his gut or the ugly thought churning in his mind, he searched the dim interior for the exit marked on Mercy's map. He tugged Lilith around a rotting, over-turned gaming table, and when another flash of light, brighter this time, lit the ruins, the barely visible opening near a cluster of old slot machines snagged his attention. When this shit was done, he owed Mercy and her blueprints a drink, or three.

He stepped into what remained of a service stairwell with Lilith at his back. Warm air slipped through the skeletal remains of masonry and carried a thin layer of dust as it sifted through the gaping hole where other floors used to stand. Once inside the dubious protection, he finally released Lilith.

She glared at him while she rubbed her wrist. "Where the hell are we going, Reaper?" She kept her voice low, which was a good thing since the stairwell was basically a vertical tunnel.

"Michael's quarters." Under the dim moonlight he picked out the missing steps between them and the first floor. "Come on."

Since he didn't trust the few rusted remains of railing, he stayed closed to the wall and carefully worked his way down, testing each step. He chose to ignore Lilith's unhappy, muttered comments as she followed him down. He pulled up short at the last step and eyed the thigh high pile of rubble that blocked the entrance. Crawling over that was going to be a bitch. "Dammit."

"What now?" From her position a step above, Lilith

leaned in and used his shoulders for balance. "Lovely." As quiet as she was, there was a wealth of disgust in her voice. "We may as well ring the damn doorbell."

He had to agree with her assessment because the pile was a treacherous mix of materials guaranteed to damage skin and shift under any additional weight. "We need to get over this shit and get in."

"Then we need a different way in," she pointed out unnecessarily.

"We don't have time."

Her grip on his shoulders tightened and a tap on one brought his head around.

He saw Lilith's frown and asked, "What?"

"Why the rush?"

"I want to be in his room before he gets settled."

Her eyebrows rose. "Hate to break it to you, but I don't think that's happening."

Frustration turned his response short. "Then we'll just have to sneak in."

She wiped a hand over her dust-streaked cheek and studied him carefully. "What aren't you telling me?"

He silently cursed her ability to see deeper than he was comfortable with. "We don't have time to get into it." He tried to pull back, but she kept him from moving forward by stepping down and around him.

She stood there, facing him, with her arms crossed over her chest and jaw set to demand, "Get into it."

He knew if he wanted out of this stairwell before dawn hit, he needed to spill, so he did. "Something's not right."

"No shit." She wrinkled her nose.

He shook his head. "Something beyond the normal fucked up, babe."

At that, her impatience disappeared and was replaced by apprehension. "Explain."

He shifted his gaze and rubbed the back of his neck. "It's going to sound crazy."

She didn't relent. "Tell me."

He braced and gave it to her. "I don't think that was Michael."

She did a long slow blink as disbelief wiped her face blank. "Say that again?"

"That asshole that Xavier and the other bastard were talking to," he curled his hands into useless fists at his side, "is not Michael."

Her shoulders snapped straight, and her eyes widened. "You're losing it, Reaper."

With every one of his instincts screaming differently, he didn't think so. The dark-haired man who called himself Michael was not the same man Reaper served with in the Border Wars. "Look, I get it—"

"Do you?" Lilith's hiss cut him off.

Temper ruffled, he leaned close and bit off, "Yeah, I do."

"Then where is this coming from?" she prompted.

"When was the last time you saw Michael?" He didn't look away from her as he kept making his point. "Face-to-face, Lilith?"

Her gaze dropped, and her brow furrowed as she thought it through. "The last meeting before we headed into Lost Angels." Her gaze jumped back to his. "Just before Havoc dragged your sorry ass to my doorstep."

"That was what? Ten, almost eleven years ago, yeah?" He didn't give her a chance to respond. "Hell, to be honest, I can't be sure when I saw him before that either. Considering the two of you move in the same circles, why haven't you crossed paths before now?"

She didn't look away as his questions created cracks in her disbelief, enough to let in the first tendrils of doubt.

He reigned in his relief that he was getting through and

sank his point home. "You interact with the others—Istaqa, Crane, hell even the Cartels—so why not Michael? Of all of them, you'd think he would use his connection to you to work his position. Ten years and no reach out? Doesn't that strike you as odd?"

She shook her head. "I figured he was keeping his distance since we didn't part on the best of terms."

"Maybe," he conceded. "But when so much is at stake, I'm thinking there's more to it than him being pissy. It's one thing for him to steer clear of me, but you?" It was his turn to shake his head. "That doesn't add up."

"Okay, I'll give you that," she admitted. "It wasn't as if you were quiet about your opinion of him."

He wasn't keen on rehashing history, but to get her to see the disturbing picture he was getting, he'd do it. "Do you blame me?"

She shook her head.

The relentless sense of urgency clawed at him and even though they kept their voices low, they wouldn't be able to remain undetected much longer. "I can't give you a solid reason why, but I swear to you, that's not Michael."

"So, you're going to what?" Her question was curt with a combination of worry and frustration. "Sneak into his room and confront him?"

As far as he could see, their options were limited. Unless... "Got a better idea?"

She visibly struggled as logic argued with vengeance and he wasn't surprised when logic won. "No." She squeezed out the denial between gritted teeth and grimaced, conceding to his instincts. "Dammit, Reaper, this is beyond stupid."

Since he agreed, he focused on more pressing concerns and motioned to the rubble obstacle in the doorway. "We need to get through that first. Then we have to get past the guards."

"Fine." Clearly despite being on board with his plan, she

wasn't happy about it, but then neither was he. She studied the rubble. "Let me go first. I'm lighter."

They switched places, and Lilith started to pick her way over the pile. He stayed close as the debris shifted, and a few minor pieces cascaded in a mini slide. Her foot slipped at one point, but Reaper stopped her backward tumble with a hand on her ass. She scrambled over the pile with a muttered 'thanks', and with a few sharp hisses disappeared on the other side. It wasn't long before her, 'Hold tight,' drifted back.

He stood there as the moments ticked by, his back exposed, his ears strained for noise, and wrestled with his frustration at not being able to see Lilith. He identified the soft hush of her returning footfalls and then came a whoosh of air when something settled over the pile with a muted thump. Reaper checked his automatic cough when a choking cloud of dust filled the air.

When it cleared, he realized she found a large board of some sort to create a ramp. It wasn't much, but it was something. He didn't need her soft urgent hiss to get a move on. He used the doorframe as he set his foot to the rubble and climbed up and over as smaller pieces rattled down the side in his wake.

Once on the other side, Lilith lifted the plank, set it off to the side, and grabbed his hand. Together they slipped into a shadowed hollow provided by a counter overhang. As protection, it wasn't much, but it was a damn sight better than nothing. They huddled in the deepest shadows and kept their breaths shallow.

They waited for someone to investigate the sounds and Reaper silently marked time with his knife in his hand. When things remained quiet at the three-minute mark, he touched Lilith's shoulder. She turned her head and even though he could barely make out the pale lines of her face, he tilted his head in the direction they needed to take. When he got her nod, he headed out, and stuck close to whatever concealment was available. Recalling Mercy's blueprints, he aimed for the most likely place Michael, or his doppelgänger, would be staying.

Back in its heyday, the hotel was attached to the casino and boasted over five hundred rooms that mixed with huge entertainment areas and large ostentatious lounges. Thankfully, time and Mother Nature gnawed the gigantic structure down to its bones and took a nearly impossible task of pinpointing livable locations to manageable.

With most of the rooms crushed beneath thousands of pounds of cement and construction detritus, it made for the perfect meeting place for less than desirable transactions but only a few areas remained where an individual would consider safely holing up for the night. One of those spots was a lounge on the west side behind a large verandah. Because it was close to the main entry, access was limited to a shallow entryway that branched off the large hall that was lined with alcoves where priceless pieces of artwork once hung.

Lilith and Reaper dodged another patrol and Reaper's pulse picked up because the heightened security meant they had to be going in the right direction. They made the most of the fact that Michael didn't have enough manpower to adequately cover the Castille's nightmarish sprawl, and used the shadowed spaces created by the surrounding rubble to make their way to their target. In fact, by the time they hit the verandah, the guards were in the middle of a shift change. Reaper and Lilith exploited the cover of a half wall to work their way to the corner of the hall and mask their presence from the guards.

Two guards stood in front of the wide mouth of the hall where scattered solar lights barely illuminated the passageway and watched their replacements come forward.

The current pair reminded Reaper of lethal bookends.

One was gray, grizzled, and dressed in a mix of black cargos and tan shirt. Even in casual conversation, he held his thick shoulders rigid and braced his legs, all evidence of military training. His partner's lean body was draped in a sand-colored uniform, complete with a headscarf that was draped over his shoulders, and his weapons were strapped like lethal jewelry at his waist and shoulders. Despite all that, he carried an air of menace as he swept his gaze with an ease born of years of practice. That one would make for a tricky opponent.

The hollow echo of boot heels hitting the stone announced the two-man relief guard and Reaper assumed the fucking new guys had pulled the nightshift. Since those FNGs emitted the shiny glow of newbie soldiers, Reaper figured their instincts for trouble wouldn't be as honed as the more experienced pair.

"'Bout time you got yo' asses here," the grizzled veteran grumped. "My stomach's about to gnaw a hole in my gut. What took ya so long?"

"Walker wanted us to ensure our guests—" FNG One's lip curled into a sneer, "—got out without a scratch."

The leaner, lethal one managed a credible snort. "Did they get lost?"

"No," said FNG Two. "They just took their sweet ass time leaving."

The veteran barked a hard laugh. "They probably knew you were following."

FNG One took the dig with telling ease and shrugged. "Walker didn't say to hide it, so we didn't." He turned to the veteran's partner. "Is he in for the night?"

Lean dipped his chin in acknowledgement. "Yeah. He's got food coming, so look alive."

The pair of FNGs snapped to and their voices sounded in unison. "Yes, sir."

"Right." The veteran slapped one of the FNGs on the

shoulder. "Well, I'm out." He shot his partner a look. "You comin'?"

"Yeah," Lean answered. "Someone needs to keep your ass out of trouble."

"And you think I'm the geezer." The veteran ran a hand over his steel-colored buzz cut. "Shit, boy, you need to loosen up."

"Fuck you, Hal," Lean said as the two men left their replacements behind.

Lilith and Reaper waited for their chance as quiet settled in and was only broken by the occasional conversation of the FNG duo. However, when the food arrived, the young guards' vigilance remained constant and kept Reaper and Lilith in place.

Reaper figured they were about to be stuck for a few hours, so he motioned to Lilith to settle in. Surprisingly it didn't take as long as expected for the guards to get restless.

About an hour in, FNG One, who didn't like the Cartels, stifled a yawn and rubbed his face. "Gotta take a piss."

"Shouldn't have had so much brew."

In lieu of actual words FNG One flipped his partner off and walked away. As soon as FNG One disappeared, FNG Two shifted further into the shadows on the side of the hall and dug his hand into his pocket. The whisper of a match being struck was soon followed by a harsh inhale and the bittersweet scent of marijuana.

Lilith grinned at Reaper and mouthed, "Dumbass."

Reaper agreed and then took advantage of the idiot's inattention. He slipped into the hall with Lilith on his heels, and then they used the deep shadows that pooled between the anemic reach of the sporadically placed solar lights to sneak down the passage.

Reaper's suspicions about the man claiming to be Michael sharpened as they moved deeper inside without detection. No way in hell would the Michael he knew surround himself with half-assed soldiers because he wasn't one to tolerate incompetence. One fuck up tended to be the last fuck up made.

Lilith claimed his attention with a feather light touch on his arm and nodded towards the thick shadows that indicated a shallow entryway. They inched closer and spotted the narrow wedge of light that seeped under the bottom of where the thick door didn't quite meet the floor. Shadows shifted along it, warning them to get out of sight quick. They split and ducked into darkened alcoves on either side of the entryway just in time.

The door swung open, and a man stepped out. Wearing nothing but a towel, he moved to where the entry met the hall. "Hey!"

There was the scuffle of feet as the pothead soldier rushed to pull his shit together and stand at attention in the middle of the hall with his hands behind his back, hiding his guilty pleasure. "Yes, sir?"

"You know where Walker is?"

"Yes, sir, he's walking the perimeter."

"Well, go and bring him here."

Panic washed over FNG's face. "But—"

Before he could finish, the dark-haired towel wearer disappeared back in the room and the door swung closed behind him.

FNG pivoted and ran his free hand through his hair. "Fuck me!" He took one last deep drag, snuffed out the end, and pocketed his joint before leaving his primary unguarded as he headed resolutely out to find Walker.

*Total dumbass.*

With time being of the essence, Reaper rushed Michael's door and stopped it with his palm before it could latch. He held his position and looked to Lilith as she joined him in the entryway. She dipped her chin in silent confirmation that she had his back and then stepped back into the shadows, her attention focused down the hall.

Reaper slipped inside and was grateful to discover that the door opened into a small, enclosed foyer. He slowly eased the door shut and stood in the space, his knife a comfortable weight in his palm. He inched forward hugging the wall. At the wall's edge, he did quick scan of the wide-open space that was filled with an oversized couch positioned in front of a cold hearth.

*Why the hell did anyone need a fireplace in the desert?*

He shook off the out of place thought and kept his steps silent as he crept further in. The room held no sign of Michael, but another doorway stood just to the right of the fireplace. Light and the sound of movement spilled from inside. Reaper glided forward, his pulse steady despite his anticipation and heard water splashing. Looked like he was about to interrupt someone's bath time.

*Oh, fucking well.*

Reaper curled into the tight corner where the fireplace and doorframe met and let a few moments pass as he trained his attention on the door's gap. The bath sounds continued, but no movement broke the beam of illumination. Confident Michael was as vulnerable as he was going to get, Reaper slipped inside.

Sure enough, an oversized claw foot tub sat off to the side, and sprawled inside, back to the door, was a naked Michael. His head rested against the tub's edge, his eyes were closed, and his arms were draped over the edge, one hand holding a glass filled with amber liquid that was perilously close to tumbling free.

Reaper calculated the best use of the scenario even as disgust filled him. *What the hell was the idiot thinking?* The paranoid motherfucker Reaper knew would never put himself in such a position—back to the only entrance and trapped in a damn tub. No way in fuck this was Michael.

Between one breath and the next, Reaper crossed the room. The rush of his passage had Michael lifting his lashes, but before he could jerk upright, the kiss of metal held him in place. Furious brown eyes met Reaper's over the blade lying against the exposed throat and widened in recognition.

"What the fuck?" The question was barely breathed as anything louder would open his skin against Reaper's blade.

Reaper held his blade steady and sank into a crouch. "Figured since you wanted to talk so bad, I'd make time for a visit." He paused and with heavy skepticism, added, "Michael."

# twenty-three

Michael's flash of fear was quickly squashed by arrogant anger. "Wasn't expecting company." His gaze flicked down to Reaper's hand on the blade. "Ease up, man."

Instead of heeding the request, Reaper pressed it deeper and took dark joy in the skitter of panic the move provoked. "In a minute." He used his head to indicate the glass in Michael's hand. "Hate to see it go to waste. Why don't you finish that before we begin?"

Michael, gaze steady despite his awkward position, slowly lifted his glass. Since Michael's ability to speak was crucial to this encounter, Reaper eased the blade a fraction of an inch. Michael threw back the drink, carefully lowered the heavy glass, and let it tumble from his fingers. It hit the floor with a dull thunk and rolled out of sight. "Now what?"

"Now we talk." Reaper studied the features under his blade from his up close and personal position. There were differences, minor ones easily explained by the passage of time, but...

Memory flickered from years past of a fight involving a

jagged edge of a broken bottle. If this was Michael, that souvenir of their feral teen years would still exist.

"Mind if I—" Michael motioned to the towel that hung on a nearby rod.

"Yeah, I fucking do." Reaper used the flat edge of his blade against Michael's jaw and forced his face towards the light.

Michael followed the silent direction even as his hands tightened on the edge of the tub and his knuckles whitened. "What the hell do you want?"

Reaper studied the illuminated profile and failed to find what he was looking for. He pulled his blade away from temptation as every muscle locked into place and he breathed through the pulsing rage when his suspicions crystalized into certainty. "How about we start with a name."

Brown eyes widened a fraction before Michael's jaw tightened. "What kind of game are you playing, Reaper?"

"I don't fucking play games." Reaper held Michael's gaze and leaned in, his voice savage. "Something the real Michael knows damn good and well."

"The real Michael?" The man in the tub managed a credible sneer even though it trembled along the edges. "What the fuck are you going on about?"

With a minor shift of his wrist Reaper opened a thin red line along the man's neck. "Got to give you credit. You got the arrogance down pat."

"You're fucking crazy." A line of sweat beaded his hair line.

"Heard it before, but don't think so."

The man under his blade scoffed. "You come here to what? Confront me with some bizarre claim that I'm not who I am, and you don't think you're crazy?" A bark of harsh laughter escaped. "You're either crazy or have a death wish."

Despite the not-Michael's protests, there was a spark of panic kindling to life deep in the dark eyes. Reaper smiled and didn't need the man's paling skin to know it wasn't nice. "Actually, I came to prove a theory."

The man's throat bobbed. "What theory?"

Instead of answering, Reaper poised a question of his own as he considered the various angles of such a complex deception. "Whose idea was it?"

True puzzlement creased not-Michael's brow. "What?"

As he began his interrogation in earnest, Reaper watched the man carefully, more interested in the small twitches that said more than words. "Who came up with the plan to replace Michael with you?"

A muscle along the angled jaw jumped. "I don't know what you're talking about."

*Lie.*

Now that Reaper had the scent, he wasn't about to lose the trail. "Had to be someone close to him, close enough to realize who they'd have to get rid of to pull this shit off." As he puzzled it out, the pieces started to fall into place and created a grim picture. "Was it Greer? Or the asshole you're working with against the Cartels?"

The flare of panic spiked, and not-Michael's throat worked as he tried to swallow.

Reaper went with his gut and murmured, "Maybe it's a group thing."

This time the man in the tub jerked. Not a wise move considering it forced Reaper's blade deeper. Blood beaded the blade and dripped down his neck. The man hissed at the sting and fell back, but nothing could hide the rapid pace of his pulse.

Reaper tangled a hand in the man's wet hair, held his head back, and pulled the blade back just enough to ensure the idiot didn't slice his own throat open. "Yeah, definitely a group thing." He stared at the stranger who wore Michael's face. "I guess it makes sense. Michael was no one's fool, so it would take a concentrated effort to take him out."

Not-Michael was panting now.

"But not by you," Reaper continued. "I'm betting it was Greer, because that pansy ass dick you're working with doesn't strike me as the kind to get his hands dirty."

Not-Michael's eyes darted away, and Reaper knew he was getting it right. "That was the easy part, because once he's out of the picture, you have to make sure no one's around to question any slip ups."

Because there would be slip ups. Seamlessly stepping into a role of that nature would be a challenge, even for the most lethal assassin. Timing would be critical. Time to perfect the target's mannerisms and tells, all those things that would give away the game to those who knew Michael intimately. But once his closest circle was taken out, it was smooth sailing.

Another piece fell into place and this time the reverberation was strong enough to threaten Reaper's icy control. His voice was a bowel-loosening growl when he demanded, "Who gave the order to take out my unit?"

What little color not-Michael clung to disappeared and left his skin a pasty white, slicked with a sheen of sweat. His eyes widened, revealing the whites as they pinwheeled looking for an escape.

Reaper's knife dug in causing a whimper and when the fucker peed himself causing the water to gain a faint yellow tinge, he sneered. He fought the urge to peel the skin from the shivering skin sack in the tub. "Who?"

"You're fucking nuts." The accusation was a harsh whisper, but it carried too much fear to be taken seriously. "You think you'll get out of here alive?"

"Who's going to stop me?" Reaper leaned close to non-Michael's ear and hissed, "You?" He pulled back as ice settled in his veins. "Who fucking gave the order?"

The man stayed silent

Reaper upped the ante. He used his hold on the man's hair and slammed the skull into the hard edge of the tub, leaving the naked idiot dazed. Before he could recover, Reaper slapped his hand over his mouth and drove his knife through the lukewarm water to sink it in the fleshy part of the man's thigh.

Under his palm, the man screamed, flopped in the reddish-yellow tinged water, and tried to escape. Reaper kept his hand in place even as not-Michael finally stopped struggling and laid back, his dark eyes wide and panicked. Moisture coated his face—sweat, water or both—and above Reaper's hand, not-Michael's nostrils flared with each harsh exhale.

Certain he had the bastard's attention, Reaper repeated his question with added emphasis. "Who. He twisted the blade deeper. "Gave." He ripped out the blade and sank it back in, ignoring the muffled scream. "The order?"

Fingers clawed at Reaper's wrists and left behind bloodied gouges. Under Reaper's palm the idiot's mouth moved. Reaper kept pressure on the knife embedded in the man's leg and lifted his hand so not-Michael could speak.

"Kane." The name came out on a sob. "It was Kane's idea, but Greer was all over it."

Kane must be the sandy-haired bastard from earlier. Reaper added the name to his list of loose ends. "Why?"

Not-Michael mistook his question and hurried to explain. "She was pissed at Michael because he ended things between them."

That was not the answer Reaper was expecting.

"The crazy bitch didn't handle rejection well." Not-Michael was all but vomiting information at this point. "Kane used that to his advantage. It didn't take much to get her on board."

Reaper once again regretted he couldn't resurrect Greer and kill her all over again. "When did you come in?"

"After Kane got Greer hooked on his dick." A hint of contempt lay under the panicked expression. "He made it sound so fucking simple. Play the king and get the benefits of the position without all the fucking headaches."

"Yeah," Reaper drawled. "How's that working out for you?"

"Fuck you," the imposter spat.

"Nah, think you're the one that's fucked now." Reaper stared into the fear-lined face. "What's Kane's end game?"

The mutinous jut of the chin should've warned him, but Reaper missed the tell and the man in the tub was done cooperating. His fist shot out and Reaper barely dodged the clumsy shot. Unfortunately, in doing so, he tore his knife free of the man's thigh. A pained grunt filled the bathroom as the man scrambled out of the tub and left a crimson trail in his wake.

It took Reaper a few precious seconds to regain his balance and then he lunged for the naked man. His tackle took them both to the floor and slammed the imposter's face into the unforgiving surface.

Reaper pushed off the limp body as a litany of curses ran through his head. He flipped the naked idiot over and pressed two fingers to not-Michael's neck. His shoulders sagged in relief when a slow and steady pulse met his touch.

*Motherfucker was out like a damn light.*

"Goddammit." What the hell was he supposed to do now? Before he could decide his next move, a low warning hiss sounded from behind him. He spun around.

The bathroom door inched open to reveal a frowning Lilith. "We've got company," she warned, then took in the bloody bathroom and the nude male sprawled at Reaper's feet. She sighed. "Is he alive?"

"For now." Reaper crouched next to not-Michael, but

Lilith called his name. He looked over his shoulder and found her shaking her head, her hand still holding the door open.

"No time. Dumbass is back with company."

"Who?"

"Walker."

He grit his teeth and looked back to the unconscious imposter. "Dammit." They couldn't drag him through Castille, not if they wanted to get out alive, but leaving him behind meant losing their only proof that this bastard wasn't Michael. Proof they would need to screw up whatever deal was in the making with the Cartels.

"Reaper, come on." Urgency rode Lilith's voice.

He turned away and reluctantly followed Lilith out of the room, his mind churning through options to expose the imposter and track down Kane.

Lilith stopped at the front door, eased it open, and checked their exit before slipping into the entryway. Reaper stayed on her heels as they darted into the shadowed recesses just as Dumbass and Walker moved into the hall. Someone called out, and the two men turned back to the verandah. Lilith and Reaper used the distraction to make tracks out of the hall and into the bowels of Castille.

They worked their way out of the old casino, and Reaper knew he was racing a clock. Once the imposter woke, shit would hit the fan and the hunt for the Vultures would kick into lethal gear. Leaving behind the proof of Kane and his deadly game grated and without the puppet, Reaper was left with only one option—going after the puppet master.

# twenty-four

As hot wind laced with dust from an incoming storm whipped through the nearly deserted streets, Lilith ducked under a ragged curtain of beads and cloth, her hand locked around Reaper's wrist as she entered the hazy confines of the smoke house where they were to meet their backup of Havoc and Mercy.

She wove her way through the clutter of seating and scattered tables as the din of voices and smoke curled around them. Their passage garnered a few looks, but for the most part they were ignored as those around here didn't want undue attention.

She spotted a barely illuminated, empty corner and dropped to the cushions, dragging Reaper down next to her. She leaned over and turned the lamp down further until its light just covered the table's surface. She sat back, hoping the shadows were enough to keep their faces anonymous, undid the tail end of her headscarf, and tugged down the breathing mask. She wiped away a bead of sweat from her upper lip and sucked in fresh air.

With a wall to their backs and tucked into a corner, the

wariness that rode Lilith's neck finally backed off. She rested her head against the wall and closed her eyes, fighting to level out her pounding pulse. The run from Castille left her revved, and not in a good way.

Their escape was too close and unsettling. Getting through the obstacle course of the crumbling building had been the easy part. Then Michael was found, and patrol activity kicked into overdrive. By the time they scrambled down the last exterior wall and into the storm that was rolling in, evading the overzealous soldiers had become an endurance test.

Behind her closed lids, the image of the bloody body sprawled over the tiles resurrected the heart-stopping moment when she wondered if Reaper's control had finally and lethally snapped. Despite Reaper's grim assurance that Michael was just unconscious, her paralyzing fear hadn't eased until she saw the unmistakable rise and fall of Michael's back.

Then there was no time to worry about it as she and Reaper ended up in a deadly game of hide and seek as they rushed back to the relative safety of the bazaar. The storm made itself known just as they hit the old, abandoned mall and slipped inside. While the city's inhabitants bunkered down in their personal shelters, the lawless late-night crowd wove in and out of the bazaar's questionable establishments.

Relatively safe inside the anonymity of the smoke house, the icy hold on her control started to thaw and left her shaky. Tonight's revelations came damn close to breaking her formidable discipline and that was a weakness she couldn't abide. It was disconcerting to realize she was closer to losing her shit than even Reaper. But listening to the two bastards discuss Tabby's abduction had erased the ruthless political leader and brought forth the dangerously furious mother. If it hadn't been for Reaper, she would've endangered everyone and everything to slake her hunger for vengeance.

She curled her fists in her lap and locked her jaw tight against the need to scream her frustration until she was empty. She was no fucking good like this and needed to pull it together. If she didn't, she'd lose everything—her people, her daughter, and the man she loved.

Again.

Reaper wrapped his arm around her shoulder and pulled her against his chest. His warmth seeped into her skin. She turned deeper into his hold and buried her face against his chest, taking his scent deep. She curled one hand into his shirt and concentrated on his steady heartbeat as she dragged the shredded pieces of her soul back together.

He didn't say anything, but simply pressed a soft kiss to the top of her head in a simple yet telling sign she wasn't alone. The weight of his touch sank past the headscarf to the emotional chill that clutched her in icy claws.

She dragged in a shaky breath, then another, until the next one was stronger and steadier. Then in a husky but calm voice, said, "Tell me."

He rested his jaw against the top of her head. "Michael's been dead for years." His voice rumbled through his chest and vibrated under her cheek.

Her muscles locked and her grip tightened as she rocked under the depth of certainty in his statement. "Who?"

"Kane, the sandy-haired bastard."

She pushed back just enough to tilt her head and looked into his face. "You're sure?"

"When we were about seventeen, Michael and I got into a fight at some roadside dive." He brushed his knuckles along her jaw. "Michael got jumped by this tiny she-devil wielding a broken bottle. It caught him just behind the ear above his jaw." He traced the spot along her skin, leaving goose bumps in his wake. "Bled like a bitch and required stitches. The bartender had a neat hand, but it still left a noticeable scar."

She tried to swallow against a throat suddenly gone dry.

Reaper's navy-blue eyes burned into hers. "There was no scar."

Her gut roiled. "Who is he?"

He shrugged. "Didn't get around to that question."

She wasn't surprised. The name of the imposter was minor in the larger implications of whatever was at play. She uncurled her stiff fingers and flattened her palm against Reaper's chest. "Who took him out? Kane?"

Reaper shook his head. "That honor was all Greer. Seems she and Michael were lovers."

That unexpected piece of information took her by surprise.

"Michael dumped her ass," Reaper continued, his voice low. "She didn't take it well. Kane made the suggestion to take Michael out, and Greer stepped up."

Lilith blinked and tried to process Greer's over the top reaction to getting dumped. Talk about a vindictive lover. "All right, that explains Greer's beef with Michael, but what's Kane's game?"

A disgusted look filled Reaper's face. "Our favorite imposter did a face plant before I could find out."

It was a hell of a story—a lethally pissed ex being manipulated by someone with a hard-on for power— if it had been anyone else other than Reaper trying to sell this bag of twisted shit, she wouldn't believe them. But it was Reaper, and he wasn't the kind to bullshit. Ever.

"This Kane," she said. "He's going to be out for blood. He can't afford for you to out him or his puppet."

Reaper ran a soothing hand down her spine and arched a brow. "Think you're giving me too much credit, babe. If we took this public, it would come down to my word against theirs. Don't think that will go over well."

His self-disparaging tone rubbed her the wrong way and

she frowned. "You're not giving yourself enough credit." She sat up and he lifted his arm, letting her settle in next to him before he dropped it back around her shoulders to keep her close.

She shot him a glare. "I told you earlier, people listen to you. You bring this to light, and your voice would carry enough weight to make people wonder." Not to mention the added pressure when she added her voice to his. He may not want to admit it, but together they could make some serious waves.

His jaw flexed but he didn't relent. "Maybe, but I get the feeling Kane's a power in his own right. Leaves me cautious to sounding the alarm without direct proof."

She stilled as Reaper's words mirrored something Belle said months ago. She tugged on the faint threads and brought the memory closer.

*"You need to watch out for that one, Lilith." Belle's witchy face was creased with concern. "I don't trust that man." Her gaze shifted to where a small trio of men stood outside the building where their recent meeting had been held.*

*"You don't trust any man," Lilith teased.*

*"True, but this one..." Belle worried her lip and tightened the strap on the saddlebag hanging off her bike. When she looked back to Lilith, there was no trace of humor in her face. "I watched him in that room. He says the right things, but he's up to something. I'm surprised the other advisers aren't watching their backs with him around."*

As the memory solidified and the pieces fell into place a knot of dread settled like a heavy weight in Lilith's stomach. Now she remembered where she'd seen that sandy-haired man before. "Kane," the name came out on a harsh whisper as her gaze met Reaper's, "he's one of Michael's advisers."

Something dangerous moved through Reaper's eyes, but his voice was calm. "You're sure?"

Unable to sit still, she ran a hand over the back of her neck. "Yeah, Belle and I had a meet with a couple of them nearly a year ago." She dropped her hand and fisted it against her knee. "We were trying to hammer out the details on a medical trade agreement. Kane was there. He didn't do anything suspicious, but Belle didn't like him." And Lilith learned long ago it wasn't wise to ignore Belle's instincts.

Reaper shifted so his body blocked hers from the main room. To anyone watching, they would appear to be taking intimate advantage of the darkened corner. His fingers stroked along her jaw, but his gaze was sharp. "Did you have Charity look into him?"

Despite his distracting touch, Lilith nodded. "Unfortunately, I never got a chance to follow up with her. The initial weapons shipment with Crane went sideways about a week later, then Crane was killed, and you know the rest."

His thumb brushed the hollow of her throat. "We need to get in touch with Charity. See if she has any info on him."

Self-recrimination swamped her, and Lilith bowed her head and blew out a hard breath. "Dammit."

Reaper tucked his finger under her chin and nudged her face back up. He pressed a hard, quick kiss to her lips. When he drew back, his lips held the tiniest curve. "Hindsight's a bitch."

*Yeah, she was.*

The soft clack of beads drew her gaze over Reaper's shoulder and the ragged curtain at the entrance danced in the rush of bodies that passed outside. Her instincts spiked and she grabbed Reaper's arm and started to shift out of the couch. "We need to leave."

He glanced back at the empty entry, then back to her. "What did you see?"

She got to her feet and refastened her headscarf, hiding her face once more. "Searchers." She pulled on his arm until he got up, tucked the tail end of his scarf in place and followed. "Michael's soldiers are going to start crawling through here looking for you."

Lilith trailed one of the staff and when they pushed through a door at the back, she followed with Reaper at her back. She rushed through the cramped kitchen and dodged a kid carrying a bucket of pans. A few half-assed yells erupted as she hit the back door, shoved it open, and stepped into the narrow space between structures.

The dented door slammed closed, and then she and Reaper headed to where it spilled into the main walkway. As they got closer, a rush of approaching feet had her ducking behind a stack of wooden crates at the entrance's edge. Reaper crouched behind her and together they watched a group of Michael's men sweep past. When the sounds of their passage faded, she shot Reaper a grim look.

The bounty just went nuclear and took their situation from bad to worse.

BY THE TIME Lilith and Reaper closed in on the secondary rendezvous point, the itch at the back of her neck had reached unbearable levels. Yet no matter how much she checked their back trail, she couldn't locate any shadows. Even Reaper was twitchy, his head swiveling as they moved through the night.

Twice they dodged the patrols and ducked out of sight to wait it out. After their second near miss, her worry escalated. She overheard a few terse exchanges and got the impression the search wouldn't stop until they returned with their quarry. The intensity of the hunt left her uneasy.

Their luck ran out when they were almost safe.

They had climbed the backside of an old building that was

refurbished into flop houses when five soldiers rounded the corner. Lilith dropped flat against the weathered fire escape, but Reaper, caught below her, was left exposed. She mentally cursed a blue streak when the soldiers spotted Reaper and filled the night with their resulting shouts.

She looked down into Reaper's face as fear skated under her skin. She inched her hand to her thigh where a nine mil was strapped, determined to take down at least two targets before the sound of the shots could call in reinforcements.

With his back to the soldiers, Reaper noted her movement and gave a warning shake of his head. He held her gaze and raised his hands over his head.

"Don't!" she mouthed and gripped the mesh of metal under her.

The cocky bastard gave her a wink and started backing out of the shadows. The click of guns filled the night as the soldiers took no chances.

Forced to watch Reaper surrender was hell. Her silent curses were locked tight as she gritted her teeth and forced her body to stay still. The smallest movement, and she'd be exposed.

One of the soldiers issued a curt order. "Down on your knees!"

Another one rand out of the alley as the remaining four took up positions.

Reaper took his time responding, but as soon as he was down, the armed soldiers closed in, their fingers on the trigger.

*Shit!*

She couldn't get a clear shot because they were clustered so close to Reaper, that if she tried one of them would nail Reaper before her bullets hit.

The soldier who ran away, came back with another heavily armed man at his side, and she amended her enemy count to seven. The newcomer was clearly in charge and sent a soldier to clear the rest of the shadows.

Lilith's breath caught because her time had just run out.

The soldier started to work his way through the shadows and stepped directly underneath her position when Reaper burst to his feet and attacked.

Shouts broke out, including the harsh bark of "Hold your fire!" A rush of feet followed as five more soldiers joined the melee.

Lilith used the opportunity Reaper provided and scrambled up and into the black hole of a nearby window. She rolled over the edge and almost dropped through the gaping hole where a floor once existed. Her breath stopped and her pulse spiked as she hung from the window's edge by her fingertips. Her weight hit the wall with a dull thud, and she winced, but the sounds outside continued uninterrupted. She ignored the bite of rough edges that cut into her palms and flailed her legs. A handful of breathless moments later, her toe found the tiniest of ledges.

She maintained her painful grip and plastered herself against the wall, her heart beating so hard it filled her ears. She rested her clammy forehead against the rough wall and sucked in a couple of breaths, forcing her body to calm.

From outside a sharp command cut through the night. "Enough!"

She froze, her ears straining.

Gravel crunched under boots and then a breathless moment of silence followed. "Reaper."

"Walker." Reaper's familiar voice was tight.

Her heart sank and her frantic gaze located a support beam just to the side of the window. Carefully, she stretched one hand out and gripped it, shifting her hold. She blew out a quiet breath when it held her weight and the ache in her arms eased with the new position.

"Busy night?" There was something in Walker's voice, but Lilith couldn't decipher it.

"Had busier."

There was another crunch of gravel. "Care to share where you've been tonight?"

"Around."

"Hmm, heard that." Walker paused. "Where's the woman?"

"Having trouble finding one of your own?"

A dull thud sounded, and Lilith had no trouble translating the sound into a fist sinking into a stomach. "You think this is a joke?"

"Am I fucking laughing?" Reaper's voice was strained but there was no mistaking the anger coursing through it. "What do you want?"

There was the sharp snap of fingers and another extended pause followed by Walker's cold voice. "Recognize this?"

Reaper's silence upped Lilith's curiosity. It was all she could do to stay still and stay hidden, forced to listen to shit go down.

"This beauty of a blade was used to slit Michael's throat."

Lilith's heart stopped.

"What the fuck are you talking about?" Disbelief roughened Reaper's voice.

*Fuckfuckfuck!*

Dread crept through Lilith's straining muscles.

"That's how you're going to play it?" Walker's question lashed out.

Reaper hit back. "Not fucking playing at a thing."

A grunt followed, then more dull thuds, the sounds painting an ugly picture for Lilith's imagination. She closed her eyes in a futile attempt to block out what was happening on the other side of the wall. Only when a coppery tang hit her tongue did she ease the grip of her teeth on her lip.

Walker's voice went colder still. "You going to tell me the blood on this blade isn't Michael's?"

Reaper's silence was more damning than a verbal confession.

"That's what I thought." Walker paused, then, "Everyone knows you've had it out for Michael, but you've never made a move until now. Which makes me wonder, who's paying you?"

"Think that should be my question." Reaper's voice was rough.

Another pained grunt sounded. "I'm not a low life mercenary."

Far from cowed, Reaper managed to pack his voice with contempt. "You keep telling yourself that, I'm sure it helps you sleep at night."

Walker ignored his taunt. "Where are the others?"

A muffled groan and then Reaper's voice emerged on a pained hiss. "Nowhere near here."

"You Vultures travel in a pack." Disbelief was ripe in Walker's voice. "You don't fly solo."

"You do when everyone's hoping to cash in on your head." Reaper managed a mocking laugh. "That's what you're doing here, isn't it? Trying to cash in by claiming I killed Michael."

"Not fucking claiming, I've got his dead body as evidence." Walker's tone was pure ice.

"I want to see it."

Lilith's breath caught at Reaper's demand. *What the hell was he up to?*

"Why? So you can gloat?"

"No, so I can make sure it's really fucking him."

*Goddammit, Reaper!*

His poking at Walker would get him killed. Sure enough the impact of a fist repeatedly sinking into flesh filled the night. By the time it stopped, Lilith's face was wet, and blood trickled from her savaged lip.

"You're a sick fuck, Reaper."

A harsh cough was followed by an even rougher groan. "Fuck you, Walker."

"Actually, you're the one about to be fucked." With that, Walker snapped out orders and Lilith was left clinging to the wall like a damn spider as Reaper was taken away.

# twenty-five

Reaper's knees hit the cement floor and he let the momentum carry him forward, rolling to his shoulder so as not to face plant. Not that the assholes behind him gave a damn. With his hands bound behind him and his ribs screaming in protest, he took his time getting to his feet. He ran his tongue over his teeth and found a couple were loose. Walker's fists were fucking heavy.

The heavy door slammed shut and left him alone in a barren, windowless room lit by a single bulb secured to the ceiling by a thick mesh of metal. Yeah, there was no breaking that and using it to cut his hands free. They were fucking smart not to give him anything to work with, and what that said about them almost made him smile.

Except Walker's accusation circled Reaper's brain and stirred up the dread shoved beneath his relief that Lilith had escaped. It chafed his ass to let Walker take him in, but it was better and less dangerous than the asshole getting his hands on Lilith. Now he needed to focus on something other than the uneasiness riding his ass and figure out how best to help his pending rescuers from the inside.

*Three against, what? Fifty? Sixty? Shit ass odds, brother.*

He snarled at his internal snarky bastard to shut the hell up and concentrated on the puzzle of who actually killed fake Michael. He played back the night, picking through the details.

Lilith's obvious worry when she saw the unconscious body, followed by relief when she noted he was still breathing. Their rushed escape out of the room and how they slipped out the door just as Walker and the idiot stoner hit the hall entrance. There had been movement in the shadows. Not much, but enough to make Walker and Idiot pause and turn back which gave Reaper and Lilith their opening to split.

Whatever delayed Walker and his sidekick had given someone time to tie up loose ends. But how would they know there were loose ends to tie up? Reaper hadn't noted any eyes while he and Lilith moved through Castille.

*So how?*

Before he could piece together an answer, the heavy door opened, and three burly men shouldered in. Reaper eyed the display of muscles and wondered if he should be flattered to be considered so dangerous. He braced his feet and grinned, confident it wouldn't take much to provoke the meatheads into something stupid.

They didn't disappoint and rushed him.

Even knowing it was pointless to fight, Reaper did, because it went against every grain he possessed. The battle was short-lived thanks to the numbers, and in the end, they had him trussed up and hooded, his body sporting another layer of bruises. As they hauled him out of the cell, the world took on a sickening twirl that left Reaper's head reeling. It was safe to say he had a concussion thanks to the meatheads' fists, but on top of that, one of his eyes was swelling shut and the cuts on his lips left a coppery taste in his mouth.

Dazed, but not completely out of it, he let his weight hang from their hands and his heels drag across the floor as they pulled him out of the cell. Hot air hit the hood and added a suffocating layer that made sucking in air more important than ever as the surface under his heels turned from hard to rough. Hands grabbed his ankles and under his arm, and with a grunted heave, he was swung into the air. His back hit the unforgiving surface that rocked and vibrated under the impact of additional weight and booted feet. An engine kicked to life and then a hard jerk followed.

Wherever they were taking him, it was by truck, and that did not bode well.

The rumble of engines was joined by the wail of the wind and despite the hood, dust still managed to coat his mouth. There was a sharp crack and flash of light that heralded the thunder that rode alongside the infamous dust storms that prowled through the Southwest.

As the truck bounced along, Reaper's reeling head took another beating. Since the journey passed in flashes, Reaper was certain he'd blacked out for moments and it messed with his perception of time, leaving him unsure how long it was before the truck jerked to a stop.

The meatheads remained silent as they hauled him down with no care, and difficult though it was, Reaper maintained his unconscious appearance. Not that it was a stretch, not with his spinning head and dry mouth. Even his muscles chimed in, screaming in protest from the combined efforts of the previous beating, the current manhandling, and the overly enthusiastic bindings. Hard hands held him, and he tried moving his fingers to ease the numbness but wasn't sure he was successful.

"Any trouble?"

That wasn't Walker.

"No, sir." The voice came from his left, close enough to be

heard over the rising wind. "We left word he was being transferred to New Seattle."

"Good. We'll take it from here."

Sand and rock crunch under foot and new hands took hold of Reaper. The next few minutes passed in a dizzying array of movement and raised voices as he was roughly dragged out of the storm and inside some structure. A faint electrical buzz sounded, and instinct made Reaper start to struggle. He didn't get far before something bit into his chest and lightning ripped through his muscles, leaving them locked and immobile.

*Where the fuck did they get a Taser?* That was Reaper's last coherent thought as things got a little fuzzy after that.

There was a sense of hand pulling and shoving him around. His back and ass landed in a chair and then the paralyzing effect of the taser was backing off, but it was too little, too late. More than one person was tightening thick straps along his arms and legs, locking him in place. Only when he was fully restrained did they yank the hood off.

He slammed his eyes shut as bright light seared his face. *Motherfuckers.*

Someone grabbed his chin, yanked it up, and slammed their palm against his cheek. The force of the hit cut the inside of his cheek against his teeth and blood filled his mouth.

He slitted his eyes open and spit a mouthful of blood into the blurry features in front of him. Not the smartest move, especially since he couldn't avoid the answering backhand that wrenched his neck and slammed his chin against his shoulder.

"Again."

Another warning hum preceded his nerve endings lighting up under the Taser's not-so-gentle touch. Curses crowded his skull because things were about to get ugly. Well, uglier.

His muscles were still twitching when the beating began. Left with no choice but to endure, Reaper locked his groans behind his teeth, unwilling to give his captors the satisfaction of his pain, and rode above it with the reminder that this was temporary.

Lilith wouldn't leave him here, neither would Havoc. This beating would be nothing compared to what those two would do once they had him back. They would be pissed at him for surrendering to Walker. Especially Lilith. He swore he could hear her even now, riding his ass about it. *"Don't you ever pull that self-sacrificing bullshit again."*

He choked on a groan as a fist sank into his gut.

*Yeah, babe, not inclined to make that mistake again.*

Another fist followed, and another, until he lost count. When they finally stopped, every inch ached. A hand grabbed his hair and yanked his head back. Reaper forced his lids to lift. One didn't quite make it, but he kept at it, bring the blurry face above his into focus.

Kane's bland features stared back.

A harsh laugh caught in Reaper's throat. *Go fucking figure.*

A sneer twisted Kane's thin lips. "If it isn't the legendary Reaper."

Unsure of Kane's game, Reaper decided to play ignorant. Hard as it was to get the words out, he managed. "And you are?"

"The one who's going to finish what Greer started." The condescension in Kane's smirk set Reaper's teeth on edge.

"Yeah, cuz that ended so well for that bitch." He knew it was a mistake before it left his mouth, but with no other way to strike back, he took his hits where he could.

Kane ripped his hand free and nailed Reaper with another backhand.

Reaper spat another bloody mouthful to the floor and worked his jaw carefully before meeting Kane's glare. Fucking-a, he needed to curb his mouth and haul his brain back in gear if he wanted to be breathing when his rescue party showed up. "What do you want?"

Kane studied Reaper, his voice ice cold. "Where's the bastard who killed her?" His voice was ice cold, but not cold enough to mask the flare of grief in his muddy eyes.

Reaper was shocked by the emotional slip. It wasn't much, just enough to indicate this bastard had actually cared for Michael's crazy ass psycho ex. As a weak spot it was almost laughable, but right now Reaper's options were thinner than air, so if Kane wanted a name, he'd keep Reaper alive long enough to get it.

Reaper grinned and felt blood dribbled down his chin. His left eye was almost completely swollen shut, which helped with the bright light, but still he held Kane's stare. "Don't know."

A reptilian coldness seeped into Kane's gaze, leaving it flat and empty, and he kept his unblinking attention on Reaper for a long moment, his thoughts hidden behind that disturbing stare. Finally, his lips curled into a cruel smile that made Reaper brace. Kane straightened and ran his hands down his shirt as if smoothing it out. He lifted his gaze, gave a short nod, and stepped back.

Searing pain ripped down Reaper's spine, and despite the restraints, his body bowed in agony. His jaw locked and his muscles screamed as a brutal wave of electricity danced through him. White edged his vision and his lungs seized.

A sharp command stopped the current. Released from the excruciating hold, Reaper slumped against the chair, his muscles jumping, his heart stuttering, and his lungs aching. He kept his head down and eyes closed and got his lungs to work, sucking in air.

Kane yanked his head back again. "Where is he?"

Despite his impaired vision, Reaper stared into Kane's eyes

and showed him there was no way in hell he was giving this asshole a name.

Something dark and sick lit in the muddy depths. "How long do you think you can endure?"

Reaper sneered instead of answering with the obvious.

Kane looked to the door. "Bring it."

He shoved Reaper's head forward and let go. Another man rushed forward with a trough of water and Kane stepped back.

Reaper got the picture quick and set his jaw, even as they stripped his boots and left him bare footed. Shackled to the chair, he couldn't evade the cold water that closed over his ankles. He glared at Kane and refused to look away even when Kane nodded.

This time the current seared through the soles of his feet and tore through his abused body. Reaper held that bastard's gaze even as his bones started to shake. Finally, the current stopped. Reaper's breath was a harsh rasp in his chest. Pain licked along every nerve ending, and if he hadn't been strapped to the chair, he'd be curled up on the floor. Vaguely he heard Kane give orders to clear the room.

The door closed behind the last of the men as the squeak of wheels rattled over the rough cement. Kane rolled a chair into position in front of Reaper and stayed to the edge of where light and shadows met. He crossed one leg over the other and tugged on the pant as if straightening an unseen wrinkle.

The pretentious movement had Reaper's lip curling.

Kane finished preening and folded his hands on his knee. "We met once, do you remember?"

Reaper wasn't looking forward to another dance with the light electric, so he played along. "No. Should I?"

Kane's thin lips curled as if he bit into something sour.

"No, I'd rather think you wouldn't." He cocked his head. "You made quite the impression with Greer though."

*Was the fucker jealous?*

Since it sure as shit sounded like it, it was time to push a few buttons.

"Did I?" Reaper shifted in his seat and choked back his groan when his ribs protested. Great, they were probably cracked. Which meant he couldn't risk another go around with the ham-fisted muscle or he would end up drowning in his own blood.

"Not a positive one, mind you," Kane continued. "She didn't like how much Michael relied on your advice." Kane's smile was one of those types that a man gives when he indulged a woman. "You have no idea how many times her advice was overridden because 'Reaper said...'."

When Kane trailed off, Reaper settled back and tried to ease pressure on his abused abdomen. "Guess it really sucked for her when he dumped her ass, uh?"

Kane's nostrils flared as he drew in a sharp breath, and his eyes narrowed as he gave Reaper a shrewd look. "Nice to know removing Lyle was warranted."

"Lyle? Guessing that's your puppet?" Hard though it was, Reaper kept his head up and his attention on Kane. The fact the bastard was eager and willing to talk proved he had no intention of letting him out of here alive. It was good to have goals. Too fucking bad Reaper didn't intend for Kane to get a chance to fulfill them. "Since we both know I'm not leaving here breathing, I got to know—why?"

"There are so many, many reasons. I could keep you entertained for hours."

*Oh, please fuckin' brag.*

As far as Reaper was concerned the more Kane shared, the more ammunition he gave to eliminating the threats he created. Reaper gave a pointed look to the chair he was strapped into before meeting Kane's gaze. "Looks as if I'm staying for a bit, so I've got time."

Kane's smile was all teeth. "Unfortunately, I don't."

That worried Reaper, because he needed Kane to stay put long enough for Lilith and Havoc to catch up.

Luckily the arrogant ass wasn't done.

Kane uncrossed his legs, leaned forward, and braced his elbows on his knees, his attention centered on Reaper. "Do you know who ran the Northwest before Michael?"

Reaper wasn't quite sure where the history lesson was leading, but he played for time. "Been awhile since I've been in class, Kane."

"Then let me refresh your memory. After the Collapse and the governments splintered, the once formidable union known as the United States digressed to an old west mentality. You're familiar with this?"

Yeah, he was, he heard it enough from the old timers that survived the Collapse and their oft repeated mantra. He repeated it now, "You're the power only if you hold it."

A benevolent smile broke over Kane's face, much like an instructor would bestow on a particularly bright student. "Correct."

*Nice to know he was exceeding expectations.* But that look was enough to make Reaper throw up a little.

Not done with his lesson, Kane continued. "The ones who managed to hold it belong to a well-off family."

*Oh Christ, seriously?* It wasn't hard to see where this was leading, and bit by bit the pieces fell into place. "Let me guess, your family."

"I knew there were brains in there somewhere." Kane's shoulders straightened with unmistakable pride and manic light lit his eyes. "My grandfather knew when to make the most of an opportunity. He made a highly respected name for himself as a weapons supplier."

"Your grandfather was the Wolf of the West." Weapons supplier was putting it nicely. More like a cut-throat dictator who hated to be bested.

Kane's smile was full of pride.

Reaper's lip curled in disgust. "He was a scavenger—picking through the decimated military bases and raiding the weapons stash. He sold inferior grade weapons to the masses, while supplying the wealthy with the best of the lots. He helped supply full scale massacres of small, self-sustaining communities, then had the balls to broker deals between the victors."

"He was an entrepreneur," Kane shot back. "He understood how to manipulate the market."

Stupid as it was to argue with the demented fuck, Reaper couldn't quell his contempt. "He was a fucking butcher."

"He was brilliant." In the first sign of his fraying temper Kane's hands curled into fists. "And his legacy would've survived, if not for my father." Something ugly crept under Kane's smooth voice. "Unlike my grandfather, my father tended to be a bit short-sighted."

It seemed someone had serious Daddy issues, but since Kane appeared to enjoy his whining time, Reaper was all about encouraging him, especially if it meant avoiding Kane's far from tender care. "What happened? He make some bad deals?"

Kane frowned. "Not him, the fool he worked with." He looked down to his hands as if finally realizing they were fists. He opened them and spread his fingers out before carefully placing them flat on his knees. When he lifted his head, his face was a stone mask.

"Father trusted the wrong man. A fact he failed to realize until a pivotal shipment disappeared, leaving him trying to soothe the ruffled feathers of his associates. They weren't so forgiving, but then neither was he." Kane's lips curved, and what they created was more a grimace than the intended smile. "My father didn't take disappointment well."

Kane rubbed one arm against his knee. The motion pulling his sleeve up just enough for Reaper to catch the edges of a ragged scar. Caught up in his story, Kane didn't appear to notice and his hands stilled, the sleeve falling back into place. "Before he faced his unhappy associates, Father decided to renegotiate the terms of his contract." Kane's gaze sharpened, an avid light sparking in the depths. "It did not end well for Owen or his family."

The name hit Reaper like a sucker punch. He knew that name, had heard it before, whispered in the dark in a voice broken by nightmares. A dark thread of foreboding wove through him and gained strength when Kane's smile turned cruel and knowing.

"I heard Owen's pretty little wife, Aurora, was quite the screamer towards the end."

Owen and Aurora, Lilith's parents.

Rage seared through Reaper, the strength of it threatening to break through his ruthless control but he held it together unwilling to give Kane any satisfaction.

Kane heaved a disappointed sigh at Reaper's lack of reaction, but he didn't stop talking. "While I admired his solution, it was too little too late. His associates were highly displeased with his failure, and they turned on him. He went down, and Michael walked over his body to take his position."

And that right here was the true root of all this twisted shit. "You couldn't find a way to take it back."

Because Michael had been a keen and ruthless strategist, one who managed to cobble the fractured powers that be into a cohesive unit. Something Kane's sick fuck of a father failed to do. Under Michael's hand, those like Kane's blood, that plagued the surviving remnants of humanity were dealt with, and that gave the rest a sense of security and safety that had been sorely lacking. It was why Reaper and those like him once followed Michael.

Kane's fingers tapped an absent rhythm on his knee. "No, I knew exactly how to get my birthright back, but it required patience. A trait father never quite got." His fingers stilled. "Patience is the key to successfully identifying opportunities. Grandfather taught me that."

Reaper's puzzle came together. While Michael rebuilt the Northwest, Kane bided his time and picked a position that would allow him to exploit any weakness. It had taken awhile, but everyone was flawed and human. Once Michael screwed up by dumping an obviously unstable Greer, Kane slithered in, honed his disgruntled weapon, and set her loose. It was scary brilliant, because the blood would stain Greer's hands, not Kane's.

Kane leaned in, his face so close Reaper could see the soul-less monster under Kane's skin. "I can be very, very patient. Every decision, every move, has been calculated for years. First, finding Michael's weak spot, then ensuring his allies began to question his motives. Even eliminating those nosy-ass Strix before they could intervene. Now, that one took some serious crafting. After that, setting the Territories at each other's throats was easy."

It chilled Reaper how well planned the entire mess was, but Kane was forgetting a very important piece of the picture. He strained against the straps to lean in and let the ice in his veins coat his voice. "Patient or not, you fucked up, Kane. You missed some of the pieces."

Like him and the other Vultures, or Math and Mercy. Even the Dogs of War could wreak havoc on Kane's ultimate plans. Even worse, all those little mistakes led to him panicking and risking it all by taking Istaqa and Lilith's kids. That move forced the two key players to come together, instead of dividing and conquering. "Now, they're targeting you."

Kane waved his words away and got to his feet. "Those mistakes are Greer's." His tone was dismissive.

Reaper didn't miss the flash of remorse Kane failed to hide and decided to use Kane's strategy against him, widening the cracks in Kane's delusional world. He aimed for a conciliatory tone and managed to convey sympathy when he commented, "It's hell to have a woman disappoint you. Ain't it?"

A frown marred Kane's face. "Mistakes are inevitable." The words were soft, as if he was reassuring himself.

"So sure of yourself," Reaper pressed softly. "You think I'm the only one turning over rocks and snake hunting?"

Kane stilled and his unblinking stare fell on Reaper. "You think your motley crew can take me down? Or those disgraced assassins?" True humor lit his face because narcissistic egomaniacs tended to be dense as fuck. "As if any of them have a chance of getting their stories heard." He gave Reaper a pity-filled look. "Even if the others know what you found in that room, no one would listen to them. Why would they?"

Relief squeezed through Reaper. Based upon Kane's comment, he believed the woman with Reaper at Castille was Mercy, not Lilith. So long as he continued to believe that, he would leave Lilith alone. Maybe long enough for her to raise the alarm. Of course, she had to get the hell out of Phoenix first.

"Not that it really matters." Kane sent the wheeled chair back into the shadows with a push. "Between you hanging from the end of a rope and the bounty, pesky mouths will remain silent." He turned back to Reaper, his arrogance once more firmly in place. "In the end, I'll still be standing." The depth of vicious delight in Kane's smile was worrisome. "You, however, may wish you weren't."

With that, he moved to the door and pulled it open. A

rush of movement signaled the guards outside coming to attention. "I need him breathing, but I want names when I return."

"Yes, sir."

Kane shot one last look over his shoulder. "I'll be back."

# twenty-six

Lilith didn't need the sound of the soldiers clearing the areas below to know it was too dangerous to stay. Panic and fear tried to gain purchase, but she locked them away in a deep, dark hole and refused to let them rise. Instead, she embraced the familiar coat of icy clarity that kept her ass in one piece for years. She adjusted her plans and carefully inched her way back to the window, her mind quickly running through her options.

First, she had to get clear of the searching soldiers below without alerting them to her presence. Since she couldn't afford to leave bodies in her wake that was easier said than done. She pulled level with the window, wedged her toes into the exposed cracks, and shifted her weight so she could peer through the opening. She hung just out of sight, her ears trained for sounds to indicate that Walker had left behind guards. There were the muffled noises from the soldiers who continued to work their way through the building, but otherwise the night remained quiet.

With no time to lose, she slipped back out to the fire escape, knowing if eyes were watching that was when she would be at her most vulnerable. With an ease born of years skulking in the shadows, she kept to the deepest darkness as she made her way back down to the street. The soft thud of her landing sounded overly loud, and she froze in her crouch, her eyes the only thing to move. A heartbeat passed, then another, before she straightened and slipped away.

Even as she wove her way through the night, taking care to avoid the roaming patrols with a skill undiminished by her years away from such covert activities, she knew she wouldn't do the smart thing—rendezvous with Mercy and Havoc, then go after Reaper. That would take too damn long, and god only knew what would happen to Reaper while she did.

Although someone wanted Reaper dead, Lilith was going to do everything in her power to ensure that didn't happen. Not just because the infuriating man—*who the hell just blithely surrendered to the asshole who wanted your blood?* — owned her heart and soul, but because she was fucking done with this shit.

Years of trying to carve out some sort of safety had resulted in endangering those she loved. First Tabby, now Reaper. Even her family had fallen under the greed of the power hungry. Was she willing to wait until she waded through Reaper's blood? The bodies of the Vultures? Of Math? Before she wised the hell up?

*No, she was fucking not, because enough was enough and she was fucking done.*

Done with the politics, done with the negotiations, done with compromising, done with sacrificing what was most important to her for the good of others. No position was worth her soul.

It was time to dethrone the Queen of the Rockies and make room for new players to enter the game, ones who didn't have weaknesses to exploit. Hell, she hadn't chosen Belle, Silas, and Everett for their sweet dispositions. The three could easily run the Rocky Mountain Territories, probably better than she could at this point. And none of them were torn between duty and family.

At that simple, yet difficult, admission, a weight she hadn't consciously been aware bearing of lifted and left behind a ruthless lucidity. She needed to get to Reaper and eliminate Kane. So long as that asshole was out there, she and Reaper and Tabby would find no peace.

It was time to go back to the basics. Kane might have maneuvered the political arena to his advantage, but when it came to the deadly, covert battlefield behind the power players, Lilith was queen for a reason.

Years ago, during the Border Wars, she built a vast network of eyes and ears that allowed her unfettered access to the world below those who held the power. Granted, it wasn't the safest world and chances were damn good many of those contacts were dead and gone, already replaced by unknown, dangerous ones. She changed her direction because there was one face she hoped still breathed. It was a hell of a long shot, but one she was willing to chance if it meant getting to Reaper.

Evading Walker's patrols made her trip to the water seller's shop an endurance test. Once she'd known this place well, but years of turmoil had left their mark. The pockets where civility once held sway now teemed with unsavory life.

At one point, she was forced to hop a cement block fence to avoid detection. When she dropped on the other side, she came face-to-face with a growling mutt held back by a thick chain. She crouched out of the reach of the light that spilled from an open doorway as its rumbling growls gained strength. Just as the first bark sounded, loud voices erupted in argument from the dilapidated house and added to the din. A crash of something shattering joined in as she dashed across the yard and scaled the other fence.

She dropped to the other side just as a looming shadow

stepped into the doorway and yelled at the mutt to shut the hell up. She left the mutt and his enraged owner behind, completed the last bit of her trip without further incident, and hit the familiar street ten minutes later.

She stood in the shadows and watched the seemingly deserted street. Positioned between two darkened buildings a lone light stood sentry part way down the street's other side. Her target was the graffiti tagged building closest to her. There was a barely noticeable edge of light that leaked around the boarded windows perched high near the flat roof line.

Someone was home.

She used the rusted hulks of old cars crouched on cracked concrete under half-collapsed roofs of rotting carports to veil her approach and crossed the street. Not inclined to take a belly full of buckshot, she didn't bother with the front entrance. Instead, she slid through waist-high weeds seeded with unidentified junk along the side of the building, and to the wall where metal and cement topped by barbed wire guarded the back.

She didn't try to scale it because anyone stupid enough to try would be in for a hell of a shock as the owner kept that wire electrified. Instead, she aimed for the pile of old tires and wooden pallets piled high at the side under a mismatch quilt of tarps. It was haphazard route, but she hoped what it hid still remained.

She slid under the tarps, and carefully shifted a few of the pieces, wincing when the wood shifted and moaned softly. She held her breath as she created a small crawl space, just big enough for her to fit. Gravel bit her palms and pressed against her knees, but when she found the grime-covered window that led into the basement, she smiled.

She used her knife to pry it open and despite the tight fit squeezed through the opening. Crouched on a pile of crates, she strained her ears as she replaced the window. Unlike most buildings in Phoenix, this one had a basement. It was a crucial convenience for its owner who used the space for storage.

Muted beams of light from the main floor filtered through the ceiling's cracks. It wasn't much, but it was enough for Lilith to pick her way through the carefully stacked barrels of water and over to the short set of stairs that led up.

She crept up the stairs, knife in hand, and tested her weight with each step. When she reached the top, she grabbed the doorknob and slowly twisted, wincing when the latch gave a soft snick. She waited a long, breathless moment with her hand on the knob, before finally easing it open.

Thankfully, as the door swung wide, the hinges remained mute. She inched into a hall, blade at the ready, and every sense on alert. A soft clink came from deeper in the house and she followed it in, stopping at an entryway to a tidy, well-kept living room lined with books. In a faded armchair positioned under a lone light, a gnome of a man had his head bent over an oversize tome on his lap.

Lilith stayed in the shadowed hall and scanned the room for hidden threats. When she found none, she moved to the arched entry, and rapped her knuckles against the old adobe wall.

The bald head jerked up, and light sparked off the thick, round lenses, almost, but not quite, concealing the wide eyes surrounded by long lashes. Stunned surprise came and went, smothered under a pleasant mask. "Lilith. It's been a while."

"Hey, Thad." She leaned a shoulder against the wall and played her blade play through her fingers in an idle threat. "I was in the neighborhood, figured I'd drop in for a visit."

Thad carefully closed the large book in his lap and positioned his folded hands on the cover. "A little late for company, my dear."

"Mmm." Her hum said everything and nothing. "I won't take up too much of your time."

Thad did another long blink before he inclined his head. "Always happy to assist the daughter of an old friend."

"I have a question I'm hoping you can answer." Once, a long time ago, Thad had dealt in much more volatile things than water. He was one of the few individuals Lilith didn't worry would sell her out. Not because he liked her, but because he had been loyal to her father. So much so, when she lost her brother Jake, it was Thad who helped identify those who betrayed the last of her family. His version of repaying old debts.

Small lines furrowed Thad's forehead. "Is this in regards to the rather esteemed guests who arrived today?"

The blade in her hand stilled and it was her turn to incline her head.

Thad sighed and murmured, "That's what I was afraid of." He stared down at his hands for a moment, took a deep breath, and lifted his gaze to hers. "I'll give you what help I can, but it may not be much."

Desperation meant she would take whatever she could get. "I need a location, someplace secure, away from curious eyes and ears."

"There are a couple that come to mind." He set the book on the floor and rose from his chair. "Which party is conducting this meeting?"

Kane's name hovered on the tip of her tongue, but he was a ghost to the world, so she offered his puppet. "Michael."

Distaste tightened Thad's mouth. "Why you didn't deal with him years ago, I'll never understand."

"It was too complicated." It was an old argument, but knowing what she did now, she wished she had heeded Thad's advice then.

"And it's not now?"

She choked back a sharp laugh. "Let's just say he's bit off more than he can chew."

"Yes, I heard about the bounty on that boy Reaper. I do hope he's planning on taking care of that." Thad didn't wait for her response but turned to one of the overstuffed bookcases.

Only Thad could get away with calling Reaper a boy. "He's working on it,' she murmured.

Thad shuffled a few books aside and pulled out what looked like bound papers. He turned, nabbed a nearby solar light, and motioned for her to follow.

She did, into a well-worn kitchen.

Thad set the solar light on a table and started to unfold his papers. "There are a few places that would fit your requirements." He smoothed out the aged paper, and Lilith noted the map was covered in handwritten notations that added color to the faded lines of what used to be the east valley of Phoenix. Without looking at her, Thad said, "I'm assuming Michael's arrival coinciding with Suárez's son does not bode well."

Strangely, she felt her lips twitch at that dry comment. "When would it ever?"

"Very true." Thad traced one arthritic finger over an unerring line to the Castille. "I'm assuming whatever business they chose to conduct was done here." He tapped the m and looked up to catch her nod. "Not surprising. It would be the best place for such parties to meet."

He drew a line south, down towards the dry riverbed that once flowed through man made canals. "There was an uptick in activity here, with out-of-town soldiers milling around and making a nuisance of themselves with the locals. Lourdes was very upset that they kept her youngest out running errands until very late the other night. If Michael's forces took a prisoner, they would keep him here. It's where they've set up camp. They asked for enough water for two days. Tomorrow is day three."

So fake Michael's comment about leaving tomorrow

hadn't been a lie. Good to know. Unfortunately, she didn't think Reaper would be there, or at least not for long. "If Michael decided he didn't want the hassle of transporting a prisoner?"

Thad's finger shifted and moved west to circle an area she knew was a cluster of abandoned high rises that lined the old riverfront. "Here."

Frustration rose because while the area was contained, it still left a massive number of spots to search. She kept her voice calm, unruffled. "Any chance of narrowing it down?"

There was a reason she had come to Thad. Not only was he well liked and highly regarded, as a water seller his interactions spanned the community. People felt comfortable sharing the comings and goings with him. Lilith's hope, slim though it was, hung on his hearing something useful.

Thad's gaze drifted as he considered her question. "Who was it?" His question wasn't for her, but for himself. "Jorge? No, Marcus." His gaze sharpened. "Marcus mentioned he'd run into a spot of trouble about here." Thad tapped a finger beside what used to be a marina. "He was upset because the noses sniffing around put a damper on his business."

A spark of anticipation lit, and Lilith sent up a silent thanks for whatever questionable business Marcus conducted. "He was sure it was city soldiers, not mercenaries?"

Thad nodded. "Marcus is quite aware of the difference as he's been very keen to avoid city militia. Seems they took umbrage with some of his earlier endeavors."

Right, so Marcus was trying to outrun a bounty, something many in this town shared. She studied the map and committed the route to memory. It would take too long to make it on foot, so she needed to find a set of wheels. Plus, she needed to get word to Havoc and Mercy because going in without backup was suicidal. And she was not that, not when she had a daughter to get home to, and a man's sexy ass to kick, once she was done saving it.

She drummed her fingers on the table. "Can you share this information with a couple of friends of mine?"

He nodded.

She quickly described Havoc and Mercy and how to reach them, then she leaned into Thad and pressed a quick kiss to his cheek. "If this pans out, I owe you."

A slight blush stole over Thad's cheeks, and he patted her shoulder. "You know I'll collect."

She gave a soft laugh. "I'd expect nothing less."

The hand on her shoulder squeezed. "You'll be careful." It wasn't a question.

She covered his aged hand with hers. "Yeah."

Thad nodded and let her go to begin refolding his map.

"I'll see myself out."

Thad didn't look up but gave another short nod.

Lilith was at the edge of the hall when he called her name. She looked back to find him standing between his living room and the kitchen, lamp in hand.

"May I suggest you finish it this time, dear."

She gave him a lethal grin. "I intend to."

<h1 style="text-align:center">twenty-seven</h1>

Close to half an hour later, Lilith shut down a bike she picked up outside a dive bar a few blocks from Thad's. Since the bikes lined along the side of the shuddering building carried various markings from the Cartel families, taking one didn't make Lilith feel guilty. Besides, based on the rowdy noises that escaped the swinging doors when she was scouting her options, she was fairly certain morning would break before the bike's owner noticed their missing transportation.

The echoes of the engine faded as she swung her leg off and wheeled the bike further into the remains of an old office building. She wasn't keen on advertising her presence to whoever lurked in the shadows and was making the last part of the trek on foot. While the bike cut her travel time down, she was still left with a good fifteen minutes, maybe a few more, to hike deeper into the treacherous maze of the dilapidated river-front buildings.

With time ticking relentlessly down, she slipped into the night to make her way in. The rancid order of rotted vegetation hung in the air from the dry riverbed. During the worse of the monsoons, the broad expanse would flood over its low shores and seep through the tangle of buildings to create a dangerous swamp of fetid water interspersed with submerged traps for the unwary.

Despite the earlier thunderstorms, her path remained relatively dry as she combed through the deserted streets, bur remained a test of nerves. She scrambled over a pile of rubble that blocked the most direct route when the hair on the back of her neck rose and the spot between her shoulders started to itch. She slid down the far side with more speed than grace and hit the ground running.

Staying low and using the partial screen of the rubble pile, she darted inside the nearest building and ducked behind a thick wall. She crouched in the shadows, pressed her back against the unforgiving surface, and listened hard for sounds of her stalker. Although anticipation thrummed through her veins, her pulse remained steady, and her breathing was soft, nearly silent.

Silent minutes stretched out until she wondered if she had been spotted and was now caught in a game of wait and see. She was prepared to shift her position to a better vantage point to find out, when she caught the soft sound of a small stone shifting underfoot.

She froze in place, her blade a comforting weight in her hand, and trained her gaze on the opening just beyond the screen of the wall. The edge of a shadow drifted forward, and slowly morphed into the solid shape of her stalker.

She waited until it drew past, noticing the lean form and broad shoulders that indicated a male before she slipped in behind him.

Two steps in, the figure paused.

Lilith lunged forward as the person started to turn. A soft grunt sounded as her weight hit and drove them both back and into the concealing shadows of the building. She used both her blade and her body to attack, and the man stumbled back, barely regaining his footing as he evaded Lilith's lethal strikes. Undaunted, she pressed forward, forcing him to retreat.

When he slammed a hand into her arm and left it numb, she deftly switched her blade to her other hand, and whipped out with a roundhouse kick. He leaned back but lost his footing in the debris strewn concrete and her kick hit his shoulder, not the temple she'd been aiming for.

A ruthless hand clamped down on her calf, but before he could shove it away, she fully committed, and used his hold as a pivot point to drive her knee into his ribs. They both went down in a tangle of limbs.

"Goddammit, woman, ease the fuck up!" The voice was muffled but the words were clear. "I'm here to help."

Her knife poised at the man's groin stilled, the lethal edge denting the heavy denim. Lilith used her other hand to yank down the obscuring headscarf and reveal dark eyes set in a menacing cast of sharp angles covered in olive skin.

Her gaze narrowed. "Am I supposed to know you?"

"Dog reached out." The fingers on her calves tightened. "Told me to keep an eye out for you and the big guy. Figured you might need assistance."

She arched a brow. "Is that so?"

"You always so suspicious?" When her hand twitched, his dark eyes grew darker, and his teeth flashed white in a grimace. "Chill, babe." The fingers on her calves carefully peeled free. "Need proof?"

She inclined her head.

"Here." His hand slowly went to his neck. He dug under the folds of material and pulled free a leather cord. "He said you'd recognize this." He turned his hand, palm up, to reveal a battered coin hanging from the cord.

From her up close and personal position, Lilith studied the inconspicuous piece of metal. The etched lines came together, and recognition clicked. The coin-sized piece was stamped with a snarling wolf head above two crossed blades—the mark of a hush-hush combat unit whispered to be utilized for the dirty work of the Border Wars who eventually became the scapegoats for a command unwilling to compromise.

She blinked. Guess that explained why Dog chose the roads. She pulled her blade back and didn't miss the rush of air as the man under her dared to take a big breath.

"Obliged," he muttered, then grunted as she pressed her hands against his chest to lever herself up and off of him.

"Name?" She got to her feet and tucked her blade away.

He rolled to his feet and rubbed his shoulder. "Lash."

"How long were you on my ass?"

"Caught sight of you just after you picked up your ride." He rolled his shoulders and refastened his headscarf until only his dark eyes remained visible. "Once I figured out where you were headed, I got in front and waited."

Which explained why she hadn't picked him up earlier. "You see anything while you've been waiting?"

"Besides a couple of coyotes? Nah."

She choked down her bitter disappointment and refastened her headscarf.

He studied her. "Know what you're walking into?"

"A fucking mess." She led the way back through the building and out to the cluttered street.

Lash disappeared, only to reappear a few moments later with a bag strapped across his chest as he matched her stride.

She raised a brow in silent question.

"Party favors."

They moved through the shadows, two pieces of darkness that melded into the night. They made it another block when Lash's low voice broke the quiet. "Since Reaper's a no show, I'm assuming he's in the midst of it?"

"Got it in one." She climbed over another pile of unidentified metal and wood pieces, grateful for the hand Lash offered on the downside. "You know who Walker is?"

"Yeah." He let her go once her feet hit the ground. "He's been running Michael's personal military force since Greer's disappearing act."

"She's dead, actually."

Lash's reaction to her statement was a slight jerk of his head, then, "Huh, couldn't happen to a better person."

For a moment amusement flickered at his dry humor, but that soon faded. "Walker took Reaper into custody."

Lash shot her a look and his hands curled into fists as he kept pace. "The bounty?"

She shook her head and braced knowing what she revealed next would hit hard. "He claimed Reaper slit Michael's throat."

"The fuck?" Lash came to an abrupt halt, wrapped his hand around her arm, and spun her around. "You telling me Michael's dead?"

"According to Walker, yes." She used the fingers of her free hand to dig into the pressure points in Lash's wrist and forced him to let her go. "But he's wrong."

Lash hissed, dropped his hand, and shook it out. "How do you figure?"

*Got to love a cynical soul.* "Because Reaper left the man breathing, which means someone else killed him."

Lash stared at her, his brow furrowed. "Sounds like I'm missing something."

"You are." She studied him carefully, knowing that what she shared next would stretch the limits of his ability to believe. The thing was, she knew in her gut that Reaper was right. Michael was long gone, and now so was his double. Maybe they wouldn't be believed, but the truth needed to be out there. "The man Reaper spoke to, the one everyone believes is Michael, wasn't really Michael."

Confusion amassed in Lash's dark eyes. "Run that by me again, but slower, because I swear you just told me that Michael isn't Michael."

"From what Reaper and I can figure, Greer killed Michael near the end of the Border Wars." Lilith quickly filled him in on the rest—Greer's vindictiveness, her twisted partnership with Kane, and tonight's frame of Reaper. By the time she finished, Lash had stalked away and wrapped both hands around the back of his neck as he processed what she shared.

Her body itched to move, but she gave him a moment, one they couldn't spare, to come to terms with everything.

He turned and came back. "You and Reaper didn't hit town alone, right?"

She shook her head.

"You get word to the others?"

"Yeah, it's en route."

He grunted. "You sure Reaper's in here? Seems damn quiet."

She squeezed through another narrow opening. "Got a tip Walker's men are down here and leaving unhappy inhabitants in their wake." She stopped where the alley opened to the street and looked back over her shoulder.

Lash shoved through the too tight opening, winced, and came up behind her. "How good's the tip?"

Together they peered down the street where bright solar lamps illuminated an old military jeep, complete with a metal containment unit welded to the back and guarded by an armed four-man team.

"I'm thinking pretty damn good," she muttered.

They ducked back into the alley and Lash asked, "Got a plan?"

Not really, but that never really stopped her before. "Go in, leave bodies, get Reaper, get out."

The lines around Lash's eyes creased. "Works for me." He

unwound the bag from his chest, crouched down, and set it on the ground. The *bzzt* of the zipper sounded and then he dug in the bag. When his hand came out , he held a small dark ball and offered it to her. "Wanna do the honors?"

With a fierce grin, she took the grenade from him. "Hell, yeah." She pulled the pin, took a stance, lifted her arm, and let it fly.

# twenty-eight

Reaper lost track of how long Kane's men worked him over as his world narrowed to the impact of fists hitting flesh and the resulting pain that bled into the all-encompassing white noise of agony. The only positive? After how long it took to revive him the last time, they had finally stopped lighting his ass up.

The beatings sucked ass, but he could deal with pain. Especially since they weren't trying to kill him, as evidenced by the fact they took breaks between rounds. The skill level of Kane's minions, which Reaper had silently dubbed Meathead and Whiny, left much to be desired.

They knew how to deliver pain, but Reaper understood how to endure and rise above. Which meant every time the fuckers meandered off for a smoke or piss, Reaper got to work and now had enough slack between the restraints locking him to the chair and his aching limbs.

The latest storm of fists slowed, then stopped. Reaper kept his eyes closed and his body limp, the perfect picture of down and out, which wasn't as big of a stretch as he'd prefer.

It wasn't long for Meathead yanked Reaper's head back

until the burn of the bright light turned Reaper's inner eyelids red. Meathead slapped the back of Reaper's skull. "Asshole's out again.".

Reaper let his head drop, chin to chest, and silently vowed to ensure Meathead's face met the concrete a couple of times before Reaper dragged his ass out of this cement box.

"What a pussy." Whiny nailed Reaper's calf with the toe of his boot, adding another bruise to Reaper's collection. The minion team was racking up points and stoking Reaper's desire to even the score. "With our luck, he'll probably keel over, and then Kane'll have our asses for killing him." Whiny gave a harsh hack of sound, followed by the impact of a wad of spit landing nearby. "Stubborn bastard ain't giving us shit. Let's take a break."

"Fuck it, why not?" Meathead grumbled. "I need a smoke."

Reaper listened to the two morons leave, and the door close behind them with a dull thud. *Fucking finally.*

He lifted his lids, and his lips curled back from his blood-stained teeth as shifted his weight and rocked the chair. The chair legs scraped against the concrete and his gaze darted to the door. He stilled, his ears straining for the sounds of rushing boots or yells.

When everything stayed quiet, he locked his jaw and rocked again, picking up momentum with each bone-jarring move. Between his body lighting up in protest and the sickening pitch of his head as he kept up the relentless back and forth action, he almost hurled. Not that it would do much good considering there wasn't much in his abused stomach to lose, but still...

Despite all of that, he managed one last surge that put him on his toes enough so he could shove backwards and slam the chair into the unforgiving surface of the wall behind him. He kept his chin tucked, but the motion still had black eating the edges of his mind. Thankfully an ominous crack signaled success.

As the chair started to splinter, his restraints loosened. Adrenaline surged and dampened his aches and pains. He rolled awkwardly toward the wall, then pushed off to do it again. The third time proved to be the charm as the chair finally gave in and broke apart.

His breath was a harsh roar in his ears as he untangled his limbs from the remnants of leather and wood. He kept a hand on the wall and dug through the shattered remains of the chair to pick out the thickest piece of jagged wood. He went to straighten, only to have to catch himself against the wall as the room tilted.

"Fuck me."

He leaned against the wall, closed his eyes, and fought to reclaim his equilibrium. Under his shoulder the wall shuddered. For a moment he thought it was him, but when a second shudder hit, and faint shouts filtered into the room, Reaper realized whatever was happening, was happening outside. Whether that boded good or ill remained to be seen. He shoved off the wall and stumbled over to the door to take up a position to the side.

Waiting was a bitch, but it wasn't like he could just waltz through the locked door. He needed someone to open it and based upon what was happening on the other side, he had a feeling it would be coming sooner rather than later.

The yells grew louder, punctuated by cracks of gunshots, and this time he could hear the dull reverberations of another explosion. Elation vied with anxiety, as it sounded like his rescue had arrived. He put his head against the wall, and barely refraining from hitting it repeatedly.

*Dammit, Lilith.*

While he appreciated the distraction, knowing who was behind it and what she faced, did not give him the warm fuzzies. In fact, he made a conscious effort not to think about it or he would lose what was left of his mind. Yeah, she knew what the fuck she was doing, but he prayed to god she wasn't going at it alone. Not for him.

*Like you wouldn't do the same?*

Not the same.

*Isn't it?*

He ignored the stupid shit inside his brain and adjusted his hold on his makeshift weapon.

Another shout went up and feet pounded closer. Reaper shoved all the messy emotions aside and focused. The knob rattled, then the door slammed open so hard it bounced off the wall.

Whiny stopped the rebound from slamming back in his face with a hand and stepped through. He spotted the broken chair and rushed forward. "What the fu—"

He didn't get a chance to finish because Reaper brought the thick piece of wood down across the base of Whiny's skull. The man dropped to his knees, the rifle he carried clattering across the floor as his hands shot out to try and avoid smashing his face into the ground.

Reaper didn't give him a chance to recover and nailed the bastard with another hit which sent Whiny sprawling face first on the floor. Reaper dropped a knee to the man's spine, ignored Whiny's groan and did a quick search that turned up a formidable blade. Claiming it, Reaper gripped Whiny's shirt and yanked him to his back and laid the blade against his throat.

The unspoken threat wasn't necessary because thanks to the purpling knot that sprouted from Whiny's forehead the ass was well and truly out. If he woke, which based upon the blood seeping from the back of his skull made that questionable, it would be with a killer headache. For now, he wasn't a threat.

Reaper pushed to his feet, nailed a couple of retaliatory kicks to Whiny's unresponsive body, and then snatched up the discarded rifle. He headed towards the door and wiped the blood that dripped from some cut up near his hairline.

Sporadic gunfire sounded, but the yells had died down or faded. Reaper wasn't sure if that was a good sign or bad. He checked the hall and found it empty.

Time to go join the festivities.

After a couple of wrong turns in thankfully deserted hallways, Reaper stumbled out into chaos, his rifle at the ready. The bitter bite of spent gunpowder drifted with the pall of smoke that hung on the air. It made his eyes sting, but he didn't dare release his weapon to wipe his vision clear.

Broken search lights lay like fallen dominoes across the ground. One was still lit, its beam cutting drunkenly through the night. Firelight from a burning carcass of a modified truck danced and added a hellish cast to the scene.

Oh yeah, his rescue had definitely arrived.

He stumbled forward and tripped over the sprawled body of a soldier. Despite his reeling head, he found his footing just as a flash from his peripheral had him spinning around, weapon up.

The sharp crack of a rifle shot followed, and he dropped into a crouch. He caught another muzzle flash through the lens of his sight. It was too far away to determine who was on the other end though. He lowered his weapon and stood up, determined to find Lilith. He got a couple of steps in before a shadow burst out of the night and barreled towards him with a threatening roar.

The lumbering shadow crossed the flicker of firelight and Reaper recognized Meathead's features as he closed in, fists swinging. With no time to get his weapon up, Reaper ducked under the punch and sank the butt of his rifle into Meathead's gut. An unmistakable grunt sounded, and he doubled over, trapping Reaper's gun.

Reaper silently cursed and with no choice, let the weapon go. Despite the bad angle, he brought his fist down in an awkward hit to the back of Meathead's shaved skull. It shoved the enraged man forward but didn't drop him.

Meathead stumbled back and knowing time was running out, Reaper stepped back, and found the blade he took from Whiny. When Meathead straightened, Reaper darted in on a rush of adrenaline and whipped his blade in a lethal X pattern. The lethally sharp edge kissed its marks and left crimson evidence in its wake, ensuring Meathead's life expectancy didn't exceed the next few minutes.

A muffled *whomp* came from behind them.

Reaper landed a punishing kick to Meathead's chest and sent him to his back. Reaper then spun around in time to catch some enterprising asshole fire a grenade at a neighboring building. His aim was for shit because the grenade dropped just above the first floor.

The impact created a rain of concrete and whatever glass shards still clung to the windows onto the knot of bodies fighting below. Shouts rose as a couple of the combatants dropped, but before Reaper could determine who was involved, the sound of his name in a familiar voice cut through the night.

Reaper turned in place until he caught sight of Lilith rushing towards him, her hands cradling a rifle. Something tight loosened in his chest and his feet were moving before it registered. As she got closer, he saw the streaks that decorated her face. Dirt or blood or both, he wasn't sure. He was sure it was blood that stained her shoulder and more darkened her shirt and pants near her hip. She moved easily, so he prayed it wasn't hers.

She shifted the weapon she carried on its securing strap

and freed her hands as they met. Her palms hovered a hair's breadth from his battered skin as if she was afraid to touch him, and a frown creased her forehead. Her jade green eyes were dark with what he thought could be worry as she studied the evidence of his interrogation. "Those fucktards."

He wrapped one arm around her waist and pulled her close. He covered her hand with his other and pressed her palm to his jaw, uncaring of the resulting sting. "I'm good, babe."

For a moment Lilith's eyes swam, and her unexpected reaction threw him for a loop. Then the threatening tears disappeared, replaced by a familiar hardness. "I can't find Walker."

There was another volley of sporadic pops—gunshots or fire hitting gas tanks, he wasn't sure—but it had him tugging her down behind the relative shelter of a nearby overturned transport. "Walker's not here."

Her lips compressed in frustration.

Seeing that almost made him smile. "It's Kane."

A predatory light dawned, and anticipation replaced her frustration, turning her voice almost eager. "Is he still here?"

"Don't know." He gave her the only answer he had since he had no idea how long he spent with Meathead and Whiny. He surveyed their surroundings. "What do we have to clear?"

She peeked around the concealing edge, waved an arm, and dropped back. She turned to him. "Lash is finishing up, so we'll find out in a minute."

Reaper grunted at the name of Dog's man but was reassured by the fact she hadn't made this run solo.

She touched his shoulder and he turned to find her eyeing him with apparent worry. "As soon as we started the noisemakers, a couple of men hightailed it inside that building." She pointed to a squat looking building tucked between two taller structures.

It clearly had served as some kind of restaurant years prior. Now it was a modern-day cave in the industrial rubble. The windows that once made up the front were long gone and had been replaced by thick graffiti-covered planks. There was only one way in, an entrance shrouded in darkness that lured the unwary inside.

It was an obvious trap, but it wasn't like they had much of a choice. Reaper checked his rifle and counted his ammunition. "Before we head in, we can't leave anyone at our backs."

Next to him Lilith was doing the same, but her voice came out calm. "Don't think it will be an issue."

Another shout was cut short and an eerie quiet swept over the night.

"We managed to catch them by surprise and eliminate most of their transports in the first couple of hits." Shadows played over Lilith's face, the shift of light and dark revealing the lethal predator that lived under the curves. "I'm betting Kane didn't get a chance to make it out but hunkered down to wait us out."

He met her gaze and held it, both of them understanding what would happen next. His voice was a growl. "Dangerous to corner a rat."

She grimaced. "More dangerous to let him run free."

True that.

A scramble of rubble had him and Lilith bringing their weapons up. The only thing riding rein on his trigger finger was Lilith's restraining hand on his rifle barrel when Lash's face came into view.

The fierce features were coated with a mix of dust, blood, and grim purpose as Dog's man gave him a quick once over, before settling in next to them. "You throw the most interesting parties, my man." Lash extended his hand.

Reaper took his offering. "I aim to entertain." He let Lash go. "How many guests are still hanging around?"

Lash snorted as he popped out an empty magazine and slammed a new one home. "The front yard's cleared, but we got a four-man team holed up inside and they aren't budging."

Reaper looked to Lilith, unsurprised to see the same grim determination in her face. Hoping she brought Lash up to date on the situation, he said, "They're protecting Kane."

Lash flashed a disturbing grin. "Welp, let's make them earn their pay, shall we?"

That worked for Reaper since he was more than ready to bring this to an end, but it would be nice if the odds were a bit better. "Havoc and Mercy?"

She shrugged, a move at odds with the tension that lined her mouth. "I sent a message, but I'm not sure they'll arrive in time."

Reaper didn't intend to watch Kane slither away while they waited for possible backup, because if that happened the bounty would not only be the least of his worries, but they could kiss any possible future goodbye. Better to nab the arrogant ass and go from there.

Since the other two shared the same opinion, they held a quick confer and redistribution of weapons. Then they picked their way through the rubble, darted around the still smoldering fires, and converged on the squat building the held their quarry. They moved around the cracked tables lying like discarded take-out across the patio and stayed cleared of the yawning entrances.

Reaper wondered who had the bright idea to hole up here because it was clear the decision was based on pure desperation since the only viable entrance or exit was the same damn doorway. They closed in, Reaper and Lilith to one side, Lash to the other. They huddled on either side of the door just under the edge of the boarded windows.

Lilith pulled a small metal canister out of one of her

pockets and handed it to him. "Tear gas. Found it on one of the bodies."

He reached for it. "You have another one?" When she nodded, he took it from her and dropped it in his pocket, happy to have a non-lethal option and hoping they'd get a chance to use it.

After an exchange of silent hand signals with Lash, they were ready.

The yawning opening stayed dark and still as they slid around the corners and inside, careful to stay low and make as little noise as possible. Lash took the forward position, Lilith the middle, and Reaper was left with the rear. They inched deeper into the shadows and relied on touch to signal each other.

When they got to the end of a short hallway that kept their approach hidden, they stopped. Lash did a careful survey and moved forward, but something crunched under his foot, the sound overly loud.

All three threw themselves to the side as gunfire ripped through the night.

Reaper rolled to his feet and kept a striped booth between him and where the shooters continued to rain bullets. He spotted Lilith huddled up and across from him in another booth.

There was no sign of Lash.

Lilith exaggerated her hand signals and indicated Lash was further in but safe. Sure enough, a deeper cough signaled Lash's return fire. Lilith waited for a pause, then popped up and added hers before she dropped back down.

Somewhere someone grunted indicating a lucky shot.

While Lash and Lilith provided distraction and forced the shooters to waste their ammunition, Reaper used the cover of gunfire, to scoot around the partition and slink toward the long counter. A swinging door to the left and another to the right, revealed the only exits from the room. Muzzle flashes lit an opening behind the counter in what was probably the kitchen. Since that was where their quarry was entrenched, it was up to Reaper to help flush them out.

Reaper went as low as possible, nearly crawling on his belly as he inched towards the opening and stayed below the overhanging edge. Above him the gunfire paused, and a rifle clicked empty.

Someone cursed.

Three shots in close succession sounded, followed by the sound of something heavy hitting the floor.

*One down, three to go.*

Reaper took the tear gas canister, pulled the pin, and lobbed it underhand towards the kitchen. The clang of metal rattled as it bounced, then a hiss followed when it ignited. A soft pop preceded a round of choking coughs.

Reaper spun left, and brought his rifle into position, aiming where they would have to exit from and left the other side to Lilith or Lash. Shadows writhed and scrambled, but Reaper's breathing remained steady as he fell into a quiet anticipatory stillness. As much as he would do his damnedest to ensure Kane was kept alive, there were no guarantees.

The seconds ticked by, then a dark figure finally burst through the swinging door nearest Reaper, while an echo came from the main door behind him. Even as his back itched, he trusted in Lilith and Lash. The figure stumbled through the opening and Reaper squeezed the trigger, his rifle barked, and the shadow in front of him dropped.

A burst of return fired erupted behind him.

A line of fire kissed the top of his shoulder as he dropped and rolled. Before he could get his rifle up, another shot sounded and the figure rising behind him jerked then dropped to the ground. He turned to see Lilith behind him, rifle raised.

Lash's cold voice called out. "Drop it or die. Your choice."

A snarl preceded a sharp crack and another body hit the floor.

Lilith held out a hand to Reaper.

He took it and let her help him to his feet. His aches and pains came back with a vengeance, but he stepped past her as she nudged the fallen man with the toe of her boot. He raised his rifle and moved toward the kitchen.

He used one hand to push the swinging door open and led with the rifle. As he rounded the corner of a rusted-out stove, he came face-to-face with a bloodied Kane. He barely had time to brace before Kane tackled him. He lost his grip on his gun as he was shoved back through the doors and into the main room.

They stumbled over the body of the dead soldier and Reaper landed a couple of blows. He shoved an enraged Kane back and reached for his rifle. Kane's back hit the wall. Before Reaper could bring his gun around, Kane snarled, darted forward, snatched up the rifle next to the body and aimed the barrel at Reaper.

A shot rang out from behind Reaper and Kane stumbled back, blood blooming dark on his chest as he hit the wall behind him and slid down.

*Fuck.*

Reaper moved in and kicked the weapon away from Kane's limp hand. He looked to see Lilith approaching, rifle in hand, still aimed at Kane. Reaper pushed his rifle to his back and despite his protesting ribs, crouched in front of a glaring Kane. A survey of the damage confirmed Reaper's first assumption—bringing Kane in alive was no longer an option.

Lilith stopped behind him, and her curse was as vicious as it was soft as she took in the scene. "Move, let me see what I can do." Her voice was hard as she nudged him out of the way. "Go get me something to cover this."

He got up, stepped over the dead soldier, and moved

further in. There wasn't much light, but the shadows weren't as deep here, softened by the shifting lights outside. He searched until he found a headscarf discarded by one of the sprawled bodies on the other side.

Lash maintained his position by the entrance, even as he split his attention between outside and what was unfolding inside.

Reaper left him to it and crouched next to Lilith.

She tore Kane's shirt open and revealed the neat hole in his chest bubbling blood. Reaper handed her the material. She bunched it up and pressed it against Kane's wound. She exchanged a grim look with Reaper, both knowing the severity of the damage belied by that neat hole.

A harsh groan sounded as Kane's lashes fluttered up. When he caught sight of Lilith, his lips curled into a sneer. "You." The one word came out on a harsh hiss.

Lilith met his contempt with icy disdain. "Yeah, me, asshole." She pressed down on his chest.

Kane winced, and his body jerked with a cough that left blood staining his mouth.

A low, warning whistle drew Reaper's attention to Lash who now stood in the doorway. "We've got company."

Reaper turned to Lilith. "You got him?"

"Yeah."

He took her at her word, got to his feet and walked to Lash. Together the two men watched as figures crossed in front of the sporadic firelight with careful precision. Reaper counted six before identifying Walker's grim features.

Looked like it was time to pay the piper.

# twenty-nine

Unable to see what alarmed Reaper and Lash, Lilith kept the pressure on Kane's chest. "Want to clue me in?" she called out.

Reaper answered. "Walker."

She muttered a curse under her breath. Like they didn't have enough to deal with.

A wet chuckle came from Kane as he continued to glare at her. "You're fucked," the dying man choked out.

She held his dark gaze, and her soul chilled at the depth of depravity that stared back. Every wrong he manipulated and inflicted played through her mind, dousing the ice under the heat of fury. Whatever it took, this asshole would go down. It was the only way to keep Tabby and Reaper safe.

Resolved, she hardened her tone and gave him a predatory smile. "Actually, you're the one who's fucked."

Behind her, the heavy tread of booted feet announced the arrival of Walker and his men. "Don't fucking move."

Since moving meant letting Kane bleed out, Lilith ignored the barked order and trusted Reaper and Lash to handle shit.

Light danced over the floor and turned the dark stain of blood to deep crimson.

"Haven't we been here before?"

With her back to the men, Lilith didn't hide her grimace at Reaper's drawled quip. The man had a talent for understatements considering last time ended up with him being hauled away by Walker's men. She did not need a repeat of that experience.

Time to be the voice of reason. "Walker, you need to stand down."

"Don't know you from Adam," Walker snapped back, dashing Lilith's hope that reason would prevail. "But I'm not going anywhere. You, however, need to step back."

Since she was still working on Kane, she wasn't sure if Walker's comment was directed to her or Reaper. Figuring it was her, she shook her head, and angled her head enough to see Reaper stood between her and Walker. "I'm more than happy to let this bastard die, but you might want to hear us out first."

"From where I'm standing the picture's pretty clear." There was the sound of feet shuffling, the creak of weapons being adjusted, and the tension in the dark space took a step up.

"If it's so clear," Reaper cut in, "why am I here beaten to shit and not on the road to New Seattle?" Everything stilled, but Reaper kept pushing, obviously determined to make Walker pull his head out of his ass. "Isn't that what you were told?"

Kane batted at Lilith's hands.

She knocked the weak attempt away and glared down.

He returned it, his skin a pasty white, but the hatred in his eyes burned with unholy fire. "You can't trust them, Commander."

For a dying man, the bastard managed to inject a convincing note of pathetic victim in his voice.

"They're in it together," He continued to inject his poison. "They're working with the Cartels."

Lilith arched a brow and added weight to her hands. Kane winced, his breath stuttering as his face inched to grey, and the lines around his lips deepened. She held his glare with unblinking, cold dispassion.

"Just noting—" Lash joined the conversation, "—those bodies out there—they don't belong to the Cartels, my friend."

"Not your fucking friend," Walker snapped, but Lilith caught the first sliver of doubt in his voice.

*Let's hear it for well-honed instincts.*

Even better she heard another rush of feet, this time heading out, not in. Hopefully Walker sent his men out to verify Lash's claim. She could work at widening that sliver to an all-out breach in Walker's surety. First though... she looked over her shoulder and found Reaper looking at her. She tilted her head in silent request and Reaper stepped back, dropped down next to her, and took over the pressure on Kane's damaged chest.

"Move back, Reaper." Walker's voice was tight and accompanied by a forbidding click as weapons were brought to the ready.

Lilith wiped her blood-covered hands on Kane's pants and pushed to her feet. Despite the rising tension, she kept her body between Reaper and Walker's threat, ignoring Reaper's soft disapproving growl. "I need him here."

Reaper shifted his glare to Walker.

*God spare her from male pissing contests.*

She nudged Reaper's foot with hers and regained his attention. She gave a small shake of her head, and slid her gaze it to Kane in a silent reminder they were running out of time.

Reaper's face darkened, but he went back to slowing Kane's imminent appointment with the grim reaper.

Kane's groan was cut off by a wracking cough that left a nasty spray of blood behind. His gaze was losing clarity, but the spiteful shit just couldn't shut up. "You can't win." It came out on a gasp, barely audible to her and Reaper, and totally escaping Walker's hearing.

Lilith took a moment to think.

No way would they get Kane to spill his sins, but she needed a way to convince Walker, who was loyal to a fault to Michael, and defang the threat of having the might of the Northwest set loose on her territory. She needed irrefutable proof. Not just for Walker, but for the others still in power in the Northwest.

Hell, if someone brought her a similar tale, she'd think they were out of their minds and needed to be locked up. She would need something stronger than a coerced deathbed confession. Something that couldn't be argued with, that proved beyond a shadow of a doubt that Michael was not Michael. If she could do that, she could unlock the entire tangled mess.

Her mind spun, and a glimmer of a solution ignited when she realized it was time to put her position to good use. She drew the familiar cloak of the Rocky Mountain Queen close, and lifted her arms, indicating she was unarmed. Slowly, feeling the unwavering weight of the gunsights, she pivoted until she faced Walker.

It didn't take long for recognition to hit Walker. A frown creased his forehead. "Lilith?"

She inclined her head in acknowledgement and shifted her gaze to the armed men next to Walker. "Unless you're prepared for the fallout, I'd suggest your men ease back."

Walker's attention went from her, to Reaper, to Lash,

before coming back to her. It wasn't hard to see his uneasiness with the situation.

Since the clock was ticking, she decided to help Walker out. "If we wanted Kane dead, he'd be dead. Seems to me, us trying to save his life is counterproductive."

Walker's jaw flexed as he narrowed his gaze on Reaper, who remained crouched over Kane. After a long, tense moment, Walker motioned to his men and the rifles were lowered, still ready to raise but no longer targeted.

Lash did them the courtesy of doing the same even as he maintained his position of guarding Lilith and Reaper's back.

The surrounding tension stepped back.

"Thank you." Lilith could afford to be gracious.

Movement at the entry drew her attention. One of Walker's men came in and as he stepped into the light, she noted he was the leaner of the two initial guards that had been watching the fake Michael's rooms at Castille. He leaned into Walker and shared his information in a low voice, one she couldn't catch. Yet, watching Walker's face grow progressively grimmer proved whatever he was sharing wasn't good.

Walker's gaze dropped to Kane. "What's going on?"

"Commander." Lilith regained Walker's attention. "He won't tell you the truth."

That earned her a sardonic look. "But you will?"

She held his gaze with a mocking arrogance cultivated over years of dealing with men who disregarded a woman's intelligence. "I've no reason to lie to you."

"Don't you?" That came from Kane, but the wet cough robbed it of weight.

Ignoring the soon-to-be dead man, she stayed focused on the man she needed to resolve this whole disaster. "Do you still have the body in custody?"

It was clearly not the question Walker expected. "You mean Michael's body?"

Lilith nodded.

"Yes," he said.

Sometimes it was just best to be blunt. "It's not Michael."

Behind her came the sound of scrabbling and Reaper's curse before Kane's hoarse cry of, "Liar."

Both she and Walker ignored him, but it was Walker who asked, "What do you mean, it's not Michael?"

"The man killed in Castille—" she kept her tone calm, rational, certain, "—was not Michael. He was an imposter, put in place by Greer and Kane.'

Walker's stoic mask cracked, and disbelief shredded his stony expression. "Why?"

"To undermine the Territories," Reaper joined the conversation. "So this bastard here could take control." A dark humor crept through Reaper's voice. "Seems someone has serious daddy issues to resolve. Though I'm betting he'll be able to resolve it on the other side soon.'

"Bastard," Kane choked out, his struggle for air becoming obvious in his frantic voice, but he kept fighting from his doomed corner. "They're lying, I have nothing t—" whatever he was going to say was cut off by another round of coughing that left him gasping and barely conscious.

Walker turned from Kane, his face dark and nailed Lilith with a hard stare. "You have proof?"

She bridled her relief as the doubt solidified in Walker's eyes. "I can get it."

"How?"

"I'm invoking code 43-10-25."

A low groan sounded from Kane.

She kept her attention on Walker. "You'll need to collect a viable sample to use, commander. It's your responsibility to get that sample to Istaqa so he can have it, and the control, sent on to the Center. You'll have unquestionable proof within fourteen days."

"What the hell's a 43-10-25?" Unsurprisingly, the question came from Reaper.

She turned and met Kane's fury with ruthless satisfaction. "Executive Identification Order. Midway through the Border Wars, at Michael's suggestion, an agreement was forged by the territory leaders to collect their DNA and have it housed in a secure location."

"The Center," Lash murmured, obviously understanding how the last bastion of scientific study played into this.

"Correct. The point of this endeavor was, should a leader disappear, and a body turn up, we needed a way to identify the remains beyond any doubt."

When panic flared in Kane's eyes, Lilith felt a dark, vicious joy burst to life and licked its lips. *That's right, asshole, you're so fucked.*

She turned away and directed the last to Walker. "This security measure is known only to the territory leaders, and we are the only ones who can invoke it."

His mouth tightened as he looked at Kane with a new awareness.

Good, it was sinking in. If Walker could be convinced, his testimony plus the results of the test, should be enough to convince those who needed it.

Walker looked back to Lilith, and his shoulders straightened. "How long?"

She wanted to be sure she was answering the right question, so she clarified, "How long has it not been Michael?"

Walker nodded.

She almost felt sorry for him. "Twelve to thirteen years."

His face blanched and in his shocked visage she saw why the EIO was vitally important. The repercussions of this situation would ripple for years to come.

"Why?" The question was harsh with betrayal and considering he was staring at Kane, Lilith knew who the question was for, and it wasn't her.

Bitter knowledge left Kane's face ugly and worn, revealing the monster he hid for years. He deliberately tightened his bloodstained lips, closed his eyes, and turned away, refusing to answer.

*Yeah, losing's a bitch, isn't it, you sniveling little bastard?* Lilith managed to keep her venomous thought quiet.

"You want the long or short story?" Reaper cut through the silent drama.

Walker sneered at Kane, then looked to Reaper. "Short."

"Greed, power, and jealousy."

Lilith was rather impressed with how well Reaper tied it up, but there were other things that needed to be addressed. "Walker." She regained the commander's attention. "Reaper didn't kill..." she stopped because Fake Michael just sounded weird.

"Lyle," Reaper added helpfully. "Michael's double, his name was Lyle."

"Right, Lyle." Lilith shook her head and got back on track. "He was still breathing when we left him tonight."

Walker didn't miss her qualifier and narrowed his eyes. "We?"

"You think I'd let someone threaten my territory, my people, my position and not take a personal interest in ensuring the end results?" There were some definite perks to political arrogance, especially since Walker didn't blink at her claim.

The soldier's mouth tightened as if he'd bit into a lemon. "No, ma'am."

She didn't care if he didn't like her, because it wasn't necessary to get what she wanted. She held his stare with unflinching resolve. "I want the bounty on the Vultures and others voided."

Walker's gaze went to Reaper, frustration clear in his tone. "You going to disappear?"

Lilith cut in before Reaper could answer. "Until the EIO is complete, he and the others have sanctuary with me."

That earned her an exasperated look. "That's not smart, ma'am."

Sometimes dealing with male arrogance was a pain in the ass. She was tired, hurt, and wanted this shit over with. "What's not smart is arguing with me, commander. You have a potential shitstorm to navigate thanks to that bastard." She jerked a finger to the limp figure of Kane, uncaring if he still had a pulse.

Now that she'd enacted the EIO, she didn't need his evil ass. If the others wanted answers, they could try keeping him alive. She wished them luck because she was fairly certain he wouldn't make it through what remained of the night. "Not to mention the fallout from Lyle's meeting with Xavier tonight. The last thing you need is to waste your time and efforts on caging in the Vultures."

Walker uttered a soft curse, turned on his heel, and stalked a few feet away. His back was stiff, his hands fisted at his side, and he stared into the night as a heavy silence filled the room while he struggled with the situation.

Watching him, she couldn't squash the flare of sympathy of what Walker would soon face. Not only did he have to go back to New Seattle with two dead bodies and explain to what remained of the Northwest's leadership that they'd spent years being played for the fool, but he had to try and keep the territory stable. He was in for a hell of a ride.

Yet that was as far as her sympathy went because she was more concerned with not being anywhere in the vicinity when the Cartels found out the truth. If they hadn't already. With the shape Reaper was in, evading the Cartels would be challenging, not to mention dodging whatever mercenaries were lurking around for that damn bounty.

Walker turned, stalked back, and issued curt orders. His men swung their rifles to their back and approached Reaper and Kane. Since they weren't directly threatening him, Lilith let them pass as Reaper stood to give them space to collect Kane.

Reaper moved up to Lilith's side.

Walker gave him a steely-eyed stare. "Revoking the bounty will take time."

Lilith wasn't about to give Walker wiggle room and countered, "You've got a week."

Next to her, Reaper grinned, not the best thing considering how frightening he looked with the battered condition of his face.

Walker's jaw flexed, his nostrils flared, but he gave her a nod, then turned on his heel to follow his men out.

Lash closed in as Reaper and Lilith moved closer to the entry. Together, the three watched Walker and his men load Kane into the back of the transport.

Lash shifted his rifle and his hands went to his hips. "Well, that was fun."

Lilith continued to watch Walker and his men but directed her question to Reaper when she felt his shoulder brush hers. "Can you travel?"

"Yeah." His voice rumbled.

Good, because the run out of here was going to be hell as they shook the Cartel shadows loose. Not to mention navigating the road back to the cabin. No way in hell would she risk Reaper, or his Vultures, being shot now when the end was so close. Better to bunker down and stay out of sight. More than that, she needed a moment with Tabby, just a chance to hold her, before Lilith upended their world.

She turned to Lash. "Need you to get a head's up to Dog."

Lash's humor drained away and left behind grim angles. "Right after I get you two back to Mercy and Havoc."

Outside, Walker stopped at the side of the truck and faced where they stood, obviously waiting on them. Lilith sighed. "Come on, let's go see the commander off."

The trio walked outside to where Walker waited, his face blank. He told her, "They're going to want to meet with you."

*They* being the remaining advisers of the Northwest, but Lilith had others she needed at that meeting. "Not just me."

"Not just you," Walker conceded.

She couldn't avoid it because before she walked away, she had one last responsibility to make sure all those with a stake in this mess were heard. "Set it up once the results are in."

Walker gave her a nod, hit the side of the transport with his fist, and then moved to the passenger side and hopped in.

Lash, Reaper, and Lilith were silent as they watched them drive away.

"I'm going to find our ride." With that, Lash left Lilith and Reaper alone, most likely going out to hot-wire one of the remaining transports.

As Reaper stood next to her, she found comfort in his presence and acknowledged the decision she'd made. It had been easier than expected, but when this was done, so was she. The game no longer held the joy and fascination it once did. She was looking forward to spending her time with what mattered most, and one of those was currently wrapping his arm around her waist and holding her close.

She let the tension drain from her body and dropped her head on his shoulder. "You okay?" This time it was the woman asking, not the leader.

She felt the brush of his chin against the top of her head. "I'll make it." He let quiet seep between them, then added, "Thanks, babe."

She gave him the only answer she'd ever have for him. "Always."

# thirty

By the time Lash left them at the hollowed-out shell tucked under an old overpass that doubled as a safe house, dawn was chasing away the night. Reaper's abused body was making itself known, and exhaustion was pressing down with a heavy hand. Sheer determination was the only thing keeping him upright and he wasn't looking forward to the arduous trip back to Colorado.

Lilith led the way around the seemingly solid cement structure and refused to scramble up the rocky incline protected by the old highway until he went first. Since he wasn't keen on arguing with the stubborn woman until noon arrived, he scrambled up. Thankfully, he didn't fall on his ass, which would require Lilith coming to his rescue.

They squeezed between the narrow blocks and made their way single file down the tight passageway. As they stepped into the hollowed interior a yellowish glow broke through the dimness. The followed it in and found Mercy and Havoc playing strained hosts to the last two faces Reaper wanted to deal with—Xavier and the lean-faced fucker who shadowed Walker no more than an hour ago.

Reaper pulled up short and felt Lilith bump into him. He couldn't stop his automatic reaction to drop a restraining hand to block her from moving out of the scant protection he could give her.

Her hands twisted in his shirt, then dropped away. From her faint movements, he figured she was going for her blades—less obvious that the rifles still slung on their shoulders.

He stepped forward and gave her more room to prepare.

"Hey, look who decided to stop by." The subdued greeting came from Mercy, who sat across a battered table from Xavier, lifted her coffee cup, a twin to the one in front of Xavier.

Behind her, Havoc leaned against the wall, go bags at his feet, his gaze locked on Xavier's man.

"Come," Xavier commanded with a casual smile as he lifted his cup in acknowledgement. "We hoped to catch you before you left."

The 'we' brought Reaper's gaze to the lean-faced man who was still trying to stare down Havoc, a feat Reaper could've warned him would be useless. He looked back to Xavier, who maintained his sharp smile. Tension curled through the room and raised the hairs along Reaper's arm, much like an impending lightning strike.

Mercy managed a serene smile. It would have been believable if not for the rigid set of her shoulders. She definitely wasn't thrilled with this situation. "Xavier caught wind of an unbelievable story and before he decided to act on it, wanted to ensure his facts were correct."

Reaper turned back to the most obvious threat, folded his arms over his chest, and braced his feet. "Which story is that?"

"The one where Michael is not Michael." Xavier's smile faded as he carefully set his cup back on the table.

Behind him, his man's gaze snapped to the movement like a snake watching a daring mouse before going back to Havoc.

It was a smart move on his part considering it wouldn't

take much to set Havoc off. One wrong move, one wrong twitch and the tension flare into catastrophic fury. Better for all involved if Reaper kept Xavier happy. "Yeah, I've heard the same one."

Xavier's flash of fury was quickly shuttered under a patently false mask of pleasantry, and seeing it left Reaper uneasy. An unpredictable heir to a Cartel family could create situations which would never end well.

Xavier's long fingers tightened around the coffee cup, his bones pressing white against his olive skin before he relaxed them. "It's true?"

To lie or not to lie? Which answer would ensure the interior didn't get a remodel in shades of red? Reaper ground his teeth and tried to decide. This was why he hated politics.

A light touch against his spine was a reminder of who stood behind him. The weight of a blade slid into the small of his back before she gave him another one-two tap. Right, let the one who knew how to play in the mud pit step in. He heeded her silent signal and stepped aside.

Lilith came forward. "Unfortunately, yes." There was no trace of nerves in her assured voice as she answered Xavier.

The Cartel heir narrowed his dark eyes and barely concealed the mocking light that rose in their depths. "Ahh, the lovely Rocky Mountain Queen." His gaze slid to Reaper, then back to her. "Strange bedfellows."

Despite the streaks of blood and dirt that decorated her face, Lilith maintained her arrogant mask of power and gave Xavier a chiding look. "No stranger than you working with Michael."

"*Es verdad.*" Xavier turned his cup in a slow, deliberate circle, but never took his eyes off of her. "Although perhaps it is not so surprising." He leaned back and used his foot to push one of the empty chairs between him and Mercy away from the table. He waved a hand towards it. "Please, sit."

Reaper stepped around Lilith, pulled the chair out, and silently waited for Lilith to take it.

Movements easy, she walked over and sat down.

Reaper took two steps back and put his back against the same wall Havoc was holding up. He was close enough to yank Lilith out of danger, but he wouldn't make the fatal mistake of hovering, no matter how much his skin crawled to have her sitting so close to the smarmy bastard.

Havoc reached up to a nearby shelf, nabbed a cup, and handed it to Mercy. She took it with a small smile, filled it, and passed it to Lilith. As Havoc resettled in position, he muttered, "Look like shit, brother."

"You should see the other guy." Reaper's reply gained him Lean Fucker's attention, but he held the empty stare with one of his own.

Lean Fucker's vicious smile broke through the empty mask before he turned back to his duty of guarding Xavier's ass.

Lilith set her cup down, the heavy mug hitting the table with a soft thunk, but she remained silent, letting Xavier lead the conversation. It was a polite game of dominance that she won.

Xavier spoke first. "Before I share the unsettling news with my father, I thought it best to get the facts straight."

Lilith flicked a glance at Lean, then back to Xavier. "Seems to me, you have your own inside source, so I'm not sure how much help I can be."

*Go, babe, call him on his shit.* Reaper kept his encouragement silent and wondered how Xavier would handle the unspoken accusation of having a mole embedded in the Northwest.

Xavier raised a brow and shot a telling look at Mercy, who was sipping her coffee. When he turned back to Lilith, his voice dripped with arrogance. "Let's just say verification from a secondary source is always... *como se dice?* ... welcomed."

Lilith sighed and sat back. "What are you looking for?"

Xavier mimicked her pose and stretched out his legs. "A way to determine how much the fallout from this, will cost *mi familia*. We had much invested."

Lilith brought one leg over the other and folded her hands on her knee. "Some losses are best left as hard-earned lessons."

Reaper understood she was talking about the weapons shipment Lyle had promised to replace. That kind of loss would be brutal to the Cartel families, so it sucked to be Xavier.

Xavier grimaced. "That is unfortunate. We had high hopes for our partnership with the Northwest."

His statement left no room for a response that wouldn't make things worse. Lilith said nothing while Xavier drummed his fingers against the table in an absent pattern. Lines marred his brow as he thought through the situation. Finally, he seemed to come to some internal decisions and heaved a sigh.

He straightened. "I would like to take some good news back to my father."

Lilith waited quietly for him to elaborate, and Reaper gave her credit for knowing how to use silence.

Once he realized that she was waiting on him, Xavier continued. "Assurance *las familias* will not be held responsible for the actions taken by this imposter would help. We acted in good faith."

The last part almost made Reaper laugh. The Cartel heir sounded like a spoiled, whiny brat. *Wah! We were duped too.*

Nothing leaked past Lilith's mask, and her voice was polite but hard. "I can't speak for the others."

Xavier leaned forward and wagged a finger in admonishment. "But you can influence them."

Lilith's smile turned predatory. "You have more confidence in my skills than I do."

For the first time since they started the conversation, a genuine emotion swept over Xavier's face. Amusement. "You've made a point to prove an intelligent, ruthless woman can accomplish much." He spread his hands wide. "I simply want reassurance *las familias* do not need to prepare for another war."

Lilith didn't rush to answer, a smart move because whatever she said could come back to haunt her. If she swore retaliation wasn't on the table and then someone decided differently, she would be left in a rough spot. She traced a finger around the edge of the cup as she considered.

Finally, she lifted her head to meet Xavier's gaze. "In my opinion, so long as you and yours don't interfere with the territories, I don't foresee an issue." She offered him a cool smile. "However, should the families decide to take up their dissatisfaction regarding their current agreements with the territories..." she trailed off with a shrug, her implication clear.

If the Cartels pushed, the Territories would push back. Hard.

Xavier gave her a nod. "I will share the information." He pushed to his feet.

Behind him, Lean straightened to follow.

Havoc and Reaper both came to attention.

Xavier gave them all a once over. "You will understand I'm not being impolite, simply cautious, when I say it may be best if you are no longer here come morning."

Reaper swallowed back his automatic snarl and instead settled for glaring. As if any of them wanted to stick around this hellish dustbowl at this point.

Ever the queen, Lilith simply curled in her lips and rose to her feet. Next to her Mercy stood as well. Reaper and Havoc moved forward and covered the women's backs as the two couples watched Xavier and his shadow disappear.

For a long moment no one spoke, then Mercy broke it. "Someone want to fill me in on what the hell just happened?"

Lilith dropped into the chair with a groan and braced her head against a hand. "Where do we start?"

"Let's go with Michael not being Michael," Havoc said.

Reaper and Lilith took turns filling in the other two on the recent developments. As they answered Mercy and Havoc's questions, the four double-checked their go bags and prepared to move out. None of them were eager to see if Xavier would change his mind or his time limit. By the time Lilith and Reaper finished, Mercy's mouth hung open and Havoc looked poleaxed.

"Okay, that's just…" Mercy couldn't find the words.

Lilith grimaced as she zipped up her bag. "Yeah."

Havoc adjusted the strap across his wide chest. "So now what?"

"Now we get the hell out of here and bunker down." Reaper positioned his breather against his mouth and tried not to wince when the seal pressed against the bruises and cuts that decorated his face.

Lilith straightened and slung her bag up, settling it in place. "Once the EIO results are back, we'll deal with the next steps."

Mercy locked down the blade at her thigh and shot the other woman a cynical look. "Which is what, exactly?"

Reaper didn't miss the exhaustion that lined Lilith's face and knew he wasn't in any better shape but seeing her drawn and pale made him itch to draw her close. Wrong time, wrong fucking place.

Lilith sighed. "There will be a meeting with the surviving members of the Northwest, Istaqa and his people, Simon and his, and me and mine."

Mercy cocked her head. "Does your people include the Vultures?"

Lilith didn't hesitate to nod. "And you and Math." She caught Mercy's surprise and added, "The surviving Strix are just as vital to this as any of the ruling powers. Maybe more so, considering what the future may, or may not, hold."

There was something in her voice that worried Reaper, but they didn't have the luxury of getting into it now. "Let's make tracks." His voice was muffled, but it was clearly an order.

They roared out of Phoenix on a cloud of dust as dawn kissed the horizon.

# thirty-one

L ilith sucked in the dust-free air and drew the cool touch of the Colorado Mountains deep into her lungs to chase away the last remnants of Phoenix. She stood at the deck's railing, feet bare, hair still wet from her shower, and just breathed. In the cabin behind her everything remained quiet, and nothing disturbed the stillness of the early morning.

They hit the cabin late last night after long, hellish hours on the road. She almost cried when she climbed the stairs from the caverns, but with Reaper's stoic silence and pale, sweating face drawn in pain, she dug deep and made it to the main floor on sheer guts.

Once she shoved Reaper into a shower, she went to peek in on a sleeping Tabby. She found comfort in watching her baby sleep undisturbed by nightmares and it was enough so she could leave Tabby's room and stumble back to where Reaper slumped on the edge of her bed.

She dragged out the first aid kit, treated the worst of his wounds, and then left him collapsed on the bed to take her own shower. She stood under the lukewarm spray and numbly watched dirt and blood swirl down the drain. She didn't remember getting out or stumbling to bed but considering that was where she woke after a solid six hours, she did.

Once she woke, stiff and sore, she shuffled through the quiet cabin and tried not to wake the others as she started a pot of coffee. Fortified with a hot cup, she headed to the deck in search of the space and the quiet the forest always brought her. Now, she stood staring into the wild as her mind churned.

She had a week, maybe two on the outside, to get her shit sorted. It wasn't much time, but she intended to make the most of it.

First would be turning the Rocky Mountain Territories over to Belle, Silas, and Everett. It hit her as she dealt with Walker that this was a decision that should have been made a couple of years back. When she laid out Kane's treachery for Walker, instead of the expected triumphant, she felt empty. No good leader should go into negotiations feeling nothing. But thanks to her EIO request, she had no choice but to attend the upcoming meeting with the territory leaders.

The prospect didn't fill her with purpose, instead it was another obligation to complete before she could get to what mattered most—her daughter and the man who held her heart. Cleary she was done with the world of intrigue, lies, and half-truths that made up the political arena. Once upon a time, it had been a challenge to be conquered. Now, it just irritated her.

Or maybe she had inherited Reaper's intolerance of bullshit.

Whatever it was, she was tired of fighting for everyone else. It was time to fight for herself. She wanted to see what living in peace really meant. Hell, maybe it would bore her to tears, but she wanted a chance to find out.

As for Reaper?

Her heart ached. She couldn't ask him to leave the

Vultures, but she wasn't willing to call the roads home. Tabby needed stability and safety, she needed a home.

A faint hope whispered maybe Reaper would choose to give them another chance, because it was obvious he adored their daughter. Plus, he said he wanted to, but who knew. Now that Michael was well and truly gone, his vengeance was done. And once the bounty was voided, there was nothing to keep him at her side.

That truth didn't do jack to dim the heartbreaking wish he would choose her and Tabby over the road. The realistic part of her doubted they held that much appeal to him. It shook its head in cynical disappointment at her foolishness, while the other, softer, well-hidden side kept a protective hand cupped over the tiny flame of hope.

Her lips curved into a wistful smile at the silly image, and she brought her coffee to her lips.

In the long run, she needed to be sure she and Tabby were okay—with or without Reaper. Financially they were fine. There was enough money from her family and her position to pursue whatever path she wanted. The cabin was hers, left to her by her mother, and hidden under layers of ownership. She and Tabby were safe here.

Only one challenge remained—finding something she wanted to do with her time. Something that had nothing to do with politics, espionage, or weapons trading. Besides, Tabby wouldn't need her forever.

*What the hell else did she have?*

The door slid open behind her and interrupted her maudlin thoughts.

The sixth sense that woke every time Reaper came near work and her heartbeat picked up. Heat closed around her as familiar arms caged her against the railing and chased away the chill edge of morning. Warm lips brushed over her neck and sent a different type of chill over her skin. She closed her eyes and savored the lick of burning heat it ignited.

"Morning, babe." The rumble of Reaper's voice curled around her, seeped beneath her skin, and soaked into her soul.

She turned her head enough to press a kiss against his bicep, then lifted her cup to shoulder height. "Coffee?"

His hand, bruised and battered, took her offering.

She leaned back and let him take her weight as they enjoyed the morning.

He handed the cup back.

She took it, cradled it, and then brought it to her lips for a sip. She swore she could taste him against the rim.

"Talk to me."

She set the cup on the railing and took a deep breath. "Thinking about the upcoming meeting."

His chest shifted behind her, and his arm coiled around her waist. "Yeah, that's going to be interesting."

Lilith winced at his understatement. "That's one way to put it."

"What do you think will happen?" There was genuine curiosity in his voice.

"The Northwest will make all sorts of excuses, but in the end, they'll turn Kane into a scapegoat. When they finish blustering, they'll retreat and bunker down. The fallout..." She shook her head, not needing to finish.

"They'll need a real replacement for Michael."

"Yeah, they will." She used her free hand and covered his that rested on her stomach. She brushed her thumb over his abraded knuckles, being careful to avoid the raw spots.

"Got any ideas on who'll step up?"

Lilith sighed. "My money's on Walker. They need a strong strategic mind, someone to navigate them through this mess without endangering their resources or losing whatever allies they have." She shrugged. "He's their best bet."

"Poor fucker."

She agreed. It was one thing to lead a military force, but to lead a territory in danger of falling apart was a whole other challenge. And there was no doubt that the Northwest was teetering on disaster.

The fact that Michael's other two advisers had failed to clue in about Lyle's impersonation, undermined their perceived authority and left blood in the political waters. The sharks would circle, uncaring about the minnows caught in the resulting feeding frenzy. That was where Walker would come in.

Lilith had Charity do some digging on the commander. What she came back with gave Lilith hope. A career military man, Walker was a harsh taskmaster, but he wasn't without mercy. He didn't belong to the scorch earth school of thought. He was disciplined, and kept his fighters under rigid control, not letting them loose on the civilians. He was a formidable foe on the battlefield and his men served him out of loyalty, not fear. It was a better leadership foundation than most.

She couldn't see him standing aside while everything he fought for fell apart, but it wasn't a role for the faint of heart. If he decided to take it on, she wished him luck because he was going to need it.

Speaking of which... "I'm stepping down," she blurted out.

The big body behind her stiffened. "What?"

Her hand tightened on the coffee cup, but she kept her attention focused forward. "I refuse to make my father's mistakes. Tabby deserves better. Hell, maybe so do I."

When he remained quiet, she continued. "I almost lost her, Reaper." Her voice shook. "It didn't matter what power lay at my fingertips or who I controlled, when it came down to keeping her safe, I was too busy playing political games that I missed the biggest threat of all—me." Raw and heavy, the guilt swamped her. God, how long would she have to struggle with this? Would it ever ease?

The arm at her waist tightened. "Lilith—"

She shook her head and stopped him. "I'm meeting with Belle, Silas, and Everett in a couple of days to plan the transition. I'll be there for the meeting, but when it's done, so am I."

Reaper's chest expanded as he blew out a loud sigh. "And then what? You'll come back here and play the stay-at-home mom?"

The sarcastic lilt to his question sparked her temper and she steadied the mug on the railing, twisted in his arms, and glared into his bruised face. "What's wrong with just being Tabby's mom?"

His navy-blue gaze roamed over her face, and whatever he saw had his lips curving. "Not a damn thing, babe, but just to say, it's just not you."

She folded her arms over her chest and set her jaw. "And you know me so well after bailing for ten plus years?"

Instead of the expected flare of anger at her accusation, he brushed his battered knuckles over her cheek. "I know the woman under the mother." His gaze moved from his hand to her eyes, and the depth of seriousness that stared back was one she rarely saw from him. "That woman will be bored out of her mind after a couple of quiet months. Downtime is not your strong suit, babe."

She bit her lip and her shifted her gaze away. Okay, yeah, maybe he had a point, but she had no intention of putting Tabby at risk, not ever again. "I'll figure it out," she muttered, stubbornly determined.

He chuckled softly. "I'm looking forward to watching you do just that."

At that her gaze jumped to him and her eyes narrowed. "You're planning on sticking around?"

His amusement drained away and left behind an unsettling intensity that had her pulse racing. "You're not the only one looking for a change."

She swallowed against a throat gone suddenly dry. "I told you before, you can't waltz in here, stay till you get bored, and leave her heart broken." *Or mine.* Not that she'd ever say the last out loud.

He frowned and caught her chin, forcing her to hold his gaze. "And I told you, I want a future. That wasn't a crock. Not sure how to convince you, but maybe after a couple of years, you'll believe me."

She couldn't explain why his repeating what he shared two days ago while they were tangled around each other struck her as true now, but it did. Hope spread, and the subtle light eased the resentful chains of the past, until she could step free.

She wrapped her arms around his neck and tugged his head down until she could take his mouth with a delicate deliberateness. She let the emotion that swirled deep inside rise and indulged in soft strokes over his still puffy lip, being careful not to bring him more pain. She wanted only to bring him pleasure, joy, the same he was giving her.

His hands slid to her hips, drew her close, and pressed her against an unmistakable hardness. Their groans mingled as his lips parted, letting her in. She took full advantage, tempting and teasing until his tongue tangled with hers in an exquisite dance. Need, lust, and love curled together until she ached.

Somehow, she found the strength to pull back. Their breaths came fast and hard as from inches away she stared into his heated eyes and gave him her heart, this time for good. "I love you, Reaper."

A beauty she thought long lost stared back. His hands left her hips and cupped her face with a heart-stopping gentleness. "Love you too, Lil."

# thirty-two

## Two weeks later in an undisclosed location

Lilith blinked in the bright afternoon sunlight, Reaper a dark shadow at her side. "Pinch me." A sharp pain on her arm ensured she wasn't dreaming. She rubbed the sting and looked to the man determined to stand at her side. "Did we really just agree to that?"

He grimaced and ran a hand over his neck. "Yeah."

"Are we crazy?"

"Fuck, yeah." His lips quirked. "But that isn't news."

She stepped into him and dropped her head to his chest. His arms closed around her. "I thought we were out of this." Her voice came out in a near whine.

He chuckled. "Should've known they wouldn't let us get away with that."

"Dammit." She thumped her head against his chest a couple times.

His hand stroked her spine. "There's one positive."

She tilted her head back and frowned up at him. "What's that?"

He grinned down at her. "We only have to deal with them twice a year."

She sighed, laid her cheek against his chest, and curled her arms around his waist.

Walker had brought the EIO results to the meeting, along with the news that Kane hadn't survived the trip back to New Seattle. Lilith was not shocked at Walker's announcement or when he revealed the EIO results.

The dead Michael wasn't Michael.

And that announcement was currently ripping across the territories like wildfire. But it would be Walker who had to get in front of the blaze because Lilith's assumption had proven correct—Walker was now speaking on behalf of the North-west. At his side stood the other two advisers, their faces drawn with unmistakable signs of numerous sleepless nights. Prob-ably because they knew their time was short. There was no doubt the Northwest would be struggling for a while.

Istaqa had listened to the retelling with his normal stoicism, and even Simon was unusually calm as Lilith and Reaper laid out the twisted details. Math, Mercy, and the other Vultures added details where needed. When everything was said and done, chaos reigned. Then came the discussion on how to avoid another such situation.

Things turned heated and voices were raised.

Lilith held back, letting Belle and Silas deflect any shots sent their way, but it was Dog who blindsided Lilith.

Dog had brought Lash and Bane. He had sat there, listening to the others with a shit-eating grin on his face, as he waited for the din to die down. Lilith didn't understand his amusement until he popped his great idea.

"Solution's simple," he drawled into a quiet pause of the overly loud discussion. "We create a Council."

Everyone had turned to him, stunned silent.

"Pick a representative." He waved a negligent hand. "I'll send Bane, he can work with Ruin. Between the two they can speak for the mercenary groups."

Bane didn't look thrilled but resigned.

Ruin shook his head.

Undaunted, Dog kept issuing directives. "Each of you, pick someone to represent your interests. Hell, invite the Cartels to send in someone, make them feel like they got some say. This way everyone's invested."

Lilith could only sit there and blink, taken aback by the simple brilliance of Dog's insight.

"You going to invite the Raiders too?" Mercy shot out with a heavy dose of sarcasm. "I can see that working."

"Don't be a bitch, darlin'," Dog shot back.

She flipped him off.

He blew her a kiss. "Not inviting those crazy fucks. Going to be hard enough keeping everyone's asses and egos in line."

That was more true than he knew.

"Mercy can represent the Strix," Math threw out.

"Boden will represent Central Territories," Simon added.

"Daniel will stand for the Free People," Istaqa offered.

"The Northwest will come back with a name." That was a grim looking Walker.

Dog nodded.

"Everett," added Silas, his smile sharp, "will represent the Rocky Mountains."

Dog frowned and shot a look at Lilith.

She shrugged. No time like the present. "I'm stepping down."

Dog grinned and looked to Reaper. "You going with her, big guy?" When Reaper nodded, he unknowingly sealed their fate. "Perfect, you two have the most experience, so you can be the voice of reason when the rest get lost."

Before Lilith knew it, the attendees had created a new Western Council to ensure the territories didn't fall into civil unrest. In six months, the first meeting would be held to hammer out the details. It was bound to be a challenge and even though she didn't want to admit it, she found herself excited about this new opportunity.

That probably had more to do with the fact that this time she wouldn't be going into it alone. Nope, Reaper would be at her side, right where she wanted him.

Voices came from behind them, and she peeked around Reaper to see Dog talking animatedly with Mercy.

Lilith looked up to Reaper. "We better get gone before they realize we're still here." She wanted some time to process the upcoming change.

He dipped his head and took a quick, hot kiss. He lifted his head, shifted his hold to turn her around until she was facing his bike, and with a smack to her ass, he said, "Let's go home, babe."

*Not ready to leave The Collapse behind? Then sign up for Jami's newsletter* **https://www.subscribepage.com/jami-gray-collapse** *and claim your copy of these alternate scenes.*

*Or, if you want to follow your heart into Jami's psychic, paranormal romance series PSY-IV Teams, start with HUNTED BY THE PAST and find out what happens when A reluctant psychic must turn to the man who walked away to escape a killer bent on revenge.*
*Now available at your favorite bookseller.*

# psy - iv teams books

*Welcome to a world where facing danger requires the unique skill set of the men and women of Jami Gray's PSY-IV Teams. As sparks, and bullets fly, love, action, and adventure will target these unique couples as they race through each breath-stealing operation.*

*Binge the series today wherever books are sold!*

## HUNTED BY THE PAST

Cyn & Kayden

*To escape a killer from their past, can a reluctant psychic trust the man who walked away?*

## TOUCHED BY FATE

Risia & Tag

*A seer's secrets become her only bargaining chip in a high-stakes game of lies and loyalty determining her fate.*

**MARKED BY OBSESSION**

Meli & Wolf

*A woman in hiding. A telepath who sees deeper than her scars. Can they forge a bond stronger than the obsession stalking them before time runs out?*

**FRACTURED BY DECEIT**

Megan & Bishop

*After a brutal attack by a telepath, Megan turns to Bishop for help, but how does he keep her safe when she's threat?*

**LINKED BY DECEPTION**

Jinx & Rabbit

*Forced to play intimate criminal partners, will Rabbit & Jinx risk turning illusion to truth as they race to untangle a web of conspiracies and lies?*

# about the author

*"This story is an emotional roller coaster, from betrayal, anger, fear, love..."* —InD'tale Magazine

Jami Gray is the coffee addicted, music junkie, Queen Nerd of her personal Geek Squad, Alpha Mom of the Fur Minxes, who writes to soothe the voices crammed in her head. Her series combine high-stakes urban fantasy and edgy paranormal romantic suspense into books you don't want to put down. Buckle up and get ready for a wild ride through the fascinating worlds of the Arcane, the Kyn, the PSY-IV Teams, and the Collapse.

Come visit Jami's website at **https://www.jamigray.com** and stay up to date on what kind of trouble she's getting into and when you can expect to join in.

amazon.com/author/jamigray

instagram.com/jamigrayauthor

facebook.com/JamiGrayWriter

threads.com/@jamigrayauthor

goodreads.com/JamiGray

bookbub.com/authors/jami-gray